DEFIANCE IN THE KEYS

A LOGAN DODGE ADVENTURE
FLORIDA KEYS
ADVENTURE SERIES
VOLUME 19

Copyright © 2023 by Matthew Rief
All rights reserved.

No part of this book may be reproduced in any form or by any electronic or mechanical means, including information storage and retrieval systems, without written permission from the author, except for the use of brief quotations in a book review.

This book is a work of fiction. Names, characters, businesses, places, events and incidents are either the products of the author's imagination or used in a fictitious manner. Any resemblance to actual persons, living or dead, or actual events is purely coincidental.

Edited by Eliza Dee, Clio Editing Services
Proofread by Donna Rich and Nancy Brown (Redline Proofreading and Editing)

LOGAN DODGE ADVENTURES

Gold in the Keys
Hunted in the Keys
Revenge in the Keys
Betrayed in the Keys
Redemption in the Keys
Corruption in the Keys
Predator in the Keys
Legend in the Keys
Abducted in the Keys
Showdown in the Keys
Avenged in the Keys
Broken in the Keys
Payback in the Keys
Condemned in the Keys
Voyage in the Keys
Guardian in the Keys
Menace in the Keys
Pursuit in the Keys
Defiance in the Keys
Treasure in the Keys

JASON WAKE NOVELS

Caribbean Wake
Surging Wake
Relentless Wake
Turbulent Wake
Furious Wake
Perilous Wake

Join the Adventure!
Sign up for my newsletter to receive updates on upcoming books on my website:

matthewrief.com

Acknowledgements

My deepest thanks to my brilliant editor, Eliza Dee (clioediting.com). Your work ethic, intelligence, and unparalleled insights never cease to amaze me.

I'd also like to thank my proofreaders, Donna Rich (donnarich@icould.com) and Nancy Brown (redlineproofreading.com), both of whom have an impressive eye for detail and provided invaluable final read throughs of this story.

ONE

Florida Strait
Spring 2012

Ten more minutes, Leon Baptiste thought as he scrambled into the bowels of the decrepit, thirty-four-foot sailboat.

The lean, strong Haitian was breathing heavily. Utterly exhausted. He'd been rushing through a series of frantic back and forth movements for nearly an hour. He was dazed. In a zombie-like state. And all his efforts seemed fruitless.

He dropped onto the bottom step of the ladder. Turned around. Was greeted by two dozen pairs of terrified eyes. Mostly women and children. All of them staring back at him. Weary and shaking. Parched throats and empty, grumbling stomachs from eight days at sea with minimal rations.

Leon landed on the deck with a splash. The water

was nearly to his knees and rising fast. The old, battered hull no longer capable of repelling the sea.

He scooped up a bucketful and heaved it topside.

Ten minutes, he thought again. *At most. Then we'll all be at the mercy of the sea.*

But he continued anyway.

Climbed back down and scooped more water and tossed it overboard. Because clinging to hope was infinitely better than just sitting and watching the sea gurgle into their vessel.

After another trip, he paused to catch his breath. Gazed out at the endless dark ocean surrounding them. Looked up at their tattered, damaged sail flapping uselessly in the wind. A perfect symbol for the state of their vessel that'd barely been seaworthy from the outset.

He turned to look at a wide-shouldered man wearing a ballcap who was manning the helm. He had one hand on the wheel, the other holding an old GPS device.

"Where are they, Marcel?" Leon said, stomping over to the man. "We were supposed to be picked up here an hour ago."

The guy shook his head. "I don't know."

"You're sure this is the right spot?"

Marcel glared back at him. "Positive. I've been running this route for over a year. We're right at the coordinates."

Leon leaned over and peered below deck. Watched with big eyes as the water level continued to rise at an alarming rate.

He gasped. Glared at Marcel. Stomped over and stabbed a finger at the guy's face.

"I paid you to get us to the United States," Leon said.

"Yes," Marcel snapped back. "And I told you the risks involved. There are no guarantees."

Leon shook his head. "So, we're all going to die? Most of them can't swim."

"Then you should probably shut the hell up and keep carrying water."

Leon swallowed hard. Stared at his old friend. Turned around and climbed back below deck. The water was well over his knees now. Most of the passengers were panicking. Climbing up onto the old benches and counters.

Leon scanned the space, a wave of pity washing over him. He approached a beautiful woman with youthful, walnut-colored skin and long, raven black hair. She was clinging tightly to a young girl fresh out of infancy. A five-year-old boy stood in front of her, clutching her leg.

Leon wrapped his arms around his family. Held them tight. Kissed his wife.

They never should have come. It was a mistake from the beginning.

But I didn't have a choice, he reminded himself. *The alternative had been slavery and death.*

Leon looked his wife in the eyes. Stepped back and surveyed the space again. There were no life jackets aboard. He'd already searched every inch of the boat.

Gazing over the frightened passengers, he motioned to the ladder. "Everyone topside. Now!"

He led the way, helping everyone up the steps. Following behind the last person.

"What the hell are you doing?" Marcel yelled. "I told you all to stay down there."

"The water's too high," Leon fired back. "They'll all drown if they stay down much longer."

The deck was crowded. Nearly every inch of it. Making it difficult to move about.

Leon returned to his childhood friend at the helm. Did a full three-sixty scan of the surrounding sea, then gazed at the GPS in Marcel's hand.

"We're at the right spot, Leon," he spat again.

"Try the radio. Hail them."

Marcel's eyes bulged. "We never use the radio. It can be intercepted and our whole operation discovered."

"We're all going to drown," Leon said, holding out his hands. "Look below deck."

Marcel ignored him. Kept his eyes forward. His face contorted with anger.

Infuriated, Leon reached for the locker under the helm. Marcel stopped him. Pushed him away.

But Leon didn't relent.

He returned harder. Shoved his old friend aside and threw open the locker door and reached for the radio.

Then he froze as the muzzle of a pistol pressed to the back of his head.

"I said no, Leon," Marcel growled. "I'm in charge. You do as I say."

Leon stared his old friend in the eyes. Glared and held up his hands and backstepped away from the helm. Marcel kept his pistol raised until Leon was ten steps away, then holstered his weapon and directed his eyes back forward.

Leon stood there, unsure of what to do next.

Time ticked away. Water bubbled into the vessel faster and faster. The saloon was nearly submerged. A woman let out a powerful, shrill cry as a wave washed right over the bow and splashed into the Haitians.

Leon ran through his options. He could swim. So could his wife. But he needed to find a way to keep his children afloat. He needed something, anything. And he needed it fast.

He threw himself back down the ladder. Made it two steps when a distant droning noise froze him in place.

He climbed back up. Squinted toward the sound. It was coming from the northeast. Getting louder. And then he saw it, the dark silhouette of a vessel cruising toward them.

It was a large boat with a high-hulled bow. With towering masts and outriggers. A shrimp trawler. The desperate passengers aboard the foundering sailboat glanced back and forth between the vessel and the water level rising dangerously toward the main hatch.

By the time the trawler reached them, they had minutes at most before the sailboat would be swallowed up by the sea.

The trawler slowed, its big engines dialing back to a low rumble. Two men stood against the port gunwale. One was Haitian. Young and casually dressed in a dirty T-shirt and shorts. The other was middle-aged, with pale skin and a thick, graying beard and a ballcap.

They were both silent a moment, just scanning over the terrified group as the water level continued to rise.

"You," the middle-aged man said, pointing right at Leon. His Southern accent was rough as sandpaper. Sounded like he'd smoked two packs a day for twenty years. "Climb up first. You look strong. Help us pull up the others."

Leon nodded. Turned to his wife and kids.

"Come on, Rosalind," he whispered to her. "You and the children." Then he smiled and kissed her. "We made it."

He helped them to the sailboat's bow. It was nearly underwater and crowded. Every lapping wave splashed onto the deck.

The men on the trawler tossed a net over the side. Leon reached and grabbed hold of it. Climbed up over the gunwale and turned around and held out a hand to his wife.

"Welcome aboard, Leon," the middle-aged man said. "I'm the captain. It's so great to see you."

Leon blinked. There was something sinister in the guy's tone.

And how does he know my name?

Leon turned and stared at the guy.

Then his mouth fell open when he realized the captain was holding a Taurus .45-caliber pistol, the barrel aimed right at him.

"That's right," the captain continued. "I know who you are. Barbossa's told us all about you. He's told us all about your wife and children."

Leon narrowed his gaze. Stared at the weapon.

The guy chuckled. "Don't worry. I'm not gonna kill you. I've got strict orders from Barbossa. He has a different fate in store for you."

The Haitian smuggler grabbed Leon from behind, then the captain turned and gazed back down at the sinking sailboat. Stared at Leon's family.

"Hello, beautiful," he said, licking his lips as he gawked at Rosalind from head to toe. "I see why Barbossa wants you back." The man's gaze drifted to Marcel, who'd moved to the bow and was leaning over the side to see what was happening. "The boss told me to give you something, Marcel. A just, due reward for your actions."

Without another word, the guy aimed his weapon at Marcel and opened fire, blasting two high caliber rounds right through his chest from ten feet away. Marcel's body jolted back and flailed in a mist of blood, splashing into the sea.

The Haitians on the sailboat gasped and cried out in shock. Leon watched the scene in horror. Looked at his family. Then snarled at the newly arrived smugglers.

"Now," the captain said, smoke still emanating from the muzzle of his weapon. "All of you aboard. Now. Unless you want to end up like him."

He turned back to Leon. "Did you really think you could steal from Barbossa and get away with it?"

Leon's heart pounded. His gaze tightened. Anger and rage and desperation taking over. He had one chance to act—one split-second opportunity to make any kind of move.

He relaxed his arms, then spun and threw an elbow

into the man holding him back. Followed it up with a swift punch that sent the wiry guy to the deck.

When Leon turned to engage the others, he was struck by a rescue pole, the steel bashing into the side of his head and knocking him unconscious.

TWO

I awoke to the sharp whistling of wind through palm fronds overhead. Kissed my wife on the cheek and crawled out of the tent. Savored a calm breeze of sea air as I emerged barefoot and shirtless.

The sky was still dark and cool. Clusters of clouds parted enough for an array of stars to poke through. Smoke wafted toward me from a dying campfire. Coconut trees rustled overhead, and soft waves lapped against a rocky shore below.

In the distance was nothing but flat, dark sea in all directions. We were far from civilization, hiding out together for a much-needed escape from it all in our own tropical paradise.

Before zipping the tent back up, I turned and poked my head inside. My wife lay in our wide sleeping bag. She was on her back. Head tilted to the side. Her blond hair a mess and strewn about, and perfect. She had one hand up and bent and touching her cherry-red lips.

I smiled. One look at her revived fresh memories of the previous day.

It'd been a day for the ages—one of the best days of my life. A day of spearfishing and snorkeling in the pristine, lively waters surrounding the island, followed by an evening of delicious grilled seafood, a bottle of prosecco, and hours completely wrapped up in each other.

The perfect way to celebrate our anniversary. Three years, and it felt like my love for her grew more each day.

I'd surprised her with a couple nights on the island of Monte Cristo, a seemingly inhospitable pile of rocks surrounded by shallows ten miles from Dry Tortugas and the outstretched fingers of the Florida Keys. It was our secret spot. Our sanctuary. A little sliver of private Shangri-la. A place to get away and to think and to have deep talks. To get right with your soul.

I relieved myself just down the slope from the tent, then returned to our campsite and stepped across a small spread of grass. Past the campfire, its red coals brightening and dimming with the wind. Past a hammock we'd strung between two palms. Right to the edge of a twenty-foot cliff.

I reached high and stretched. Glanced down at the lapping waters below, then up to the horizon. Closed my eyes and breathed deeply in and out. Opened them and scanned the world around us. The flat Gulf to the north and west. The flat Straits to the south and east.

As my eyes neared the completion of the circle, I spotted something in the distance. Far off to the southwest. A dark object bobbing in the blue. I blinked and squinted. It was far off. Five miles at least. It was small and floating low. Appeared to be a sailboat.

Curious, I turned and ambled back to the tent. Knelt down and reached inside and grabbed my backpack. Ange was still asleep. Motionless and angelic.

I paused a moment, just looking at her. Enraptured. Completely enamored by her.

I smiled and heaved out my bag. Unzipped the main compartment and grabbed my monocular, then set the bag on an unfolded camping chair. Picked up my pace a little as I returned to the cliff's edge.

I reached the corner. Held up the optic and adjusted the focus. The blurry, distant vessel cleared and took shape. As I'd guessed, it was a sailboat. Looked around thirty feet long. Old and battered and dirty. A damaged sail raised, flapping along the mast.

All of my attention swiftly homed in on the main deck. It was littered with people. Had to be over a dozen of them, all huddled together and holding on as the vessel bobbed up and down on the open sea.

A fraction of a second later, I noticed the waterline.

It was too high. Well over the vessel's portholes, and waves were lapping over the bow and splashing to the deck.

It was taking on water. Soon to be claimed by the sea.

A sharp, distant cry tore across the air. A woman's cry. And in that moment, I realized that I hadn't been awoken by the wind whistling through palm fronds.

THREE

It took me all of three seconds to turn and bound across the knoll to our campsite. I slid to a stop beside the tent's partially unzipped door. Ange was awake when I poked my head in this time. Up on a knee and clutching her Glock 17.

Neither of us were strangers to danger and high-risk situations. We'd both lived in a world of violence with potential threats waiting at every turn. It was a time gone by, but the instincts remained—ingrained facets of our being we couldn't shake even if we wanted to.

The switch was immediate and total. The mood going from calm and relaxing and tranquil to battle ready in a blink. I told Ange what was happening. Rapid-fire. Necessary words only.

Sinking boat.

Roughly five miles southeast.

Passengers in distress.

I grabbed my bag. Unzipped the main compartment and checked my sat phone. The device's screen was dark, and it wouldn't power on.

Of course, I thought.

I'd owned the reliable long-range communications device for years. Taken it on daring ventures all over the world. And it'd been a brief dip in the water the previous day that'd seemingly fried it.

I stowed the sat phone. Grabbed a first aid kit as well and zipped back up the main compartment. Hustled down the steep path to a hidden lagoon and beach. Untied our Zodiac, slid it into the water, and jumped aboard.

I fired up the eighty-horsepower engine and nosed us through a tight zigzag in the rockface. Once free of the island's natural fortifications, I throttled wide open, bouncing us across the water at thirty-five knots.

Ange crouched at the bow, keeping low to minimize drag. She had my bag beside her and our sat phone removed. Was holding it to the side of her face and waiting impatiently. Intermittently smacking it. Trying to will its revival as wind whipped past us and swells sprayed up and over us.

Her mouth wasn't moving. Clearly the device still wasn't working.

I held tight. Kept the throttle shoved and my eyes forward. Fought to catch a glimpse of the sinking vessel with every roller we crested.

From up on the cliff, we'd had a much better vantage point. Thirty feet up meant a line of sight of roughly six and a half miles, as opposed to less than half that standing at sea level.

Two minutes later, I saw it. Dead ahead. The waterline was significantly higher, the sea lapping over its foredeck. The passengers were moving about frantically, heaving buckets of water topside and splashing them overboard. But it was a futile effort.

The clock was ticking now. Every second crucial. Simple physics. Boats sink faster the more water they take on. Weight and air displacement and buoyancy. Soon it would be gone, vanished and plummeting toward the seafloor.

"It's still not powering on," my wife called out, holding up the sat phone.

I squinted as water sprayed over the bow. Shook my head in frustration.

"Keep trying," I shouted back, but Ange was already on it.

Thick clouds rolled in over the moon, darkening the sky even more. Monte Cristo shrank behind us while the sailboat got bigger and smaller at the same time as it sank more.

We were half a mile away when Ange shifted, grabbed my monocular, and aimed it toward the sailboat. I realized she was aiming it fifteen degrees off the vessel's bow, then I saw a second boat appear. This one big and fast. Closing in on the sailboat from the northeast.

It was a shrimp trawler, and it was nearly upon the sinking boat. Ange glanced back and smiled. I let out a long breath and relaxed a little.

We watched as the trawler closed in on the distressed sailboat, then pulled right up alongside it. I reached for the throttle instinctively and dialed us back to twenty knots.

As we approached, we saw more people climb out and crowd the sailboat's deck. There looked to be at least two dozen of them. Migrants, no doubt. Judging by the state of the vessel and their frail, worn appearances, they'd been at sea for at least a week.

We watched as they flooded toward the sailboat's bow. Saw fishermen scrambling on the trawler. Tossing a net over the side and helping a man aboard.

We were two hundred yards away when the mood of the interaction shifted dramatically.

Ange and I watched in horrific shock as one of the fishermen pulled out a dark handgun. He took aim from barely ten feet away and opened fire, blasting two rounds into one of the migrants and tossing him into the sea.

FOUR

The two gunshots were thunderous. Cracking in rapid succession and echoing across the dark, empty world.
 Changing the nature of the encounter.
 Changing everything.
 There was a minuscule, nearly nonexistent moment of disbelief. The sort of mental shell shock that follows witnessing something so unexpected that your mind can't comprehend it.
 But then the moment passed. The reality of the act took over, and our instincts kicked into their highest gear.
 Immediately after the bullet-riddled man splashed and bobbed in the sea, a quick scuffle broke out on the trawler's deck. A migrant was knocked out of sight. Then the foundering vessel's passengers were no longer ushered respectfully onto the bigger boat. They were forced. Prodded along at gunpoint from the sailboat to the trawler's deck and toward the doors

of its pilothouse.

The shrimpers hadn't seen us yet. Their big diesels idling and drowning out our little outboard, and their attentions fixed on the migrants. But it was only a matter of time, and Ange was ready, her Glock 17 clutched in her right hand.

We had no idea what was going on. All we knew was we'd just witnessed a man being murdered in cold blood. Then a group of frantic, desperate foreigners being loaded up and tied and forced below deck.

The switch had been flipped.

These weren't Good Samaritans cruising by after a night of fishing, in the right place at the right time just by happenstance. These were killers.

I eased back on the throttle and turned slowly to starboard, motoring to try and be on a line with the trawler's bow and out of sight of the shrimpers on its deck.

Suddenly, a man along the forward section turned and stared in our direction. Then he grabbed a handgun and raised it.

"Logan!" Ange shouted as the weapon was trained our way.

Taking evasive action, I completed the turn as sharply as our momentum would allow, then shoved the throttle all the way forward. Gunfire rattled off again. Bullets soared past and splashed into the sea behind us.

The quick maneuver had bought us maybe two seconds, but they were precious seconds. And Ange used them to take aim with her pistol. She didn't hesitate. There was no margin for it. She opened fire the moment her barrel locked onto its target. Pelted the front of the trawler with a rapid storm of 9mm rounds.

The man dropped down for cover, vanishing from view behind the gunwale.

In the heat of the moment, my wife glanced back at me between shots. Shot me a look that said, *What the hell is the plan now?*

My mind ran through the upcoming encounter. I thought about strategic attack points. Thought about the angles.

My mind calculating. Strategizing.

The first priority was keeping our mode of transport intact. I was piloting an inflatable craft. Susceptible to puncture by even a poorly placed shot. If that happened, we'd be done for. Dead in the water.

I couldn't minimize the size of our enemies' target, so instead I continued full speed, then immediately cut left, heading straight toward the vessel's bow. The maneuver resulted in less deck space that Ange needed to cover, and she fired intermittently as we continued our charge. A round every couple seconds, just to keep the criminals honest. Pelting the wheelhouse. Cracking glass. Sparking lead off the hull.

The second priority was proximity. We needed to eliminate the distance between us, so I kept the throttle pegged.

As we neared the trawler's bow, I came up with a quick plan. Whistled to get Ange's attention, then said, "I'm going for a swim."

She nodded. Fired off another cover shot, then stepped backward, knelt down, and gathered my freediving fins, mask, and weight belt. We'd left the gear in the Zodiac the previous evening, and she piled it all together beside the starboard pontoon.

When we were twenty yards away from the trawler, I reined in our speed, letting our RHIB idle right up to the vessel. Ange had been creeping backward steadily toward me, her weapon aimed toward the deck above.

The trawler's bow rose high out of the water and angled upward, giving us a natural cover. I kept the engine idling, then moved out of the cockpit.

I grabbed and swiftly donned my freediving gear, strapped my holstered Sig Sauer P226 pistol to my thigh, then straddled the starboard pontoon as Ange took the wheel. She fired another shot to cover me, then gave me a quick nod as I sucked in a deep breath and slid headfirst into the Caribbean.

Submerging completely, I kicked roughly ten feet down, then angled parallel with the surface and finned along the boat's port side. Parting clouds allowed the moon's glow to break free and illuminate the water with a silver tint. The glimmer reached down through the translucent water, dying off in the black abyss below.

I finned my way along the trawler's barnacle-encrusted hull and sliced under its aft section. My lungs began to throb a minute later as I reached the stern. I surfaced along the aft port corner of the vessel. Nice and slow, my head barely breaking free enough to take in a breath and look around. From that vantage point, I could barely see the back half of the sailboat.

It was nearly completely swallowed up by the

Gulf. It was a sight to behold. A dying vessel, gurgling out bubbles from its final pockets of dry air as the sea took over. The remaining migrants moved about frantically on its deck. Splashing and taking advantage of the boat's final moments of buoyancy before they'd be forced to tread water. Some already were, thrashing and struggling toward the trawler with everything they had. The only other means of liberation in sight. Either grab hold or drown.

I watched as many of them were pulled up out of the water and flotation rings were thrown. In the short amount of time it'd taken for us to close in with the Zodiac and for me to freedive along the trawler, the criminals had already prodded a handful of the migrants out of my sight below deck.

Turning, I kicked along the starboard side to a trio of tires tied off to the trawler's side. I unclipped my weight belt, letting it sink, then kicked with everything I had and grabbed hold of the nearest tire. Sliding off my fins, I let them go as well, then climbed up and removed my mask and peered through a hawsehole at the main deck.

It smelled. This was where all the muck and excess shrimp and seaweed were shoved off the deck. It was a working trawler. Nets bundled about. Wayward shrimp here and there. Big coolers resting side by side. A working shrimping boat.

There were two men on the deck. One was along the port side of the pilothouse. He was a short, sprightly Latino wearing pants and a cutoff shirt and clutching a pistol and taking intermittent glances around the corner toward where Ange piloted the Zodiac ahead of the bow. The other guy was reaching over the starboard side to haul someone I couldn't see up onto the vessel. He had tanned, tattooed skin and light, scruffy hair and dirty working clothes. Looked like one of hundreds of fishermen I'd seen at marinas over the course of my life.

Both men looked anxious, their movements frantic and jittery.

As I scanned the deck, I noticed a third figure. A young, lean Latino lying motionless barely ten feet in front of my face. He was shirtless, with tattered denim shorts and had blood dripping from a fresh blow to the side of his head. His malnourished physique and threadbare attire made it clear that he was one of the migrants. The one we'd watched get assaulted on our approach to the trawler.

Continuing my rapid scan of the deck, I noticed that the thick iron door leading into the pilothouse was propped open, and there were muddy footprints leading across the deck into it. Shouts emanated from inside, and I spotted blurry movement through the pilothouse windows. An obscured figure with a thick beard and a ballcap.

There was no time to sit tight and wait for the opportune moment to strike. With the sailboat submerged, many of the migrants would soon be drowning.

I withdrew my Sig and took aim through the hole. The guy on the left found himself in my sights first. He had priority. He was armed and ready, and alert. The guy keeping watch while the others dealt with getting the migrants below deck.

The vessel swayed with the open sea rollers. The guy shifted his body all around, fighting for an angle on my wife beyond the bow. Frustrated at his inability to obtain one.

I opened fire. Two rapid shots. One burst through his upper left leg. The second caught him in the lumbar spine as he collapsed forward. His weapon fell and he face-planted and flailed on the deck.

Before he'd collapsed, I was already making my next move. Hands firmly gripping the rusted metal edge of the gunwale, right leg swung and hooked. Center of gravity thrown up and over and my feet hitting the damp deck.

The second guy still had his back to me as he reached over the starboard side. His head snapped around for a look toward the commotion as I charged toward him. I'd already decided not to shoot the guy. Not then. Not at that angle.

He was pulling someone up from the water. My 9mm parabellum would tear clear through his flesh with little effort and punch right out the other side of his body. It'd continue on its trajectory, and it'd still have enough velocity to do serious damage to whatever or whoever was behind him.

When I was halfway across the deck, another man burst out from the propped-open door. He was big and muscular, and my peripherals caught him just before he'd emerged. I whirled around and realized he was gripping a shotgun.

The moment my eyes homed in on the firearm, I stopped and pivoted on the next planted foot. Slipped on the deck at the sudden change in direction and was horizontal in a blink, my hip colliding with the deck.

The mishap saved my life.

The guy opened fire immediately, blasting a storm

of pellets into the empty space where I'd been fractions of a second earlier. If we'd had greater separation between us, I'd have been toast. But we were barely five feet apart, and the projectiles hadn't had sufficient distance to spread and widen their impact radius.

Before the brute could redirect his aim and attempt a second shot, I rolled off my impact with the deck, closing the distance between us, then whipped my right leg into the side of his shin. His lower body flew out from under him, and he smacked into the deck. I was geared up for a second strike the moment he landed. Tucked my right knee in, then drove my heel forward, bashing it into his left temple and smacking him into the corner of the thick iron door.

Whipping around, I came up onto a knee with my Sig at the ready, taking aim at the criminal at the starboard gunwale. In the brief span of time it'd taken to subdue my shotgun-wielding opponent, the guy had finished lifting his victim up out of the water.

It was a girl.

She was tiny. A toddler. Maybe two years old. Terror-struck and screaming at the top of her lungs. Her face coated with tears. Her short, unruly hair wild and her eyes big.

The guy had her held up, using her small frame as a human shield to cover his upper body and head. His left arm was tight across her. His right gripped a knife that was pressed to her neck.

"Drop the gun, hero," the man spat. "Or she dies."

He was maybe thirty and had a distinct Southern accent.

He wasn't an experienced killer. That much was

clear by the way he held the knife, the shaky fear lacing his voice, and the lack of confidence in his posture.

His legs were exposed from the thighs down, but a shot there was too risky. The guy would jar and buckle forward. The girl would fall with him and likely be thrown right into the tip of the blade.

With my attention wholly fixed on the man and the little girl in his arms, I heard Ange fire up the Zodiac and race toward the sailboat. In my peripherals, I could barely see any of it. Just a blurry white vessel, completely submerged. Soon to be nothing but a memory. And the frenzied, thrashing movements of terrified people just trying to stay alive.

I glanced over and watched my wife slow and help the drowning foreigners, reaching over and fishing them out of the sea. They quickly flooded into our little boat. A dozen of them at least.

"Now," the guy snarled, tightening his grip on the little girl. "Or she dies."

He pressed the blade deeper, drawing blood.

She was still screaming. Her voice cracking and her body shaking. Sheer terror in her eyes.

I shot a glance toward Ange. Saw her watching our interaction.

Bending my knees slowly, I lowered my weapon and set it on the deck. My eyes remained locked on the guy. My body ready to charge at a moment's notice.

"Let her go," I said, standing tall once more.

"Kick it over there," he snarled, gesturing toward my weapon.

I did as he said, nudging the weapon with my foot

and sending it sliding far out of reach.

The man smiled. "Now, get the fuck off my boat."

He lowered the knife. Turned and hurled the terrified girl overboard. She flailed and spun and shrieked, then vanished from my view.

I was already moving. My legs and arms driving into a full-on sprint. I blurred right past the guy and dove over the gunwale, soaring and splashing into the Gulf right beside the girl. She was bobbing up and down frantically. Gurgling water by the time I reached her and wrapped my arms tight around her.

With my right arm across her chest, I swam us both toward the Zodiac ten yards away. The trawler's engine growled a moment later. The propellers churned and the vessel picked up speed.

I stole a glance over my shoulder and watched as the man who'd held the young girl at knifepoint moments earlier sprang up, pistol in hand. The trawler was swiftly accelerating away, already twenty yards from where it'd started.

Ange was taking aim from the Zodiac with her Glock. She opened fire on the guy before he could level his weapon. Managed to strike him in the shoulder. He cursed and staggered forward, but somehow maintained control of his sidearm as he bent over the gunwale. He let loose. Just random spray and pray in our general direction.

There was no time to tell the young girl to hold her breath. No time to do anything but suck in air myself and close my eyes and throw us both beneath the surface. I held on tight to her and kicked with everything I had. Bullets streaked past, torpedoed and slowed, and then sank into the darkness around us.

We surfaced to the sound of intense shrieks of pain. The little girl gagged and coughed uncontrollably, her eyes still big as the night sky.

The gunshots had stopped. I saw Ange standing on the nearby Zodiac, aiming her pistol at the trawler. Our attacker tumbled off the shrimp boat, a fresh gunshot wound to the side of his head barely visible before he splashed into the sea.

As I focused my attention on helping the gagging young girl, another sound reached my ears. The distinct loud and steady hissing of air.

FIVE

The world around me was a whirlwind of confusion. A flood of tragedies all manifesting themselves in one chaotic moment. A cacophony of noise.

The shrimp boat grumbling, its massive diesels propelling it north. Powerful cries of pain and fear. The gurgling and coughing of the young girl clutched in my arms. The release of pressurized air, our vessel's source of buoyancy seeping out into the atmosphere.

We had a list of problems on our hands.

When the toddler cleared the water from her lungs and managed to catch her breath, I closed my eyes and focused. Brought up the damage control manifesto in my mind.

Tackle the direst, most pressing matters first.

If the Zodiac deflated, we'd all be forced to swim for it. At the mercy and whims of a strong current way out in the middle of those notoriously temperamental waters between the Gulf and Florida Strait.

I kicked with everything I had. Holding tight to the girl and keeping her head above water. She was struggling. Still coughing and fighting for every breath. But she was getting air in. She was surviving—going to be all right.

I reached the Zodiac.

It was flooded with people. Over a dozen of them. Most of them women and most of them young. The starboard pontoon was already halfway deflated. The port was intact and barely keeping everyone afloat.

Ange was helping a woman out of the water who was crying and bleeding out profusely. She'd clearly been shot in the chest and was shaking and going into shock. I helped Ange slide her up into the RHIB. Found my backpack and pulled out the first aid kit and handed it to her while I dug deeper for the Zodiac's emergency patch kit.

As I tore into the bag and pulled out the equipment and went to work, a memory flashed in my mind. Sixteen years earlier. Small Craft Instruction and Technical Training School in Mississippi. My forte in the Special Forces had been small boat operations and explosive ordnance disposal, and I'd spent four separate eight-week stints undergoing various specialty small craft training programs there.

One of the courses involved inflatable boat repair. Patching up a damaged RHIB. Only the training was designed to put students under as much stress as possible. We had been kept awake for forty-eight hours, then tossed into a pool of ice water for ten minutes. Exhausted, body shaking from the cold, I'd been handed a patch kit and a damaged pontoon and told I had sixty seconds to save the squad or eight letters were going to be sent home to family and loved ones.

All of it on my shoulders.

Like I had years earlier, I went to work. Hyperfocused. The task at hand warranted nothing less.

The leak was easy to spot. A large rupture. Over an inch across, and with a matching hole out the opposite side. Two gashes that were just barely within the limits of the patch's ability.

I dried the area as best I could, then ripped the clear cover over the sticky side of the patch and positioned it over the hole. Held it with strong pressure. Then I grabbed a second patch and repeated the process for the exit side. It was harder. The loose Hypalon folded over and was tough to work with.

I completed the patching tasks in just under a minute, then grabbed the emergency pump, shuffled aft and connected its adapter to the pontoon's valve. Ange was working quickly, doing everything she could to help the woman who'd been shot.

Once it was locked into place, I switched on the pump. Sent the compressor droning and spitting air through the hose. The tube inflated and the patches held and another minute later, the pontoon was revived.

After restowing the emergency gear, I crawled over and dropped beside Ange. She already had the woman's wound exposed. It was gruesome. Ange had opened a bag of QuikClot, the absorbent gauze pressed over the crater and slowing the bleeding.

I helped her apply more and secure it with bandages. Applying pressure and doing our best to calm the woman. She'd already lost a lot of blood. It'd flowed and splashed over the deck.

With Ange taking care of the woman, I checked on the young girl. She was huddled right beside us. No longer coughing or screaming but still shaking and sobbing. A hand draped over the woman who'd been shot.

"It's going to be all right," I said, then repeated the words in Spanish.

Then I turned and addressed the group. There were fourteen of them. All scared and wide-eyed. Some crammed onto the vessel, some holding on to the side and floating in the water.

"You're all safe now," I said.

My eyes shot to the north. The trawler was still racing away at what I assumed was its max speed. Cruising into the Gulf and getting smaller and smaller.

"Dominica?" I said to one of the men.

He paused, shook his head. "Haiti."

His accent was thick. Haitian Creole.

I nodded. Said, "Seven hundred miles." Then I pointed northwest. "Ten miles left. Let's go."

With Ange still tending the injured woman, I helped the rest aboard. Spotted the shrimper Ange and I had shot floating on his back in the water. He was motionless and bleeding out, and had drifted right up to the side of our boat. Ange's shot had barely grazed his skull—just enough to knock him unconscious. But somehow the guy was still breathing.

Unable to stop myself, I leaned over, grabbed hold of the criminal and hauled him into our boat. Left him curled up on the dock.

The Zodiac was pushed to its limits, the water rising up to the handles. I threaded through the migrants and crouched beside the engine. We were overloaded. Enough to capsize if hit with a decent swell. But the morning was calm and the rollers had waned.

We could make it.

We were going to make it.

I fired up the engine and eased us up to ten knots. That was about as fast as we were gonna reach. Last thing I wanted was for the bow to rise up too high and the stern to take on water or for the engine to overheat.

I fumbled for our sat phone. Sighed when I realized it still wasn't working. Then I pulled out my cell phone and switched it on. No signal. Not even a bar.

"Logan!" Ange gasped.

I peered through the group and saw the injured woman shaking violently. Convulsing and crying out. Eyes bulging and limbs thrashing.

"Hold it steady," I told the man beside me, then gave him the wheel and crawled back to Ange.

The young girl was still partly draped over the woman's side. And a young boy of maybe five was draped over the other.

"Hold on," I said to the woman, kneeling beside her. "We're almost there."

I asked her name. She coughed and winced and said, "Rosalind. Rosalind Baptiste."

She looked young. Early twenties, maybe. Pretty and strong. Fighting with everything she had. Her children there. Willing her on and crying out. The sight was hard to watch. Horrific and devastating. We'd done everything we could. She needed the care and equipment and medical staff of an emergency room, and fast. But all we had was the meager supplies of our first aid kit.

I grabbed my sat phone again. It still wasn't working, its screen blank. I closed my eyes and squeezed tight on the device. Smacked it against the console again and again, trying to get it working through physical agitation. But the screen remained dark.

I crawled back around to the stern and kicked up our speed, accelerating us to fifteen. It strained with the effort, letting me know that we were flirting with failure. And even at that pace, we were still at least half an hour away from the Tortugas and the nearest stationed rangers.

Rosalind was hitting the next stage. Right on the verge of death.

Frustrated and desperate, I smacked my sat phone against the console once again. The screen remained blank.

I cursed and chucked it to the deck, the device hitting hard and settling sideways against the port pontoon. As I turned forward, squinting into the strong breeze, I noticed a glow in the corner of my eye. My head tilted back and I saw that my sat phone's screen had illuminated.

It happened in an anticlimactic, blinking flash. No warning or audible indication. Just liberation in the form of a brightening LCD.

I bent down and scooped up the phone and placed a call to the Coast Guard station in Key West. Just over eighty miles to the east of us, and just up the coast from where I kept my boat moored at Conch Harbor Marina. I'd been there a couple times. Met many of the personnel there. Knew their response times and reputations and level of expertise.

I gave the operator a quick rundown, setting the clock into motion. I pictured the trained on-duty experts rushing out of their quarters and lounges, throwing on their gear with the rapid, fluid movements of firefighters when the fire bell sounds. They'd be in the air in less than two minutes, I guessed. Then it was full-speed west. A hundred and eighty miles per hour. No wind or foul weather. They'd be there in just under thirty minutes.

My second call was to the Border Protection office. Then to Key West's chief of police, Jane Verona. Not only did I want them to assemble and send whatever help they could our way, I also wanted every law enforcement agency out looking for the smugglers' vessel that had escaped and was tearing into the Gulf.

They'd all contact the park rangers on Garden Key to let them know to be ready for our upcoming arrival.

The moment the call ended with Jane, my sat phone went blank again. As if fate had intervened and shined a wink of good luck in our direction.

The engine was struggling and sputtering. Smoking a little. The little RHIB pushed right to its limits, but no further. There was nothing more to do, and an eerie quiet came over the group. Quick, scared breaths. And the woman struggling for her life as her children held her, willing her to keep her eyes open and to keep breathing.

I aimed us straight for the distant dark walls of Fort Jefferson, then handed the helm back over to the young man and returned to Ange and Rosalind.

She was no longer shaking. Her body was motionless and her head was resting back on a lifejacket. Her eyes were as big as ever, and she was gasping slowly in and out.

"We're almost there, Rosalind," I said. "You need to hold on. A couple more minutes."

She looked away, staring up into the night sky. The distant stars. She was fading. Weakening with every passing second.

As her children continued to sob, she reached up a jerky hand and touched my shirt, beckoning me closer. I leaned over, my head barely a foot above hers.

"You... are a good man," she gasped. She closed her eyes. Opened them and glanced at Ange and added, "You both have good hearts."

She closed her eyes again. Angled her head and wheezed.

She dropped her hand and reached into her soaked pocket. Pulled out a crumpled piece of paper. She held it out to me and I unfolded it. It was a picture. The woman with the two kids beside her. They were all smiling and well dressed. Happy. Full of hope.

There was a man in the picture with them. A man I recognized immediately—the same one who'd been lying unconscious and bleeding on the deck of the shrimp boat.

"Leon," she said, pointing a shaky finger at the photograph. "My husband."

She coughed. Fought for a breath.

"Promise me...," she gasped again. "Promise me you'll look after my babies." She reached out her right hand, dropping it over the young girl. Then she reached out her left, resting it on the boy.

"Olivier and Esther deserve a chance...," she said, the words barely strong enough to escape her lips. "They deserve a chance."

I looked into her eyes and said, "I promise."

She gasped and closed her eyes just as the distant but intensifying sounds of helicopter rotors echoed across the air.

"It's coming," I said, pointing to the east. "It's right there. You need to hold on a little longer. You have to. For your children."

But her eyes remained sealed. Her body went limp and she said, "I... have nothing more." She opened her eyes a final time. One last teary glimpse of her babies, then closed them and uttered, "No strength left."

SIX

The Jayhawk reached us twenty-six minutes after I'd made the first call. Even faster than I'd expected. I idled the engine as it swept in and descended and hovered right over us. Earsplitting and powerful. Its slipstream beating down and rippling the water around us as we huddled and covered our faces. The side door opened, and a line slithered down and straightened.

A rescue swimmer rappelled down, slowing just before splashing into the water off our port side. Smooth and professional. A second Guardsman descended as well, and they held steady to the pontoon as an orange basket stretcher was lowered and positioned right beside them.

One of them climbed aboard and we helped heave Rosalind into the stretcher. She was motionless. Not breathing and had no pulse. She was gone, but they needed to do all they could to help her regardless.

Hold on to the sliver of hope that she could be revived by an AED.

The unconscious shrimper who'd been shot was lifted up next. The guy had been motionless since Ange had blasted him into the sea. Incapacitated and trickling out blood, but somehow still alive. Then another injured migrant was hauled up last.

I kept the two children with me. They'd already witnessed their mother perish right before their eyes. They didn't need to stare at her motionless corpse for the ride to the Lower Keys Medical Center on Stock Island. And I'd promised her. Stared into her dying eyes and promised that I'd look after them.

Once the four were aboard, the Guardsmen were lifted back into the craft. They gave a thumbs-up to me and Ange, then the Jayhawk took off, soaring back to the east.

Silence returned aside from the humming engine.

I pushed aside the emotional ordeal we'd just been through. Focused on the task at hand and returned to the engine and throttled us back up to ten knots. The motor was struggling less. Less weight and demand at the dialed-back speed.

It took ten more minutes for us to reach the outskirts of the Dry Tortugas, rounding the thin mile-long Loggerhead Key and heading straight for the forty-foot red brick walls of Fort Jefferson. Always a sight to behold. A hexagonal structure covering sixteen acres and sprouting up from the blue surrounding it.

There was a group of park rangers waiting for us along the stretch of beach on its southwest side. And a group of visitors and campers were nearby, watching as we motored to the beach. The steady groan of the engine was broken up by intermittent gasps and cries. Emotional sobs that reached a crescendo when the Zodiac's hull pierced the beach and scratched partway up onto the white sand.

What happened next blew me away.

The weary, starving, dehydrated Haitians spilled out, vaulting over the pontoons and dashing and dancing their way up from the surf. They let out triumphant, passionate cheers. Cried out uncontrollably, savoring the respite of dry land for the first time in what probably felt like a lifetime. They cheered and wept and fell to their knees. Reached their hands high into the air. It was an incredible, moving sight.

One I'll never forget.

A dramatic culmination. The grueling days at sea filled with dangers and unknowns. An eventual shoot-out that'd left multiple dead. And now they'd arrived. What happened next didn't seem to matter to them in that moment. They'd made it.

The following minutes were a blur of activity. Park rangers hustling over and providing aid. Ushering the Haitians into the fort and giving them bottles of water along with protein bars and apples. Lines of tourists watched and documented the arrival with their phones and cameras. Even though it was still dark out, I threw on a hat and sunglasses and angled my head away from the lenses as I helped however I could. Ange did the same, neither of us wanting attention.

I knelt down beside Rosalind's two young children and gave them sips of water and slices of banana.

They were still shaking. Still silent. Eyes big and staring out into nothing at all. They clearly couldn't get over the shock—couldn't get their mother's dying face out of their minds. I knew they'd likely never be able to. They'd both experienced a horrific, traumatic experience if ever there was one. And Ange and I stayed right there with them, keeping them close and offering them more food and water.

I borrowed a sat phone from the rangers. Wiped tears from my eyes as I strode to the nearby ferry dock and placed a call. Got the Customs and Border Protection office on the line again and gave them a full description of the trawler. The operator said they had all of their boats dispatched, and every other office from Miami to Texas had been notified and were on the lookout.

Then I called Captain Rinaldi, the CO of NAS Key West. Let her know what was happening to keep her in the loop.

When we ended the call, I stared at the device's screen a moment, then glanced over at the distant group of migrants. Ange was at the edge of the cluster with the two little ones, both of them getting much-needed nourishment.

Then I turned and gazed north. Squinted at the horizon, feeling equal parts antsy and angry. Forced to be patient. There was nothing else I could do. Nothing else to do but wait as the men who'd tried to kill me and my wife motored farther and farther away.

SEVEN

Captain Robert Heinrich stood at the helm of the shrimp trawler, his eyes forward and his heart still pounding from the unexpected encounter. They were motoring full speed, thundering through the dark sea. They headed north for three miles before turning east, keeping their distance from the Tortugas as they made their way toward the Lower Keys.

The trawler's hull had a more aquadynamic design than most shrimp boats. Combined with its two oversized diesel engines, the vessel had an impressive top speed, but less hauling capacity than most trawlers.

But that didn't matter. They were never worried about overloading the vessel. Even during their largest runs, when they transported over forty migrants in their hold, they were far below the vessel's max weight.

Heinrich closed his eyes and fought to control his

breathing. The experienced mariner wiped the sweat from his brow. He'd spent most of his life at sea. Had grown up in a small coastal Alabama town. Lived on a shrimp boat. It'd been a family business going back to his grandfather. A difficult but lucrative family business.

But things had changed, and the profits had shrunk and funds were tight.

He'd spent his life working his fingers to the bone. His hands were raw. His skin scarred and spotted from the sun. His hair thin and gray.

And for what?

Only to find himself on the verge of being broke in the twilight years of his life.

It was then that opportunity had presented itself.

He knew the sea. Knew the regulations. Knew how the Coast Guard and Border Patrol agents operated. And for the last year, his skills had been put to use. No longer just hauling in shrimp. He was smuggling far more precious cargo, and it'd paid him well.

But reality was setting in.

It'd been barely ten minutes since the incident when he pulled out his sat phone and placed a rapid call. It was three thirty in the morning. He'd be waking their boss up. Irritating the hell out of him. Something to be done only in emergencies.

But this was an emergency. A damn big one.

"What is it?" a rough voice said after the third ring.

Heinrich relayed what'd happened. It came out between rapid breaths.

"What did you do with their bodies?" the voice said. "The ones who attacked you?"

The captain paused. This was the hard part to say. The worst part. The rough news.

"They're still alive," he said. The words tasted bitter. Were painful just to utter. "But we popped their Zodiac and it was deflated and overloaded with Haitians and—"

"You left them alive?"

"They weren't ordinary people. The guy was quick and armed. So was the woman. Both well trained. They came at us hard. Took down two of our men before I could bloody blink. Then Declan tried to shoot them more as we made our escape and was instantly shot overboard. It was insane. We barely made it out alive."

There was a short pause. One that grew more uncomfortable the longer it lasted.

"We have rules," the man said. "Barbossa has laid out a strict system that keeps our operation running. And what's the most important rule?"

The captain sighed. "No one witnesses a pick up and lives to tell about it."

"That's right."

The captain swallowed. "We couldn't kill him. We tried."

"Why did you initiate the grab with others nearby?"

"We didn't see them. They appeared out of nowhere. We kept checking the horizon and saw no one. We were miles away from the Tortugas. No one and nothing out there."

"You grabbed the children at least?"

Heinrich hunched lower. "No. But we got Leon, and we'll deal with him as was previously instructed.

Like I said, these strangers were brutal. We'd all be dead if I hadn't throttled us away."

There was another pause. Even longer than the first.

Finally, Heinrich said, "What are we gonna do about this, boss? I have us running at max speed, but we're barely chugging fifteen knots. We'll be discovered. Hunted down and searched and they'll find our goods."

"Let me handle it."

"How? How can we—"

"I said, I'll handle it. Just deal with the bodies. And do the usual routine."

"We'll be searched," Heinrich said again.

"Yes. So, get the hell off the boat as soon as you dock. We'll switch out the crew."

"We'll be searched," he said a third time. Like the boss hadn't heard him.

"I know. But it doesn't matter. They won't find the cargo. We've been searched before and no one ever does."

The line went dead.

Heinrich swallowed hard, then gave an order to his only remaining crew member.

"Time to tidy up, Dennis," he said.

They dealt with the bodies of their two dead associates first. That part didn't take long. A rusted old chain. Thirty pounds of links wrapped around the corpses from head to toe, making them both look like some kind of junkyard mummy. Then they heaved them off the deck and hurled the bodies overboard into two hundred feet of water.

Once their fellow crew members were dealt with,

they dragged Leon Baptiste's unconscious body down into their hidden cargo hold and locked him away with other migrants they'd managed to haul aboard before they'd made their escape. Then they went right into their usual returning-from-sea routine. Removing a metal plate that'd blocked the vessel's name and home port. Tidying up and rearranging the deck. Cleaning away all the excess grime and stacking the frozen bags of shrimp they'd caught in the cargo hold.

The thirty minutes of changes made the trawler look like a different vessel.

When all the tasks had been performed and the smuggling hold was properly concealed, Heinrich returned to the helm. It'd been a long, stressful night, and the hardest part was yet to come. They'd had close calls before, but this was a new experience entirely. And he wondered how in the hell their boss planned to get them out of this one.

For a moment, the man on the other end of the phone had wondered the same thing.

He'd ended the call and stared off into space, running through everything in his mind.

He wasn't the boss. Not really. He was just the guy in charge of all pick-ups and maritime transportation within US waters. Just one link in a long chain of command. Which meant he also had someone to answer to. Barbossa, the powerful and violent leader of their operation. A man who wouldn't be too happy to learn that the latest shipment had been compromised.

Especially considering the special cargo that was supposed to have been reclaimed.

The guy's initial reaction was that it was a damn shame.

He'd organized hundreds of successful trips. Thousands of young, healthy, manipulated migrants delivered to happy customers. And millions in revenue.

And now the jig was up.

He knew that. Without a shadow of a doubt, he knew it. It'd been a good ride, but the end was near.

He immediately began making the necessary preparations. The ultimate exit strategy that would set him up for life. And ensure no trails from the operation ever led to him.

But first, they had to make it through the morning. And to do so would require immediate action on multiple fronts, so he picked up his phone and dialed number after number, calling in all favors and using every resource at his disposal to ensure they made it through unscathed.

Then, once he'd done everything he could on the damage control front, he called Barbossa to relay the bad news. And to give the notoriously vengeful crime boss the names of the locals responsible.

EIGHT

Two hours after arriving on Garden Key, I watched as my dark blue forty-eight-foot Baia Flash came tearing around the northwestern edge of the fort. The sleek speed demon raced toward where I stood at the base of the dock, my best friend manning the helm, his messy blond hair flapping in the wind and his eyes fixed on me through a pair of sunglasses.

He slowed and drifted up to the dock. Scarlett, Ange and my sixteen-year-old daughter, stood at the bow and tossed over a couple of fenders, then I tied them off.

Atticus, our energetic yellow Lab, said hi first, leaping onto the dock and jumping into me and covering me with licks. Scarlett climbed over and threw her arms around me.

"Where's Mom?" she said, worry in her voice.

I motioned toward the beach. Ange was walking toward the dock, carrying the young girl in her arms and holding the boy's hand. Scarlett ran over to them, and I patted Jack on the shoulder.

"Thanks for picking us up, Jack," I said.

"What are best friends for?" He gazed toward the beach. "Where are the others?"

"In the fort. Waiting to be taken to Key West."

He nodded, and we walked toward the beach.

"You guys sure got the islands in an uproar," he said. "I've never seen so many law enforcement boats patrolling our island home."

I was about to respond when I saw a familiar face strolling toward us from the fort.

I walked past Ange and the kids as my wife introduced them to our daughter, heading straight for Key West's Chief of Police Jane Verona.

"They find the shrimp boat?" I said when we were within earshot.

The serious, athletic Latina didn't reply right away, which was as good as a negative response.

"Based on the last update I received," she said, "the vessel is still at large."

I shook my head. "There's no way you're telling me that they didn't find that thing. A sixty-foot shrimp trawler chugging away at barely over fifteen knots into the Gulf."

"They've found dozens of them. Nearly a hundred."

"What?"

"It's May, Logan. And shrimping isn't what it used to be, sure. But the pinks are prized. Everyone knows that. And there are shrimp boats from all over the Gulf and Atlantic coast here to net them up."

I sighed. Looked around, then toward the fort's

walls. "What about the Haitians?"

"There's a bigger boat on the way," she said. "And a bus will take them to the Customs and Border Protection station in Marathon."

I fell silent. Jane looked back at me and said, "You and Ange did a good thing."

I shrugged. "We saw people in trouble and tried to help."

"Well, neither of you had to," she said. "I can't thank you enough for what you guys did."

"Maybe you can," I said, turning and gesturing toward my family and the two kids. "I'd like to sponsor them. Just for the time being."

She nodded. "I'll see what I can do. Talk to CBP. It shouldn't be a problem given the circumstances. But you'll have to swing by their office downtown so the kids can be put in the system."

"Of course."

"Their parents?"

"Their mom died in my arms. She was airlifted by the Guard."

Jane fell silent. "I'm sorry to hear that."

"Can you do me another favor?" I said. She nodded, and I added, "What's the protocol for what will happen with her body?"

She thought a moment. "Usually, in a situation like this, after a full autopsy, the body would either be sent back to the country of origin or cremated if unclaimed. From my experience, it's typically the latter."

I glanced at the kids again and shook my head. "She should be buried in Key West Cemetery. So her kids have a place to visit her."

Jane bit her lip. "There's no way I can get that approved. I'm sorry, Logan."

"We'll pay for it," I said.

She thought again, then patted me on the shoulder. "All right. I'll make sure her body's taken to the mortuary. You'll have to make further arrangements with the cemetery."

"We'll take it from there. Thanks, Jane."

She headed back to the fort, and I turned and joined my family and Jack. The eastern horizon glowed yellow and orange, then the sun rose up beyond the island, streaking brilliant, warm rays across the sky.

We helped the kids down the dock and onto the Baia. Both of them were clearly nervous about the idea of boarding another boat, but once they were below deck, their fears subsided. The Baia was far from spacious but had a comfortable interior that probably seemed like a suite aboard the *Queen Mary 2* compared to the decrepit sailboat they'd been aboard the past few days.

We dragged the Zodiac back into the water and tied it off to the Baia's stern. Cast the dock lines and motored away from the island. I cruised us west. Passed the northern tip of Loggerhead Key and continued another seven miles before returning to Monte Cristo.

Jack had brought along our two-person sit-on-top kayak. After unlashing it from the gunwale, Ange and I paddled across the shallows and back through the narrow slit in the rock. Neither of us said a word as we entered the lagoon, beached the little craft, and trekked up to our camp.

We broke apart and stowed our tent. Collapsed our camping chairs. Untied and bagged our hammock. Doused the lingering embers of our campfire. Then we lugged everything down to the kayak.

When the camp was cleared, I stepped to the edge of the cliff. Slowly. Reverently. Stopped right at the same spot I'd stopped at four hours earlier. Shielded my face from the morning sun and gazed southeast. Right where the sailboat had foundered. Then I closed my eyes and visualized the incident. The whole thing playing out in fast-forward. Then I pictured the trawler making its escape, heading due north. Vanishing. Like it'd never existed at all.

NINE

It was nearly eight in the morning by the time we'd covered the seventy miles back to Key West. There were over a dozen shrimp boats idling just outside the opening into the bight. Two Border Patrol boats and a Coast Guard patrol were making their way down the line, officers boarding the trawlers one at a time.

"Any of them look familiar?" Jack said as we motored close

"Yeah," I said. "All of them."

Most of them looked nearly identical. Roughly sixty feet long. Old and worn. Tall outriggers. Nets hanging about. Many of them had chipped, sun-bleached white paint jobs just like the one we'd seen. But some were blue and red, so we could rule them out at least.

"It was dark," Ange said. "And we didn't exactly have a lot of spare time to thoroughly examine the thing. What with our being shot at and all."

"What about the names?" Scarlett said.

"It didn't have one," I said. "Must've been covered or something."

As we neared, I watched a group of Border Patrol agents pull up to a nearby shrimp boat. It had a rich crimson-colored hull.

I turned the wheel and brought us up close to the patrol boat.

"No need to search that one," I called out. "You're looking for one with a white hull."

The agent craned his neck to look at us. He appeared to be maybe forty. Looked to match my height of six two, but probably weighed twenty pounds more than my one-ninety. Wore a ball cap and sunglasses, along with his tactical bulletproof vest.

"We're on official business," he said, waving us along. "Please keep moving."

"I'm Logan Dodge," I said as I eased us closer. "I'm the guy who called in this morning. My wife and I are the ones who engaged the group of smugglers."

The agent froze. Stared at me a moment. Then turned to the lawman beside him.

"I've been trying to get a hold of you guys," I added. "To ask for an update on the search."

"Well, we've been a little busy."

"I can see that," I said, eyeing the armada of shrimp boats.

I gave Jack the helm, then glanced over at Ange.

"I'll take care of these two," she said. "Handle whatever paperwork we need to."

I nodded and climbed up onto the sunbed.

I was tired. Worn down from the lack of sleep, the shoot-out, and the bombardment of psychological strain that comes with having a woman die in my arms with her children draped across her.

And I was tired from not hearing good news regarding the search's progress.

I read the guy's name tag, then said, "Permission to come aboard, Agent Briggs?"

"Granted," he said.

Instead of waiting for our vessels to reach each other, once close enough, I stepped on the rail and vaulted over the side. Threw myself across the five-foot gap and landed on the bow of the Border Patrol boat.

The agent just stared at me. Gave a slight shake of his head as he approached me.

"That's one way to do it," he said.

I waved to Ange and the others, then Jack piloted the Baia into Key West Bight, heading for our slip at Conch Harbor.

"You're wasting your time searching this one," I said again. "Like I told the operator at your office, it had a white hull."

"We're searching all of them. That was the order I was given."

I stepped to the port bow and stared at the line of shrimp boats. All of the vessels had their crew members topside, loafing about as they waited to be searched.

"You recognize any of the shrimpers?" the agent said.

I shook my head. "They won't still be aboard." He eyed me curiously, so I added, "It's been six hours since the incident. These trawlers might be slow, but other boats aren't. If they're not moved off, switched out with other shrimpers by now, then these guys are amateurs. And they're not amateurs."

I'd engaged them, and they weren't all dead. Which meant that they'd possessed a certain level of competency.

"You law enforcement?" he asked me, lowering his sunglasses.

"No."

"Military?"

"I spent some time in the Navy."

"Doing what?"

"We're wasting time," I said, then motioned toward a boat two vessels down. "I'm gonna search that one."

I climbed onto the nearest shrimp boat, then strode across its deck and made my way to the white-hulled vessel. The agent followed right behind me.

We reached the white one, and I was on it all of thirty seconds before I ruled it out as well.

"Not this one," I said.

The drain hole along the starboard side was a slightly different shape and size from the one I'd held onto while shooting the first criminal. There were certain things that could be changed relatively quickly. And, again, given that they weren't amateurs, I operated under the assumption that all those changes would be made. But major changes to the metal gunwale weren't on the list, even if it were possible in such a short amount of time. It was a subtle thing most would overlook.

The second white-hulled shrimp boat had a drain hole just like the one I'd boarded. But as I stepped toward the pilothouse, I stopped again. The door was on the wrong side. I remembered that clearly, too. A simple task when someone barges out, shotgun raised, and opens fire at you from inside it.

The third white one was the most promising. Same drain hole, same door position. It looked similar to the one I'd boarded, though most of the equipment was oriented differently.

Like most of the trawlers we'd searched, its cargo hold was packed with forty-pound bags of frozen shrimp. Mountains of the clearly recently caught crustaceans stacked over eight feet high. Though it was promising, after nearly an hour of searching, we realized that there was nothing and no one suspicious aboard. There seemed to be no place where you could hide a single person without us having found them, let alone multiple.

We finished searching the final white-hulled boat thirty minutes later. Standing aboard the vessel, I turned to Agent Briggs. "These are all the shrimp boats that were nearby?"

He shook his head. "There are more congregated over in Safe Harbor on Stock. Another team has been searching all morning. Hasn't found anything yet." He sighed. "You should go home, Mr. Dodge. You've done enough. We'll handle this. We're trained to handle this."

I thought over his words for about two seconds. Then I turned and stared east.

"We should head over to Safe Harbor," I said. "I know you guys are trained for this, and trained well. But I stood on this boat. I have the best chance at identifying it."

The agent eyed me a moment, then said, "You don't stop, do you?"

I didn't reply. Just held my gaze east.

The agent nodded. Fired up the engines and blasted us around Key West, heading for Stock Island.

TEN

We were at it all day, the sun sinking into the western horizon by the time we finished up the final search. Shrimp boats had been funneling in and out of Safe Harbor since the early morning. I stood at the bow of the final vessel to be searched. Looked down the line of the two dozen other gathered vessels, watching as they headed back out to open water.

Then I faced west and watched the sun as it hid behind the wall of mangroves, its brilliant beams poking through and streaking across the evening sky. It'd been a long day. An early morning, a tumultuous first couple of hours, and a whole lot of waiting and searching and disappointment after.

I checked my phone. Saw two messages from Ange, asking me how it was going and letting me know she had a grouper dinner prepared. I replied that I'd be on my way home soon, then approached Agent Briggs.

He'd been in contact with agents up along the Gulf and Atlantic Coasts all day. Checking in and inquiring if anything suspicious had been discovered. Hoping for good news.

None had come. There'd been no sign of smuggled aliens aboard any of the trawlers searched.

We stood beside each other in silence a moment, then he said, "You all right?"

I nodded.

"You look like there's something on your mind," he added.

I nodded again. There was something on my mind. But not something I was going to share with someone I'd just met. I needed to voice my thoughts to my wife. I needed the ear and mind and opinion of the one I trusted most.

"Only frustration," I said.

Not a lie. Just an omission of the full truth.

"I know the feeling," Briggs said. "You get used to it, unfortunately. Been at this job for twelve years. There's a lot of sea and we're always short-manned."

"You guys finished?" a crusty, white-bearded shrimp captain who looked to be in his seventies said. "'Cause we've got a long night ahead. Long couple nights."

Briggs thanked the mariner for his compliance. Then we climbed over to the Border Patrol boat and motored in silence back out of Safe Harbor, cruised west for five miles, then cut north past Fort Zachary Taylor. We cut between the cruise piers and Sunset Key, then skirted along Mallory Square. We'd just missed the famous sunset celebration, but the downtown party scene was just warming up, with flocks of tourists and locals alike filling the promenades, enjoying a meal or drinks, and marveling at the various street performers.

As we motored around the breakwater into Key West Bight, I turned to Briggs.

"I know you don't have to, but I hope you'll keep me in the loop," I said.

"Of course," he said, keeping his eyes forward. They eased up to the end of Conch Harbor Marina's longest dock and dropped me off. "And, Logan," Briggs said after I hopped off. "You did good today. You and your wife."

I nodded, then turned and strode down the planks. Past Jack's Sea Ray at slip forty-seven, and then the Baia at twenty-four. Our twenty-foot Robalo center-console was tied off to the dock beside it, Jack having borrowed it for a couple days. I waved to a few familiar faces, then passed the marina office and slipped out the gate to the harbor walk.

A block inland, I caught a whiff from a corner pizza joint and realized I hadn't eaten anything all day. I bought two slices of pepperoni and devoured them on the move. I debated calling Ange or getting a cab but decided that I needed the alone time. I needed quiet and solitude. Space and stillness for my thoughts to form and to try and make sense of everything that'd happened.

Earlier that day, I'd tried to get ahold of Elliot "Murph" Murphy, a notorious hacker and old friend. He was my go-to guy when it came to online intel gathering, and I hoped he'd be able to get some insight on human smuggling operations off the coast of Florida. Hopefully some involving shrimp boats.

But I'd yet to hear back from the busy tech wizard.

I'd also yet to hear back from Homeland Security agent Darius Maddox, another good friend who I'd worked alongside many times before. Since one of Homeland's key responsibilities was border protection, I knew he'd be able to help.

Hearing nothing back was frustrating, but it also gave me time to formulate my own conclusions and make my own estimations. To organize my thoughts into something resembling coherence.

I reached our driveway just before nine. A seashell lot spilling out onto Palmetto Street situated on the fringes of New Town. I walked the drive slowly, the shells crunching beneath the soles of my shoes.

Our property was flanked by palm trees and cocoplum bushes. The living room lights were on in our gray stilted house, washing warm light over our wraparound porch. The side door opened before I reached the stairs, and Atticus came running out. He tore down the steps and jumped into me. Tail wagging like mad. I dropped and hugged him. Patted his head and looked up as Ange appeared.

My beautiful wife was wearing gray lounge shorts and a white tank top. She met me halfway up the stairs and leaned into me slowly, head right into my chest, arms wrapped tight around me.

"No news is bad news," she sighed.

I squeezed her tighter. Kissed her cheek.

"You all right?" she said.

The second time I'd been asked that question in one evening.

I gave her the truthful answer. "Infuriated. And I…" I glanced up toward the house. "How are they?"

She loosened her grip on me. "Asleep. Both of them have been out for a couple hours now."

"I'm sure they need it. They talking at all?"

"A little." She gestured inside. "Come on. Have some dinner and relax a bit. Then we'll talk."

Ange warmed up a plate of grouper, broccoli, and Spanish rice. I'd scarfed down the two slices of pizza on the stroll over but was still plenty hungry enough to clean up the plate. It was delicious, but I barely tasted it. My mind was elsewhere.

Scarlett stepped out in pajamas, then sat across from me as I finished eating.

"Excluding the incident today, did you guys have a good time celebrating your anniversary?" she said. She was like her mother in many ways, and one of them was her inherent ability to see and focus on the positive.

"Yesterday was amazing, Scar," I said, clasping Ange's hand in mine. "One of the best days of my life." I smiled and kissed my wife. Turned back to our daughter and asked, "How's school? You finish that essay on Sam Houston?"

She nodded. "Yeah. And it feels like cruise control."

There was only a week left, but I didn't mention that. Usually, the end of the school year and the beginning of summer vacation are a cause for celebration, the most exciting and monumental and sacredly cherished day of the year for school-aged kids. At least, it sure always was for me.

But the end of the school year was bittersweet for Scarlett. Her longtime boyfriend, Cameron Tyson, was graduating. A highly recruited quarterback, he'd gotten a full-ride athletic scholarship to the University of Florida and would be heading to Gainesville to begin summer training camps the day after graduation.

As if that weren't bad enough for her, Isaac, Jack's nephew, was also finishing online college courses and heading even farther away to the Georgia Institute of Technology to wrap up the final year of an accelerated degree program. The bright teenager had been skipping grades since kindergarten and had a special knack for computer programming.

Scarlett's boyfriend and one of her closest friends, both leaving around the same time.

But she was handling it well, and she'd already found new ways to keep herself busy over the summer. She'd be running cross-country in the fall, and she was working with me, Ange, and the coach on an intense training regimen. And she'd volunteered to work a couple days a week for Reef Relief, spending time out on the water helping to restore our underwater world. And she'd also agreed to work off and on at the Turtle Hospital in Marathon as needed. On top of that, Ange had plans for some international travel this summer, her eyes particularly set on Europe.

Scarlett glanced down the hall toward our study. "How long are they going to stay here?"

Ange and I exchanged glances. I finished the final bite and wiped my lips with a napkin. "I don't know. This is gonna be hard for all of us. But it's the right thing."

Our daughter smiled. "Oh, I don't mind them. It's nice having them here, and they can stay as long as they want as far as I'm concerned. I know what it's like not to have a home." She paused and added, "I just hope they warm up to us at some point."

After dinner, I headed down the hall. Our home had three bedrooms. Scarlett's bedroom and our master room. And we'd added the third to be used as our library and study, and Ange had the space cleared and an inflatable mattress and blankets and pillows set up for the two children. They were curled up together. Nestled close, their faces relaxed. Their little stomachs bobbing up and down. An old teddy bear Jack had scrounged up from the marina attic tucked under the young boy's arm.

I couldn't stare at them for long. The emotions stirring within me were too powerful.

I left the door cracked. Turned and stared off into space a moment. Scarlett kissed my cheek and headed off to bed. Ange and I settled into our wicker couch on the back balcony. The backyard was my favorite part of the house. The lush lawn leading right up to a waterway that fed east out into Cow Key Channel. There was a boathouse where our twenty-foot Robalo was typically stored, the convenient proximity allowing us to walk barefoot from our house and motor anywhere in the Lower Keys in no time.

"It's a sixty-foot, eighty-ton shrimp trawler," I said. "How does a boat like that just disappear?"

She didn't answer. Let my question linger there in the ether.

"A boat and a crew that'd evidently had a lot of practice and experience with evasion," I added.

She nodded. It was a key component to anything resembling a logical explanation.

"Something's off here," I said, shaking my head. "Something big." Then I turned and looked my wife in the eyes. "Operation like this, they must be getting help."

"The CBP agents?" she said.

"Maybe. Or someone else. I'm getting the feeling this thing's been going on for a while. It seems to run like a well-oiled machine." I ran a hand through my hair and leaned back. "How else could a boat like that just disappear?"

Ange let out a deep breath. "And disappear with a group of migrants hidden aboard."

I reached into my pocket and pulled out the picture Rosalind had given me moments before her death. Stared at the creased, damaged photograph. Four smiling faces. Two who were asleep in our house. One who was dead. The wife and mother. The woman who'd died in my arms.

One of the most emotionally charged moments of my life.

And the fourth person in the picture. A man who I'd seen bleeding and unconscious on the shrimp boat. Dead too at worst. Imprisoned somewhere at best.

I thought about the people we'd saved, and their emotional landing on the beach on Garden Key. The American beach. How they'd been overwhelmed with excitement. I thought about how we should wake every day with that joy. That level of gratitude. The fights and struggles and wars and blood our ancestors had shed so that we could have the life and the world we have today. The comforts. The freedoms. The opportunities. All of the incredibly good things we have to enjoy and that have been earned by our ancestors' countless sacrifices.

Then I thought about the people we hadn't been able to save. The ones who were imprisoned somewhere at that very moment. I also thought about the thousands that'd likely already been smuggled by the operation, and the countless more that would become their victims if they weren't stopped.

The anger and frustrations all culminated in a powerful resolution. Wherever the shrimp boat had escaped to and whoever had helped them do it, I'd figure it out. As sure as the sun set in the west, I'd get to the bottom of it all and I'd make everyone involved pay.

ELEVEN

Later that night, the two surviving shrimpers idled side by side in front of a fenced compound ten miles south of Miami. It was dark and quiet. No movement nearby aside from a wandering cat and palm leaves swaying in the ocean breeze.

They waited there. Patiently. Anxiously.

After being ferried to shore via a brand-new, blazingly fast fishing boat, Heinrich and Dennis had driven the hundred miles up out of the Florida Keys and into the mainland of South Florida. They'd taken different vehicles and left at different times.

If their boss was anything, he was cautious. They'd had their share of troubles in the past. Close scrapes and near tragedies. But this was something entirely different. This was a catastrophic failure. The kind of incident that would make serious waves and make the news. A story that would garner loads of interest from the public and spread fast and put the entire operation at risk.

And so they were in damage control mode.

They waited there until a man dressed in black pushed open a nearby gate and emerged from the shadows behind it. He waited there briefly, then the two shrimpers stepped out of their vehicles in unison and headed through the gate.

The man shut it behind them without a word.

They were led past rows of trailers and boats and heavy machinery to a warehouse wedged between a small shipping facility and a commercial fishing marina. It was relatively small compared to the structures on the flanking properties. A lone building that had once been used for boat maintenance with a dock and a pair of monster-sized overhead doors in front where vessels used to chug right in in order to be serviced.

The two men headed inside, led by Captain Heinrich, and were met by three armed criminals who stood with their arms crossed, eyeing the shrimpers. One of them was tall, with a shaved head. He had a tattoo around his right eye and wore sunglasses, even though it was dim in the warehouse.

He was the distributor. A man Heinrich knew only as Kane.

No words were spoken for a solid thirty seconds.

"That was a close call," Heinrich said.

Kane remained stoic. "You could say that again."

"At least we managed to save some of the cargo."

The man nodded.

Heinrich swallowed. Scratched his beard. "How upset was the boss when you talked to him?"

"He was stern. But no more so than usual. He said we'll brush this off. Continue with business as usual in a week or two when this thing dies down."

Heinrich nodded. Let out a long, relieved breath. Blinked and felt a little better.

A voice crackled through a radio in Kane's right hand. He replied in Spanish, then nodded to one of his men in the corner. They pressed a button, and one of the big overhead doors rattled up into the ceiling, revealing a rectangular view of the heart of Biscayne Bay. The shrimp boat had made the voyage north and chugged right into the pen.

Heinrich and Dennis helped tie off the trawler, its big engines weakening and then shutting off entirely. Once its stern was clear, the overhead door rattled back down where it'd been, completely shielding them and their work from the outside world.

Heinrich and Dennis boarded the vessel. Met with the interim crew down in the cargo hold as they were heaving forty-pound bags of frozen shrimp off a spread of wooden pallets. They focused on the northeast corner, the spot farthest from the stairwell where the tallest pile of shrimp had been.

They removed the mountain, then grabbed and pulled away four of the pallets, revealing a deck coated in a thin layer of mud. Heinrich dropped to his knees. Placed his hand on the far-right edge and slid it along a barely noticeable seam. A tiny sliver between the sheets of metal. Nothing unusual. Nothing that would catch anyone's eyes.

He ran his fingers forward until he felt a slight deviation. It was subtle and coated in dirt and mud. He brushed away the grime to reveal a tiny metal latch. It was perfectly flush and barely the size of a dime. Something you'd only notice if you happened to get down on your hands and knees and clean and inspect from less than a couple feet away that minuscule section of deck in the entirety of the shrimp-laden cargo hold.

Heinrich cleaned away more mud and pried up the latch using the nail of his index finger. It was small but made of solid titanium. Once the loop was free, he curled his index and middle fingers under it and pulled. Heaved up a three-by-three-foot section of deck. Once there was enough separation, he dug his entire left hand under the hatch, then his right, then he muscled the metal plate up. Its hinges were mounted on the underside and completely hidden from view from above.

Dennis clicked on a flashlight and shined it inside, the beams revealing nine bound and terrified young migrants. Heinrich aimed his pistol at the group. Ordered everyone out. It took five minutes to get them all out of the cargo hold, up the two sets of steps to the main deck, across the gangplank, and into a seated cluster on the warehouse floor.

As with every shipment, inventory had been taken during the cruise over. The information had been relayed to their various buyers, and distribution decisions had been made.

Kane made a quick call, then stepped toward the nine Haitians. They were all tired and shaking. Hands secured behind their backs with duct tape.

"There's no need to be scared," he said, his words calm and friendly. "Your journey is over. You're on US soil, and you're safe now."

Kneeling beside the nearest Haitian, he slid out a knife and sliced the tape securing the woman's wrists.

Then the rest of the migrants were freed, and bottles of Powerade were brought in and dispersed.

"You must be thirsty after your long voyage," he added.

Many of the criminals involved in the organization, including Kane, knew the nature of the business and the trip the Haitians had just taken. Most of them had embarked upon the same trips themselves. He knew the terrified people in front of him had been thirsty long before they'd been fished out of the sea. Long before the tedious journey north in the hot, dark, cramped trawler's hidden cargo hold.

Seeing the suspicions in the migrants' eyes, Kane uncapped a bottle and took a long pull. Wiped his chin and let out a satisfied gasp. Then one of the Haitians joined in. Then two more. Pretty soon they were all drinking and relishing the beverages. Quenching their thirst. All of them except Leon.

He stared back at Kane, defiance in his eyes.

"That's Leon," Heinrich said. "He gave us some trouble."

Kane smiled. Strolled over. Raised a pistol and aimed it at the captive's head.

"Time to drink up, Leon," he said. "Or I'll blow your brains all over this floor."

Leon stared fiercely back at the man, then relented. Uncapped his Powerade and downed its contents.

Kane looked around the group. Every one of the migrants had drained their bottles dry.

He smiled.

Thirty seconds later, the first Haitian's eyes closed, and then she curled up asleep on the floor. Within a minute, every one of them had passed out, lying motionless on their backs or their sides. The empty bottles were cleared away, then the nine prisoners' wrists were all taped again.

Kane slid out his phone. Gave a quick order. A minute later, an overhead door on the western side of the warehouse opened, and a box truck rumbled into view. It backed in and braked to a stop ten feet from the group of unconscious Haitians.

Two men got out. A big musclehead. And a lean average-height guy with a short black mohawk and a gray polo shirt. Neither of them spoke at first. They strode right up to the group of prisoners. Then the smaller one held up his phone and read a message.

"Payments for seven for prostitution, two for labor, and one for organ harvesting." He motioned to the big guy, who slid a plastic grocery bag filled with stacks of bills off his shoulder and held it out.

The smugglers didn't need to count it. They had a long and successful working relationship. Besides, the buyers knew what would happen if they were caught trying to screw them over. And it was a fate they feared far more than any capital punishment the judicial system could dish out.

"There are only nine," Heinrich said.

He pointed his finger at each of the migrants as he counted them for what felt like the hundredth time. Just making sure. It'd been a long damn night after all.

Kane leaned over and whispered something to the mohawk guy. The buyer just nodded. Checked the screen of his phone again, then said, "My mistake." He gestured toward the bag of cash. "You keep the extra. Call it thanks for years of cooperation."

They loaded the prisoners up into the truck. It was mostly filled with boxed refrigerators, the two-hundred-pound appliances packed solid. The buyers muscled and slid two of the fridges out of position, revealing a dark hollow space behind them.

The sleeping Haitians were dragged through the opening and dropped in the hidden space. There was plenty of extra room. They'd been expecting significantly more prisoners.

Once all of the migrants were inside, the appliances were repositioned, the door was rattled shut and locked, and the two buyers climbed back into the box truck and drove out without a word.

The warehouse went silent. Kane opened the grocery bag and divvied the cash, handed Heinrich and Dennis a wad each.

"I was worried," Heinrich said.

"Mistakes happen. The boss understands."

"I thought he'd fire us for sure."

"Boss wouldn't do that."

Heinrich and Dennis flipped through the cash in their hands.

"Don't blow it all," Kane said. "You'll need it to last a couple weeks. We'll be in touch."

Heinrich nodded and the two shrimpers turned around. They both took one step for the door, then the man dressed all in black who'd opened the gate for them raised the Desert Eagle in his right hand. Without a word, he took aim and blasted a round into the side of Dennis's skull. The man shook and toppled over and smacked into the warehouse floor.

Heinrich cursed and threw his hands over his ears and dropped into a crouch while spinning around.

Eyes wide and mouth agape, he gazed up at the man's pistol, its smoking barrel aimed right at him.

The space fell silent again following the thunderous report.

Kane strode forward and stared at the corpse for a moment. A cold, unaffected look.

He pulled out his phone and sent a quick message. Twenty seconds later, the western overhead door opened again. The box truck reappeared and backed up ten feet from the corpse. The buyers climbed back out. Strode over. Kane motioned toward the dead body.

"One for organ harvesting," he said.

Kane smiled and let out a chuckle as the corpse was zipped into a body bag, heaved into an industrial cooler, locked and rolled up into the truck to be stowed with the others. The door rattled down and locked again, and the box truck drove off.

Captain Heinrich was still on his knees. His eyes immense. His mouth hung open.

He hadn't uttered a sound. He was shell-shocked. In utter disbelief at what he'd just witnessed.

Kane strode over casually. Leaned down and grabbed Dennis's stack of cash. Dropped it back in the plastic bag with the others, then glared at Heinrich.

"Mistakes happen," Kane said. "The boss understands." The smuggler withdrew his own pistol and crouched down. Aimed the barrel right at Heinrich's head. "But he wanted me to make something unequivocally clear. You make one more mistake, and this will be your blood puddled on the floor."

TWELVE

I awoke naturally just after five. Turned onto my side and grabbed my phone from the nightstand and angled the screen toward me. There were no new messages. No missed calls. Just a happy picture of Ange and Scarlett smiling back at me while relaxing on the beach at Bahia Honda State Park.

Ange was still asleep, so I rolled out of bed slowly. Pushed the sliding door open a crack and exited sideways. Stole a long glance at my sleeping wife, then nudged it shut.

I stepped to the railing. Stretched and gazed out. Flashed back to the previous morning, when I'd done the same thing, awoken by a noise and fumbling out of the tent and eventually making my way to the top of the cliff. There was no sinking vessel this time. Just the narrow, dredged channel and our boathouse. Dew on the grass twinkling in the moonlight.

The cool air felt good. And I stood there a moment, eyes closed. Breathing in and out slowly.

After a quick meditation, I downed two glasses of water, then laced up my shoes and went for a run. Atticus came with, my Lab jumping up and down when I asked if he wanted to come. It was heads or tails with Atty and my morning runs. Sometimes he felt up for it, other times not, but this morning he was about as excited as I've ever seen him.

We did one of our usual routes, heading south to the waterfront and then west, eventually passing the southernmost buoy and continuing down Whitehead. Breezing by the lighthouse and Hemingway's old residence. We cut onto Duval and I picked up our pace when we hit Buffet's famous Margaritaville restaurant, then on past Sloppy Joe's and then to the waterfront.

The place was quiet and still. I once read that Key West was a city that woke up like a cat after a nap. Slow and leisurely, and then alive and energetic. But it hadn't woken up yet. It was still in that brief period of time between the night owls out on the town, and the early risers getting up to clean and restock and keep the whole place running.

I expected to see Cameron while jogging along the boardwalk to Mallory Square. He and I had been working out together for a while now. After an unfortunate and heated interaction had led to a fight at a traffic light, I'd intervened and protected him from a potential beating, and he'd asked me to show him some moves. So, we trained and sparred. Ran and worked out. And though we usually planned our sessions ahead of time, we often ran into each other in the early hours. But he wasn't there.

I kicked us into a higher gear as we finished the

downtown route and looped back home, covering the final miles as quickly as I could and returning to our driveway coated in sweat.

My heart pounded as I reached the backyard and fell onto the damp grass. Atticus plopped down beside me, and we lay there and caught our breath as the early dawn glowed.

I eventually rolled onto my side and rose. Used a nearby hose to fill Atticus's water bowl. He collapsed right beside it, his face falling into the dish and his tongue licking up big gulps of fluid.

I went right into a set of pull-ups and Indian club mobility movements and kettlebell swings in the makeshift gym under our house, and then beat the living tar out of our heavy bag. The pounding it received could often be directly correlated to the level of frustration brewing deep within me.

As Ange had pointed out, we'd saved many the previous day. And we'd taken down a couple vile men and brought attention to a serious issue taking place right under our noses in our paradise.

But we hadn't saved everyone.

And the criminal smugglers had gotten away somehow. Not in some sleek, expensive, modern craft, or some go-fast boat, or a narco submersible of some kind, but a big, sluggish shrimp boat. Some of the most advanced military and government organizations in the world were actively scouring the area, and yet the trawler had somehow slipped through the cracks.

And the fact didn't sit well.

As I struck my fists into the bag again and again, my mind flashed images from the previous day. I pictured the brief standoff on the shrimp boat's deck, and the criminal tossing the two-year-old girl into the sea. Wondered what sort of human being could behave like that.

Breathing heavily, I stopped a moment and checked my phone again. Nothing.

I stepped back to the bag and pounded it with a final barrage before collapsing to the ground with my back against one of the stilts. My upper body hunched over and my chest heaved up and down. Utterly exhausted.

Atticus stepped over. Brushed up against me and licked my face.

"I'm all right, boy," I said, petting behind his ears. "I'm all right." I said it a second time, though I didn't believe it.

The truth was I was anything but all right. I wanted to break loose and crack skulls, but I didn't know where to go. I felt like a marksman without a target to shoot.

Shoving my frustration aside, I headed upstairs. Whipped up a blueberry, banana, and acai smoothie using coconut water as the base. Enjoyed it on the balcony, then showered and cooked stone crab and avocado omelets for breakfast. Brewed a big pot of coffee.

Scarlett arrived first, beckoned by the smell of the sizzling melted butter mixed with chives and parsley.

"How long you been up?" she said, rubbing her eyes. She was wearing purple pajama bottoms and a Beach Boys T-shirt.

"Too long," I replied.

I served up the omelets with slices of toast from

Old Town Bakery, Ange arriving as I plated the food.

We ate breakfast out on the balcony. Before digging in, I checked on the kids. They were still asleep, snuggled up together in the study with the old teddy bear still nestled against them. They looked like they hadn't moved at all since the night before.

After breakfast, I checked on them again. They still hadn't moved.

I tried my best to put myself in their shoes. They were in a strange house in a strange land. No familiar faces. Nothing resembling the life and the world they'd left behind. And they were in an adult house, with nothing for children aside from the teddy bear in their arms.

Still having heard nothing back regarding the prior day's incident and the whereabouts of the shrimp boat, I swiped my keys from the counter and headed for the door.

"I'll be right back," I said.

Ange took a sip of coffee, then asked, "Where are you going?"

"Just got a quick errand to run. I'll be back in thirty."

"Could you pick up some diapers?" she said. "We'll need those. And wipes. And baby soap. And baby formula and milk. We can get clothes for them later."

I ran a hand through my hair. "Could you message me a list?"

She smiled and kissed me on the cheek.

I climbed into my Tacoma. Fired up the V-6 and cruised north and east two miles to the Key Plaza Shopping Center. New Town Key West is an incredible contrast with Old Town. It was like they were on different islands entirely. One side old and weathered and classic, the other big and shiny and commercial. Like the big-name chain stores had charged as deep as they could into the island paradise.

I swung by the Winn-Dixie and picked up everything Ange had messaged me to buy, then pulled into the Home Depot. Parked at the outdoor garden center and relished the aromas of all the flowers and greenery as I made for the interior doors. They parted open, blasting me with a wave of cool air carrying the smells of power tools and fresh lumber.

I grabbed a flat cart and navigated the colossal assemblage of home improvement products. I'd spent a good deal of time there over the years, so I knew where I was heading. Found what I was looking for two rows over and three-quarters of a row down. Scanned the selection a moment, then found one I liked and heaved it onto the cart and rolled it to the register.

Ten minutes later, I was back at the house. Folding down the tailgate and sliding and heaving that same big box out of my truck and carrying it under our home. I leaned it against a stilt, then wheeled out and set up two big umbrellas in the yard, along with a portable workstation. I didn't have an impressive collection of tools by any means, but I had enough. Ange, Scarlett, and I had helped out with portions of our new house, so I had some essentials.

Tearing into the tape securing the cardboard with a box cutter, I removed all the pieces and put them in a neat arrangement on the shaded grass.

Ange arrived with lemonade ten minutes later. She

angled her head to see the image of the product taped to the box's exterior, then smiled.

"Gotta say, that's not what I was expecting."

I kissed her forehead and thanked her for the lemonade. "Woman like you, I gotta keep you on your toes."

I wiped a bead of sweat from my brow and glanced upstairs. "They're still asleep?"

She nodded. "Need any help?"

I accepted her offer and we went to work. We had the playground set up in just over two hours. It was a simple two-story wooden number, with ladders and monkey bars, a slide, and a little rock-climbing wall. Seemed smaller than I'd expected, but I figured it would suit the two little ones perfectly.

We headed upstairs to check on them. They were still fast asleep, and it didn't look like they'd stir anytime soon. They clearly needed rest after all they'd been through, but a new, chilling explanation entered my mind. That there was no doubt a part of them that didn't relish the idea of waking up. Like their new reality following the loss of their mother had become a nightmare they couldn't bear to return to.

As I moved into the kitchen to make some lunch, my phone buzzed in my pocket.

A call from an unknown number.

I answered, and a familiar voice came through the tiny speaker.

"Sorry for taking so long to get back to you, Logan," Murph said. "I'm on GMT plus five, and it's been a long couple of days."

"I know the feeling," I said, then Ange followed

me out to the balcony. "You able to find anything?"

"Is Ange there?"

I dropped into a wicker chair. Ange sat beside me and scooted her chair closer. I clicked my phone on speaker and set it on my armrest.

"I'm here, Murph," she said.

"All right, based on the information you provided, we can draw a couple major conclusions. First off, it's obvious that the men aboard the shrimp boat you guys encountered were professional smugglers. This was a planned meeting between the two vessels. The smugglers must've been informed of the migrants' position, which means that there was likely a professional smuggler aboard the sailboat as well."

Murph coughed, then added, "This sort of thing has been an ongoing problem for a while now. Generally, operations like this charge desperate foreigners for passage into the United States via land routes. The Darién Gap and then up all the way to the southern border. But the sea route is often utilized as well. It's a great business for the smugglers, and the vile men who run their operations."

"Because they get paid beforehand," Ange said. "So, they make money whether their clients make it to the States or not."

"Exactly," Murph said. "And, as you two witnessed, the smugglers clearly don't waste money on seaworthy vessels because there's always a decent chance that they'll be caught by a patrol."

There was a short pause, then Ange said, "One thing I'm trying to understand, Murph. If these criminals don't have anything to gain by delivering on their promises, why was the shrimp boat there to pick them up? Why not just let the boat sink or drift into an island somewhere and forget about them?"

Murph sighed. "That's where this thing really gets evil." He cleared his throat and added, "I may have stumbled into the Department of Homeland Security's classified records database. There I discovered a report of a beautiful young Haitian woman who hired professional smugglers last year. She paid the fee, did everything she was told to do, and was successfully snuck into the States. Then the smugglers had her record a message and send it home to all her friends and family, letting them know she was safe and happy in America. That she was thriving. And she pleaded with all of them to do as she'd done and give themselves opportunities they'd never dreamed of. She was well dressed in the video. Designer clothes. Showered and wearing makeup and lipstick. And she had an expensive purse in her lap and a pool behind her."

"Propaganda at its finest," I said.

"Of course... she was never heard from again after that. Vanished into the black-market human trafficking machine."

We all went silent at that.

"So, let me get this straight," Ange said, "these desperate foreigners pay to board these old, rickety boats. Many of them don't make the passage. Many of them die or are taken in by patrols. Then, the ones who do make it are smuggled into the US and sold into various forms of slavery?"

"That's pretty much it, yeah," Murph said. "Multiple sources of profits. They win regardless, but they win big when they get their victims into the country. Especially when it's big groups and when multiple migrant boats arrive at the same time."

A discomforting thought entered my mind for the first time. Maybe the sailboat hadn't been the only vessel the trawler had rendezvoused with that evening. Maybe there'd already been dozens of foreigners stowed away in their cargo hold.

At face value, it'd been one of the vilest operations I'd ever encountered. Hearing about the nuts and bolts of it somehow made the whole thing even worse. Inhuman beyond imagination. Corruption and greed and utter depravity, and nothing more. Pure evil.

"What should we do, Murph?" I asked. "Where should we start?"

He sighed. "It's tricky because, based on what I've read, these operations are frustratingly liquid. The key players don't change much, the ones running things, but the ones on the ground doing the actual smuggling are constantly replenished. This makes it hard to get a foothold on their operations. And they're constantly shifting and evolving. Changing with the times and adapting. Always trying to keep one step ahead. And these Haitian crime lords running these operations have some key assets at their disposal."

"Money?"

"That, but even more so, manpower. There's no shortage of desperate young men looking to make quick, good money. So, they've got an endless supply of eager and energetic young soldiers. And they can dispose of and replace all of them with ease if things go south. No skin off their noses."

He went quiet again. Neither Ange nor I said

anything, both of us sensing that the genius was working something out and wanting to give him space to do it.

"You asked where to start," he finally said, "and I think the focus should be on shrimpers. Many of the traffickers are likely disposable, but they must have at least some locals involved. Boat captains and crews. People who know the vessels inside and out, and know the waters, and know the protocols and methods Coast Guard and Border Patrol agents utilize. The first phase of the con doesn't require any particular skills, but sneaking migrants into the States via shrimp boats sure as hell does. There's no way an operation like this could function successfully without knowledgeable mariners. And, whoever these people are, they're making a lot. Caught transporting an illegal immigrant for profit? You're facing at least a couple years in prison if you're lucky and have a phenomenal lawyer. But more likely with something on this scale it would be closer to ten years. So, they must be getting a substantial cut of the profits to make the risk worthwhile."

He cleared his throat again. "So, if I were looking to track these criminals down, I'd find someone who's really plugged into the shrimping community down there. Someone who knows everyone. People talk. Rumors often contain a shred of truth. Things spread around. Start asking all sorts of questions and you might figure things out. And you might hit some trip wires. And your questions might make some people uneasy. And they might just try and do something about it."

"I like the sound of that," Ange said.

I smiled. When and if they did something about it, we'd do something of our own in response. And then we'd have them. Members of the criminal group at our mercy. Then the real, truthful answers would likely follow.

I thought over Murph's words. A local who was plugged in. A mariner. Someone who knew everyone.

I happened to know just the guy.

THIRTEEN

At a quarter past eleven, I pulled into the parking lot of Salty Pete's Bar, Grill, and Museum. The lot was nearly empty, but I parked in the back corner, knowing it wouldn't be that way for long and wanting to give patrons the prime selection.

Atticus came with, never one to turn down a car ride, and trotted over to his favorite spot in the shade of a gumbo-limbo tree beside the establishment's front door. I filled a water bowl and petted his head, then strode for the door.

The familiar sound of a bell greeted me as I stepped inside. The main dining area had booths at the sides and tables in the middle. The entire place's walls were covered with photographs, many of them black-and-white, the images accompanied by various maritime memorabilia the proprietor had collected over the years.

Mia, the head waitress, was positioning chairs and

setting out ketchup bottles and napkin holders when I arrived. I expected the young, dark-haired woman to point me upstairs. Pete could often be found up there tinkering with one artifact or another, or lounging in his small corner office. But Mia pointed instead to the back left corner of the dining room, where a short hall led to the bathrooms, a utility closet, and an emergency exit.

"He's back there," she said with her usual happy smile.

A splash filled the air, followed by a thud, then a loud grunt. Then a parrot came flying into view, gaining altitude as he entered the vaulted space and settling on the corner of the upper rail of the stairs. Tiko, Pete's colorful and easily excitable pet bird, cocked his head and eyed me curiously.

"Follow the chaos," Mia added with a chuckle.

I smiled and thought that could be a decent name for a heavy metal band. I followed it, the commotion getting louder with every step. The hallway's walls were lined with more images and relics—pieces of history from throughout the island chain. I'd spent my share of time standing there on packed nights, waiting on the can. Ogling at the spread of history on the walls.

The place was like a window into the island's past. A wealth of archives and, as Pete often reminded us, surprises. It was literally built from the remnants of bygone eras. Furniture from some of the oldest restaurants on the island. Stairs built from the timbers of a wrecked English merchant ship. Floorboards salvaged from a long-ago-torn-down house that'd once been owned by Pardon C. Greene, one of the island's founding fathers.

When I neared the end of the hall, I saw a pair of rubber boots and tanned, scarred legs poking out of the door leading into the men's room.

"How's that?" Pete said, calling out toward the propped-open emergency exit door.

There was a length of thick hose snaking out and around the corner. Leading beyond my line of sight.

"Try it again," a voice called. "We're making progress."

Pete grunted. I stopped. Waited. Didn't want to interfere with their work.

I heard the twist of a creaky knob. The hiss of water. The hose expanding. Then another hiss and a grunt.

"All right, you're good," the voice called.

But Pete kept on twisting.

"You're good, Pete!" the man yelled.

Seeing Pete still hadn't heard him, I leaned around the corner and repeated the man's words.

Pete was wearing a torn-up yellow raincoat that was probably older than I was, along with two surgical face masks and rubber gloves. He had a bucket beside him and an open toolbox and was curled up under the sink. The place was a mess and filled with an inch of standing water. And it reeked so bad, I fell into full retreat after delivering the message. Backtracking all the way to the end of the hall before finding clean air again.

I caught my breath and coughed. Gagged a little, then looked up at Tiko the parrot.

"Now I understand your enthusiasm," I said.

Pete crawled out of the bathroom and stood. The

seventy-year-old owner turned and gazed at me with big, wild eyes. He said something I couldn't hear to the plumber, then stepped toward me and removed his masks.

"I can come back," I said.

"He doesn't need me anymore," Pete bellowed. "I already saved the day, right, Timmy?"

"More like flooded the day," the man replied, striding around the corner. He was in his fifties. Dressed in gray coveralls and had a belly that was even bigger than Pete's.

"Well, the floods would've never happened if you'd done your job right the first time," Pete jabbed back. "I can't believe I'm the one paying you for this experience."

Tim chuckled, then shook his head. "You're the owner of a restaurant that's gonna open in fifteen minutes. You really want to piss off your plumber?"

"What, you gonna lose your last loyal client on the island?" Pete joked. Then he patted the man on the back. "All right, that was the last one." He gestured to the floor and bathroom. "Can we get it revived in time?"

"I've worked harder miracles. But only if you stay out of my way for a change."

They both laughed, then Mia threw Pete a towel and he slid off his boots and removed and hung up his raincoat.

"Owning a restaurant in paradise isn't all conch fritters and tequila shots," he said while drying his hair. "Sometimes, you gotta deal with crap. Literally."

I laughed and gestured to the stairs. "Should we go

to your office?"

"Here," he said, striding across the dining area, "let's take your booth."

We slid onto the padded bench seats. It was the same table I'd sat at when I'd first entered the restaurant over four years earlier. I'd been a stranger then. Drifting in through the doors, just fishing for information about a wreck south of the Marquesas Keys. Asking the old seadog for advice when it came to treasure hunting and searching for a lost wreck. What sort of equipment I'd need. Stuff like that. Four years later, the booth was nearly the same. But much of the dining area had changed. It had the same rustic, authentic Key West feel. Just a little cleaner and tidier and in better shape.

Mia dropped off mugs of coffee, and we both thanked her.

After taking a sip, I led off, "I'm sure you've heard about what happened yesterday."

He nodded. "Small island. And the Coconut Telegraph's as active as ever. Yep. I've heard some things. Glad you two made it out all right. Sounds like it was a terrible incident."

I nodded. Then cleared my throat and shifted the topic on the tightest turn I could manage.

"How much do you know about shrimpers around here?"

He folded his hands and leaned forward. "Nearly as long as there's been shrimp boats here, there's been captains using them for smuggling," he said, getting right to the crux of my question. "But it all amplified when tourism exploded and the dock rents went through the roof. Then the cost of shrimp went down, fuel costs went up, restrictions increased. You name it." He shrugged. "It made the business nearly impossible to run in the green in the Lower Keys. So, many of the shrimpers left, and many turned to smuggling. You could make a single run of marijuana north from Colombia and make more in that one delivery than in ten years as a shrimper. Talk about a tempting, hard-to-pass-up opportunity."

I leaned closer. Lowered my voice. "The temptation ever convince you?"

He shook his head. "I'd be lying if I said it wasn't hard to turn down. It was just some reefer, after all. At least at first. And I certainly had friends who made some nice fortunes for themselves. But no. I never did." He stared off into the distance a moment, then added, "Then cocaine became the new smuggled product of choice, and I closed the book on the idea entirely. That poison ruins lives. I wouldn't have felt right with my conscience."

I rubbed my chin. "Ever hear of shrimpers smuggling, say... people?"

He nodded. "A couple times, over the years. Not on a large scale, though. Not routinely. That's usually a job for the blistering, heavy-horsepower vessels. And the subs. Or, my understanding, most are taken to Central America, then brought in by land up north."

He rubbed the back of his neck. "But I got out of the shrimping game years ago. Before the pink rush ended. Started this restaurant while it was still humming away, and there were still armadas of boats dropping their catches off in the harbor. Not that I was ever really in the game. Just dipped my toes, I guess. I was far more interested in the prospect of real gold than pink. At least, from a commercial standpoint."

I leaned back and held out my hands. "I'm sure you know people who are. Still in the game, I mean."

Pete turned his head and glanced up at the wall across the room. Then he held up a hand, said, "Wait here a moment."

He lumbered back down the hallway. Grabbed a ladder from the utility closet and returned. Threaded through the empty tables and chairs and spread it open and climbed nearly to the top step.

"You trying to get yourself killed?" Mia said.

Stabilizing himself with his hook of a right hand, he reached with his left and grabbed a framed picture. He lifted its back wiring off a nail, then pulled it away. There was a faint square outline left behind, the shadow of its years hanging there. The picture having protected the wall from discoloration.

He climbed down with the photo. Left the ladder there and returned to the booth. Wiped away a layer of dust with a rag from his back pocket, then set it on the table in front of me.

It was black-and-white. Three boys smiling with big grins by a dock. A fleet of shrimp boats behind them. Packed so tight you could barely see any water. Two of the boys looked to be maybe twelve. The third was an infant of maybe two or three.

One of the twelve-year-olds was barefoot and wore a raggedy cut-off shirt and torn-up shorts. The other wore a nice formfitting outfit with a hat and sunglasses and clean dress shoes. The toddler was wearing just a diaper and a little sun hat.

"Care to wager a guess as to which one of these kids is the crusty seadog sitting across from you?" Pete said.

I looked back at the photo, then pointed at the kid in tattered clothes.

Pete laughed. "Lucky guess."

"You still have the same style," I said.

He looked down at his dirty, worn attire and nodded. "And I don't think it'll ever change."

He coughed and leaned forward, gazing at the photograph and clearly thinking about all the memories it brought back.

"This was taken in Key West Bight in the early fifties during the peak of the rush," Pete said. "We used to play there all the time. And back then, you could run clear across the bight without getting wet. Just hopping from one shrimp boat to the other. Millions of pounds of the little crustaceans were hauled in every year. It was a sight to behold, I tell you. Truly unbelievable. I ate more shrimp as a kid than you could imagine."

He stared longer at the grainy picture and smiled again.

"The kid dressed like Andrew Carnegie beside me is Red Delaney. His dad owned the biggest fleet of shrimp boats in the area. A real shrewd businessman. The little one in front of us is Kevin O'Malley."

"As in Officer O'Malley?" I said.

Pete nodded. "That's right."

I'd met Officer O'Malley a couple of times in passing. He was a sergeant with the Key West Police Department. One of the most senior members of the precinct, though he apparently hadn't been sworn in until he was in his forties.

"O'Malley's dad owned a lot of boats as well," Pete said.

"And your dad?"

He smiled. "Pops was a deckhand. I come from a line of men with collars bluer than the sea. I was the poor kid of the bunch. My dad may have been short on monetary wealth, but he was one of the wisest men I've ever known. And he gave me the most precious gift any parent can give their children: his time. If he wasn't working, he was taking me island hopping and exploring on our old skiff." He closed his eyes and grinned. "Those were some of the best times of my life. And I've led a good life. But, I guess you could say that I had to start from the bottom when it comes to finances."

I looked around the establishment. "I'd say you've done pretty well for yourself."

He smiled. "Well, it was years and years of work and risk. Stress and worries and unknowns. Blood, sweat, and tears, as they say. Literally. And even with all the sacrifices, I'd be broke right now in all likelihood were it not for that wide-eyed, adventurous, and aspiring young man who stumbled into my run-down joint four years ago, inquiring about a shipwreck."

"You'd have found a way without me." I glanced back down at the photograph.

"Delaney lives on Stock Island," Pete said. "Runs a little boat maintenance operation there. But he's been more plugged into the shrimping business in the Florida Keys than anyone alive over the past fifty years. If there's anyone you could talk to who might've heard something, I'd say he's the best bet."

"You two still friends?"

"We are, but I don't see him much."

"He doesn't come by here?"

"He doesn't go much of anywhere, far as I know. He's a hermit if ever there was one. I doubt he leaves Stock Island more than once a year. His island's a hundred yards away from mine, and he hasn't walked through these doors in over ten years. Not since Clive Cussler stopped by for lunch."

I blinked and shook my head. "Clive Cussler ate here?"

Pete smiled, pointed at the wall just above us. I squinted and saw a picture of the Grand Master of Adventure himself standing right in that dining room and surrounded by Pete and his staff.

"Like I always say," Pete added, "this place is a trove of secrets and history. Red didn't want to be in the photo, but he was here. I called him the moment Clive walked in. We'd always been big fans. Read every Dirk Pitt book. I knew he wouldn't be able to turn down a visit with the author."

Pete cleared his throat. "Anyway, I haven't seen the man since. It's been over a decade. And it's interesting, 'cause Red's family used to nearly run the place."

"They ran this restaurant?"

Pete shook his head. "They ran Key West."

I stared at him a moment, my mouth hanging open a little.

"I think you may be underestimating just how much shrimp they brought in," he explained. "We're talking millions of dollars' worth. Back in the fifties, sixties, and seventies. Back when that was a whole hell of a lot of money."

"And now he does boat repairs?" I said, raising my eyebrows.

Pete folded his arms. "Well, that's a bit of a long story. And everyone has their versions, including Red."

"So, he used to be rich. Now he's not. Animosity there?"

"He's not exactly destitute. Just not exorbitantly wealthy by any means. But I won't say anything bad about him or his family. Hell, it was his dad who gave me the loan to help buy this place. There'd be no Salty Pete's were it not for him." Pete pointed across the room, toward another hanging picture. This one of a twentysomething Pete and a middle-aged man in a business suit and top hat. "That's Joseph Delaney. Red's dad."

I stared at the distant picture a moment, then turned back to Pete. "You don't think Red could be involved in something like this?"

He paused a moment, then said, "I don't think so, no."

"Were they involved in the drug smuggling?"

He was about to answer, then stopped himself. Kept silent a beat.

He was trying to be diplomatic. Trying to have an old friend's back.

The delay in his reply was really all the answer I needed. But he eventually said, "Many shrimp boats were. Especially the successful ones."

I nodded. Satisfied with the answer.

Pete leaned forward. "Red's not the man and boy I

once knew. He went off to fancy schools after high school and came back different. Talked differently. Walked differently. And definitely treated me differently. Our relationship essentially ceased to exist aside from passing pleasantries. It was rekindled somewhat later on, but now... I just don't see him enough to call him my close friend anymore. He's just an acquaintance now. An unfortunate changing and growing apart."

Pete looked up as Mia flipped the sign hanging from the front door from closed to open, then a group of waiting patrons flooded inside.

"I'll call Red," Pete said, sliding out of the booth. "Let him know you're coming and put in a good word for you. Whatever that's worth to him anymore."

He rose, and I followed suit.

Turning back, Pete added, "Just be warned, he's a little rough around the edges. Rubs more people the wrong way than anyone I've ever met. Just don't take it personally if he insults you, 'cause he's good at insulting people. Whether intentional or not."

FOURTEEN

I thanked Pete for everything and left just as more hungry visitors were starting to file in. There were half a dozen vehicles now parked in the first row as I ambled out and whistled to Atticus. My reenergized Lab hustled over and stuck with me across the lot. He hopped into the Tacoma and settled in beside me, head up, eyes and ears alert, excited to be going somewhere again.

"One more stop to make," I said. "Then we'll get some lunch."

I kept the windows rolled down. Let the tropical afternoon breeze in as we cruised the old streets. Turned up Pirate Radio and blared "Come Monday" as we drove north, then east. We cut across the bridge to Stock Island. Turned onto MacDonald Avenue, then crisscrossed to Front Street, which leads all the way down the eastern side of Safe Harbor to the southern tip of the island right at the mouth of the port.

I followed it about a quarter mile, then slowed, hunting my turn. When I found it, I pulled onto a pier and cruised past a restaurant and a dive charter company. My destination was the very tip of the wharf, where there was a small lot beside an old three-story structure surrounded by palm trees. The structure was right along the water's edge at the corner of the pier, and an assortment of boats were tied off around it. Three of them were shrimp trawlers. Two were relatively new and seaworthy. The third looked ancient and was built of wood. Looked like it was ready to sink at any moment.

I flashed back to the previous afternoon, when I'd searched dozens of boats alongside Border Patrol agents right in front of that very structure.

I parked beside an old, battered pickup truck that looked like it didn't get used much and killed the engine. Sat there a moment in the silence, just looking around. The pier jutted out maybe two hundred yards, and to the southwest, I could see the Perry Hotel and Marina just across the water. Its beautiful swimming pool and two big docks packed with everything from multimillion-dollar yachts to fishing charters.

That part of the harbor was shiny and sleek, and immaculate. The side I stood on was far more rugged. Less polished and cleaned up. A glimpse of what all of Stock Island and Key West had looked like about forty years earlier.

As I surveyed the area, my eyes fixated on the third floor of the narrow structure ahead of me. It was built like a crow's nest—just a small protruding room with a little balcony. A table and two chairs. One of the chairs had a man sitting in it. And he was staring right at me.

He was far off, but I had a strong gut feeling that this was my guy. And I'd seen him before. He'd been perched right up in that crow's nest the previous evening, watching as we'd searched the shrimp boats.

I scanned the area again, then peered back at the man high above. He was still staring at me. His body fixed. No glances away. No attempt at subtlety. No normal human reaction of blinking and looking away when someone catches you staring at them. Apparently, he'd never learned that it's not polite to stare. Or he just didn't care, because he held his stare long after I'd opened my door and stepped out.

"Wait here, boy," I said, reaching through my window and patting his head.

He'd be all right. Windows down. Some cloud coverage. A nice breeze off the harbor. He had been raised in the islands and was used to the climate.

I strode casually toward the structure, hugging the seawall, then stopped right between one of the tied-off shrimp boats and the base of the structure. I lowered my sunglasses and looked up. The guy had adjusted his position and leaned forward a little. He was still staring, his head angled to look nearly straight down.

The man three floors above me wore a ball cap and sunglasses and had a big, graying red beard. He looked to be in his late sixties, but it was difficult to gauge.

"Red Delaney?" I said.

The man didn't reply.

"I'm Logan Dodge. I'm friends with Pete

Jameson."

Still nothing. Still staring.

"I was here last night searching the shrimp boats. I was looking for a smuggling boat I ran into yesterday morning."

Still nothing.

I let out a breath. Held his gaze.

Time to get a little more proactive.

"I saw you here last night," I said, a sliver of hostility in my voice.

I folded my arms and held my own stare.

"I live here," he said. "Anyone who wasn't blind would've seen me."

He sounded defensive. He was educated, clearly, but it was a long-ago education, and time and seasons had roughened his mannerisms. Like an expensive, polished-up vase that'd been left out in the elements for years. Like his truck.

"You work with shrimpers?" I asked.

He angled his head and looked at the three trawlers tied off.

"Maybe you are blind," he snickered.

He seemed like he wanted me to get to the point of my visit. So, I happily obliged.

I peered at the trio of boats as well, then said, "Any of them involved in this crap?"

"This crap?" he said, uttering the words slowly.

"You gonna need me to spell everything out for you?"

He scowled.

Two can play the sarcasm game, buddy.

"Smuggling's damn near the oldest occupation around here. Part of the islands' history. I'm sure Pete told you that."

"So, yes. How about illegal alien smuggling? Heard anything about that?"

He paused a beat. Adjusted his hat. Took a sip from a can of Guinness and leaned back. "I told the agents I haven't."

"And now *I'm* asking you."

"And who the hell are you?"

"Logan Dodge. I'm—"

"I'm not telling you anything."

"Why not?"

"Because I don't know you. And you're not a conch. And I'm leaving soon."

"Where you going?"

"Vacation."

"Where to?"

"None of your business."

"All right."

I stood there silently, staring up at him. A good thirty seconds. Then I sighed and scanned the harbor.

"Pete said your family used to run the town," I said.

"Ancient history," he grumbled. "Now all my family's got is this tiny speck of real estate."

I nodded. "You bitter about that?"

He laughed and pointed to shore. "I think it's time for you to take a hike."

He leaned back and looked away from me for the first time since I'd driven up. I noticed a game on the table beside him. Small black and white figures. A chess set.

"How about this, Red?" I said, "I beat you at chess, you tell me everything you know."

The man laughed. Shook his head. "One problem there, guy." He leaned forward, grinned, and said, "You have nothing I want. Haven't you ever wagered before?"

He laughed.

I sighed and checked the time instinctively. Thought back to something Pete had said and got an idea.

Raising my hands, I rested them on the top of my head. Angled my left wrist just enough for it to catch the afternoon sun and reflect rays toward the man above me. He turned his head away, then leaned even farther forward. Squinted and stared.

"That a Doxa?" he said, gesturing toward my timepiece.

I slid my hands off my head and inspected my watch like I'd forgotten it was there.

"You can see it from up there?"

"I'm old, but I'm not blind yet."

"Orange dial," I said with a nod. "Same one Dirk Pitt wears."

He went quiet a moment. Glanced at his chess set, and then at me. "You any good?"

"I'm terrible," I said. Then I folded my arms again. "But I bet I can still beat you."

He clicked his tongue. "I've been needing a new watch. Let's get this over with."

I was hoping he'd let me in so I could take a quick peek around his place, but he gathered the board and pieces and headed downstairs. Met me at his front door and shut it quickly behind him and pointed to an old picnic table in the shade of the palm trees.

He was all business. Set up the board and

positioned all of the pieces in a blur of muscle memory.

"This looks old," I said, running a hand over the worn hardwood. "Where'd you get it?"

"It was my grandfather's." He pointed over his shoulder to the old, battered shrimp boat and added, "It and the first family trawler are all I ever got in a will."

He grunted. Then looked up and shot me a frustrated look. Like he wished he hadn't opened up a little about his life.

"You can be white, Hogan," he said. "You're gonna need all the help you can get."

"It's Logan," I said.

He waved a hand. "Whatever. Your move."

I sat across from him. Grabbed the e4 pawn and slid it forward two spaces and we were off. He was good. No doubt about it. And fast. I could barely let go of my positioned piece before he'd make his next move. And he liked to smack their felt bottoms against the board. Like he was making some kind of primal, authoritative statement with every move.

He was better than me. Far better. I got off to a decent start, but the tide quickly swayed when he snagged one of my rooks. Then a knight. And then my queen.

He smiled as he set it aside. Shook his head and eyed my watch like it was already his.

I focused up and managed to make a decent comeback. He wasn't the best I'd played, but he was close. Regardless, he left the door open a couple times. But I didn't take advantage of the opportunities and he quickly had me beat. It was an across-the-board move of a bishop that did me in, and he slammed the piece home and exclaimed, "Checkmate."

I knew it was over, but I took a moment to scan over the board anyway. Mumbled some things to myself like beaten players usually do. Then sighed, letting him see that I knew it was over.

"Tough break, Brogan," he said, holding out his right hand.

I turned over my left wrist. Unclasped the watch and stared at it a long moment before handing it over. Red swiped it eagerly and inspected it.

He laughed. "To Logan, the love of my life," he said, reading the inscription on the back. "Not only did you make a stupid wager, but you lost a gift?" He shook his head. "You're some kind of a moron, aren't you?"

I ignored the remark. Leaned forward and looked the man in the eyes. "You'll let me know if you see anything suspicious at least? I'm trying to help innocent people here. Don't you care at all?"

He shook his head again. "I don't know you. And you're not a conch. I won't tell you anything." He cleaned up the board, putting all the pieces into the set and shutting it and coming to his feet. "Like I said before, it's time for you to take a hike."

He disappeared back into his little sanctuary. Less than a minute later, he was in his crow's nest. Watching me while sipping his beer.

I stared back at him a moment, then turned and headed for my Tacoma.

"Pleasure doing business with you, Rogan," he shouted. "This thing's a beauty. You looking for a new watch, you might want to swing by the Dollar Tree."

I ignored the jab. Bowed my shoulders a little and let the guy bask in all the glory of his victory as I drifted to my truck.

I'd met a number of irritable people in my life, but I had to hand it to the guy. He was near the top of the list. Perhaps even alone at the summit.

I thought about how many names rhyme with Logan. There aren't many. And they're all relatively obscure. But the guy had managed to find them regardless.

Pretty impressive, really.

Then I thought back to my talk with Pete and how he'd described his old friend.

Hermit. Rough around the edges. Good at rubbing people the wrong way.

Check.

Check.

Check.

FIFTEEN

Striding along the seawall, I stopped a moment. Turned around and stared at the house, then the docks, then the three shrimp boats, then the rows of sparkling million-dollar yachts and the sprawling resort across the harbor. All developed to the nines. All on land Red Delaney's family had apparently once owned.

The guy was sitting up in the crow's nest. Still watching my every move.

I turned east and saw Atticus staring at me through the rolled-down driver's-side window. I made it halfway back to my truck before I realized that Delaney wasn't the only one watching me.

I angled my head to the left slightly and saw a parked vehicle in my peripherals. It was a Key West police cruiser parked in the shadows of palm trees on the opposite side of the pier maybe fifty yards ahead of me. It was partly blocked by a dumpster, but still visible. The windows were rolled up and dark. Its engine idling.

I reached my truck and leaned through my window.

"Couple more minutes, boy," I said to Atticus. "I promise."

He sighed and nestled back into his seat. He looked starving, the treats Mia had given him back at Pete's clearly not cutting it. My stomach was growling as well, but my curiosity was stronger.

I turned and strode toward the idling cop car. My hands were empty and swaying casually. I made a wide turn around the dumpster so whoever was inside could clearly see me, then approached leisurely.

The driver's-side window rolled down when I was maybe ten feet away, and I nearly froze midstride, taken aback by the man in the driver's seat.

It was Officer O'Malley. A sergeant and the little boy from the photograph Pete had taken down from his wall and dusted off earlier that day. It struck me as incredible that I'd now seen all three boys from that photograph within an hour.

I'd met Officer O'Malley a couple of times in passing, but we'd never spoken long. He had short, solid gray hair, and a trimmed goatee. He was tanned and in good shape for a man any age, let alone in his early sixties.

"Hey, Logan," he called out in his friendly voice. "I was just cruising by and saw your truck. What brings you here?"

He seemed a little off. And it struck me as odd that he would pull into the pier just because he saw my truck. And it struck me as odder still that he just so happened to be the third person from Pete's old picture.

I stopped beside his door. Motioned toward Delaney's place. The angle and trees prevented us from being able to see him, but he nodded, clearly knowing what I was saying. He'd been there the previous evening as well. He along with Chief Verona and other members of the Key West Police Department.

"He say anything?" O'Malley asked, lowering his sunglasses.

"Not really. He insulted me a couple of times. Then told me to leave."

The officer laughed. "Sounds like Red. At least he didn't drive you off his property with a pitchfork."

"He'd need more than a pitchfork to drive me away."

O'Malley nodded. Then his radio crackled to life. He picked it up, triggered the mic and gave a rapid, mumbled response. Then he slid his sunglasses back into place.

"Good to see you, Logan."

I nodded to him and he put the cruiser in gear and accelerated off. He was down the pier and around the corner ten seconds later.

Turning back, I shielded the sun from my eyes and saw movement in the eastern-facing window blinds in the crow's nest of Delaney's house. They were cracked open maybe an inch. A tiny slit. Like two fingers were prying them apart. Just enough for an eyeball.

A moment later, the blinds closed and the slit vanished.

I shook my head as I strode back to my Tacoma.

There was something fishy as hell going on there. It was rancid. And it wasn't the dumpsters full of fish guts across the harbor at Charter Row.

SIXTEEN

I called Ange on the drive back to Key West. The two kids had apparently just woken up, and I told her I'd pick up lunch for everyone. I swung by Old Town Bakery and boxed a variety of favorites.

I didn't know much about toddlers, but I knew they could be picky. And headstrong. And difficult to convince that sustenance would be beneficial for their continued existence. Anyone who's been to a busy family-friendly restaurant or a theme park knows that much by simple observation.

So, I put together a platter of options. A real smorgasbord. Different types of sandwiches on freshly baked bread along with muffins and pastries.

I returned home just after one.

The two kids were playing with toys in the living room when I stepped through the front door. They were both cleaned up, with Olivier wearing a tiny blue T-shirt with a triceratops on it and Esther wearing a floral sundress. Ange sat cross-legged on the floor beside them.

Both kids were silent as I entered, gazing over at me. But they both smiled as Atticus led the charge, bolting into the living room, jumping everywhere, and covering them both with licks. Esther even giggled as Atty's tail wagged into her face.

I noticed bags of clothes by the door, and before I could ask about them, Ange said, "Apparently, word got around pretty fast that we're looking after these two. I've had four different people stop by to drop off clothes and toys and children's books."

I smiled, no longer surprised by conch hospitality. It was one of the many things that made our island home so great.

I knelt down and greeted both of the kids, but neither said anything back. They remained silent as I opened the bags of food and plated everything on the dining table. They watched me while playing with their new toys. Ange ushered them over, and when they saw the spread, they climbed up onto chairs and dug in.

Neither of them turned out to be picky. They wolfed down anything and everything we put it front of them. From the muffins and pastries to bowls of blueberries and apple sauce.

After lunch, Ange and I led them into the backyard and showed them their new playset. They were hesitant at first, but within five minutes they were both climbing and swinging and sliding. And smiling.

It was good to see their spirits improving, but there was still a dark cloud hanging over both of them. They still seemed suspicious of us and our home and everything. It was natural. They didn't know us. But we did everything we could to ease the transition and make their time as easy and enjoyable as possible.

They especially liked playing with Boise and Atticus. Loved watching our six-toed calico chase a toy mouse at the end of a string, and our Lab dash across the yard to retrieve a tennis ball and return with the orb between his teeth, his slobbery tongue hanging out.

They were both still shell-shocked, but it was waning a little as the afternoon passed.

While we all played and relaxed, I cracked open a watermelon and sliced it up. They were still dehydrated, so we offered all the fluids they would drink. Water with electrolytes dissolved in it. And coconut water. We kept a close eye on both of them and were ready to drive them to the hospital if need be.

Scarlett and Cameron showed up later that afternoon, and as the two teenagers played with the toddlers in the yard, Ange and I migrated to the upstairs balcony. From up there we could observe all of the activity below, while having enough privacy to catch up on what I'd been up to that day.

"Weren't you wearing your watch this morning?" Ange said, eyeing my bare left wrist.

"Yeah, I may have lost it in a bet." She raised her eyebrows at me, and I added, "A game of chess against one of Pete's old friends."

I told her the story, about my conversation with Pete and then with Delaney and then with Officer O'Malley.

It took a couple minutes for me to get it all out,

and she fell silent after, mulling everything over.

"You've got a plan here, I hope?" she said.

"A rough one, yeah. Just based on gut instinct. I don't know. There's something about this Delaney guy. At face value, he's an obvious suspect. But Officer O'Malley seems plausible as well."

"What about the CBP agents?" Ange suggested. "Hard to believe shrimpers have been routinely smuggling people into the States right under their noses."

I nodded. "Could be. Hell, they all could be involved. For all we know."

Ange rubbed her chin. "Heard anything from Maddox?"

"Yeah," I said.

The Homeland agent had called me just after I'd left the bakery. A quick chat, just catching me up to speed.

"He's spearheading a major investigation. They've already visited three of the major shrimp ports along Florida's Gulf Coast. They're making their way here."

Ange went silent again, then said, "So, what's the next step here?"

I motioned toward the two kids playing with Scarlett and Cameron. "Take care of them as best we can. Then help Maddox and his team when they arrive."

"You're not gonna talk to Delaney again? Or Officer O'Malley?"

I shrugged. "Maybe. Not sure what good it'll do. Neither would tell me anything if they were involved. And it's not like I've got any evidence linking them to this mess."

We watched as Scarlett uncoiled a hose and dragged it to the center of the yard. She screwed a sprinkler to the end, then gave Cameron a nod. When the young man twisted the valve, water sprayed out in the shape of a giant mushroom, the sun's rays creating a rainbow in the mist.

We focused on enjoying the rest of the afternoon as much as we could. Taking turns running through the sprinklers and cooling off from the tropical heat. Later that evening, after giving the kids baths and putting them in fresh clothes, Ange and I were just starting on dinner when Scarlett approached us.

"I have a proposition," our daughter declared.

Ange and I exchanged glances, and I said, "Uh-oh. We've heard that before."

"Don't worry about it, Scarlett," Cameron said from the living room. He was sitting amongst a spread of toys and listening to "The Bare Necessities" while Olivier and Esther played beside him. "We'll go out some other time."

Scarlett ignored him, and said, "Cameron's planned a date for tonight, and I was hoping we could go."

"We should stay here and help out," Cameron said. "Kids are a lot of work."

I pulled out pizza dough, marinara sauce, and a bag of mozzarella from the fridge, and said, "It's a school night, Scar."

"Barely. There's only four days left. Most of my classes don't have any more tests or assignments. And we'll be home by ten."

Ange grabbed a bag of pepperoni, along with

mushrooms and onions, then shut the door.

"Fine by me," my wife said with a shrug.

"It's really fine," Cameron said. "We can go out another time."

But the truth was that the number of evenings left for them to go out was waning. And very soon they wouldn't be able to at all.

"Have fun," I said, kissing Scarlett on her forehead. "And ten o'clock sharp. I'll hold you to that."

Thirty yards from the Dodge house, two men sat in an idling black Chevrolet Impala parked along the curb. The guy in the driver's seat sat still, keeping a watchful eye out his window and the corner of the windshield. The man in the passenger seat tapped the grip of his Smith & Wesson pistol on his knee.

They both watched as a blue Ford Bronco bounced out of the driveway. Its windows were rolled down. They each caught a brief glimpse of a young man in the passenger seat and a teenage girl in the driver's seat as they turned left onto Palmetto, giving them a quick side profile view.

The driver reached for the shifter to put their vehicle in gear.

"Not them," the guy in the passenger seat said, holding up a hand. "We want the big dogs."

Silence a beat.

"Should we go now?" the driver asked.

"Not yet."

"When?"

"Soon," the hitman replied, still tapping his weapon excitedly. Eager to fire it. "Very soon."

SEVENTEEN

Scarlett and Cameron drove across town, landed a parking spot along Fleming, and strode into Margaritaville. The place was packed, mostly with happy tourists. Just like it'd been on their first date. And, also like their first date, they both ordered cheeseburgers and washed them down with ice cold cokes.

Scarlett was unusually quiet the entire meal, looking around and off into space and appearing dejected.

"What's wrong?" Cameron asked as they finished up the last of their fries. "You didn't like the food?"

She patted her lips with her napkin. Said, "No. It was fine."

"What's wrong?" he asked again.

"I'm just thinking about Olivier and Esther. And their mom." She bit her lip. "It's really sad."

"Your parents make any headway with all that?"

"Some. The shrimp trawler disappearing somehow makes the whole thing both incredibly strange and difficult. But I overheard them mention a potential suspect. Some guy named Delaney."

"Red Delaney?" Cameron said.

Scarlett shrugged. "I don't know. But I heard them mention Stock Island."

Cameron nodded. "That's Red. My uncle knows him. From what I hear he's become something of a hermit. Your parents think he's involved?"

"He's one of their suspects, yeah. And Officer O'Malley's name was mentioned for some reason."

Cameron rubbed his chin. Shook his head. "I sure hope they're wrong. Officer O'Malley's a good man. Used to be a star athlete in his day and he helps out with the team."

They went silent again.

Cameron squinted at her. "You sure there's nothing else bothering you?"

Then she tilted her head at him. "You know there is. We've only got a couple more nights like this. I guess I'm just bummed out all around."

Cameron leaned back. Shrugged. "We should make the most of it then." He pinned two twenties under an empty coke bottle then pushed his seat back. Sauntered around the table and held out his hand to her. "The night's still young."

She smiled. Slid her seat back as well and rose and they strode hand in hand out of the restaurant. Duval in all its evening glory hit them like an avalanche. A blast of sensory overload. The noise. The flooded sidewalks. The cacophony of smells. And the rambunctious energy in the air.

"What do you have in mind?" Scarlett asked as they strode back toward her Bronco.

"I was thinking a tour. See some old favorite locales. Maybe see some new ones."

Scarlett checked her watch. "It's getting late. We don't have much time."

"Last I checked Key West has a tour train."

She chuckled. "Too bad for us it stops running at like what, five?"

Cameron smiled again. This one with a hint of sly. "And good thing for us, I know a guy."

They rounded a line of gumbo-limbo trees and a tiny parking lot came into view. It was mostly full, and parked in the middle between the rows of cars was the Key West conch train. A lanky, pimple faced teenager wearing a straw hat sat in the locomotive.

"You know Jeremy Hinkley, right?" Cameron said.

Jeremy was a sophomore at Key West High. Soon to be a junior, just like Scarlett.

"His dad owns the tour company," Cameron explained. "And he happens to be a big football fan. I promised him a signed ball in exchange for a private tour tonight."

"And a jersey," Jeremy said. "Gonna be worth a fortune one day."

Scarlett joked around with Cameron while being chauffeured around the city. Jeremy took them to a couple typical spots, cruising past Truman's Little White House and Mallory Square, and then detoured to memorable locations Cameron had chosen.

First was a new café along Duval in a commercial space that used to be an Italian trattoria called

Bonetti's. On his and Scarlett's first date, things hadn't gone according to plan, and Cameron had ended up proving that pigskin wasn't the only thing he could hurl with velocity and precision.

Next, they swung by Tropic Cinema, where they'd watched many classic and independent films together. Listened to a couple live songs by Jack Mosley at Smokin' Tuna while drinking nonalcoholic margaritas. Checked out the Key West Island Bookstore, where Cameron had bought her a book written by the legendary basketball coach John Wooden, and she'd gotten him a copy of her favorite novel, Jane Eyre.

They ate shrimp from the Conch Republic Seafood Company. And a slice of Key Lime Pie from Blue Heaven. Cameron had called ahead and everything was ready for them on arrival.

"You planned all of this?" Scarlett said.

"I wanted to make it count."

She batted her eyes, then kissed him.

Then the alarm on Scarlett's phone went off.

She pulled her mouth away. Silenced her phone without looking. Sighed. "Time to head home."

Cameron nodded.

"I've got to get this train back anyway," Jeremy said, listening in on their conversation. "My dad said if it's out after ten, I'm grounded all summer."

He turned them back onto Simonton Street, heading for the turn onto Fleming to take them back where they'd started. Just before hitting Southard, Cameron glanced hastily over his shoulder. Blinked and turned back forward, his eyes big. He blinked again and shook his head slightly.

"What is it?" Scarlett said.

He looked back over his shoulder. Stared off, his mouth agape.

"Weird," he muttered.

"What's weird?"

He swallowed. Rubbed his eyes, then peered back forward. "Nothing I just... I think I just saw Delaney."

"What?" Scarlett gasped. She turned around and scanned the street and sidewalks behind them. "Where was he?"

Cameron pointed behind him. "Back there. He turned inland. Kind of strange. You just mentioned him earlier." He shrugged, checked the time. "Anyway, you should get back plenty early. I—"

"Stop the train!" Scarlett exclaimed, leaning forward.

Jeremy jolted and shoved a foot onto the brake, bringing them to an abrupt stop.

"What is it?" he said, spinning around in his seat.

"Turn us around," Scarlett said after catching herself against the handrail. "Back to the previous intersection.

Jeremy shook his head. Pointed at his watch. "No can do. I gotta get this train back to the garage."

Scarlett turned to Cameron. Stared into his eyes. "You're sure it was him?"

He nodded. "Pretty sure, yeah. It's dark, but he's got a distinct look."

She slid off the seat. Pulled Cameron with her and they landed on the concrete.

"Thanks for everything, Jeremy. See you at school."

The young man stuttered unintelligible words as they rushed back the way they'd come.

"Wait, what are we doing?" Cameron said, stopping and holding a hand up to her.

She pulled away from him and rushed to the end of the street. Poked her head around the corner and caught her first glimpse of the man. He was wearing shorts and a long-sleeved shirt. A light blue fishing buff around his neck under a thick red beard and a ballcap angled low over his face. He moved quickly in the shadows, and his head swiveled from side to side.

Cameron caught up with her. Was about to say something, but she cut him off.

"That Delaney?" she said, pointing at the guy.

Cameron nodded.

"He never leaves Stock Island, right?" she said, keeping her voice low.

"It was a figure of speech. I mean, he's got to leave sometime. No one's that much of a recluse."

"But he's here now. And he's rarely here."

Cameron shook his head. "I'm not following, Scarlett."

"He's up to something," she said, keeping her eyes on the guy. "And we're going to figure out what."

Cameron swallowed. "I don't like the sound of this."

"Then you should head home," she said. Then she kissed him on the cheek. "Really, you should. Thanks for the great evening."

She turned and crept around the corner. Moved into the street and kept low, concealing herself behind the rows of parked cars along the street. Cameron was back on her six moments later.

"You really think I'm going to leave you here alone?" he whispered.

"No. But you have the option, of course."

They followed Delaney for another block, keeping their distance and moving low. He turned onto Mangrove Street, and then stopped and looked around a moment before sauntering another fifty yards and cutting into a small gravel lot.

"That's Salty Pete's," Scarlett said.

The teenagers picked up their pace. Spotted Delaney again as he reached the other end of the lot. The place was packed. Music and chatter and the sounds of clattering dishes emanating from inside.

Delaney didn't head for the front door. Instead, he skirted around the right side of the restored Victorian style house. Scarlett and Cameron followed, sticking to a tight ribbon of grass between the farthest row of parked cars and the hedge.

Pete had a modest yard out back, with overgrown bougainvillea bushes, and buttonwood and pigeon plum trees along an old wooden fence. And there was a small shop where he kept a restored 1969 Camaro he'd been working on for years.

Scarlett and Cameron tip-toed behind the garage. Leaned out the other side and saw Delaney standing on the lawn.

"Get down," Scarlett whispered. "We're gonna have to crawl."

She dropped onto her chest and shuffled along the shop, crawling right into a thick bush. She brought them as close as they could without being spotted. They were just ten feet away from him, just within earshot. Both still and silent. Slowing their breathing and listening.

They caught a brief glimpse of Delaney's face in the glow bleeding from the balcony's strand lights above. The man looked furious. His face red and scrunched. His eyes narrow and intense. His right hand was in a tight fist as he turned around abruptly.

Then Pete appeared from the opposite side of the restaurant.

EIGHTEEN

Pete Jameson headed upstairs after making his usual rounds in the main dining area of his restaurant. He was a man of many interests and facets. Enjoyed spending his days out on the water, relishing the quiet and tranquil nature of remote parts of the island chain. Fishing and exploring. Keeping an eye out for the occasional lost antiquity or two.

Evenings were for socializing. Catching up with old friends, making new ones, and swapping stories. Drinking and eating and listening to great live music and laughing the night away. The life of a modern-day pirate.

He reached the top of the stairs, Tiko perched on his shoulder as he strode past rows of glass cases filled with artifacts toward a big sliding glass door. It led out to the balcony, which featured more tables along with a stage on one side and a bar on the other.

There was no live music and it was not quite a packed house. A slow, quiet night, by the establishment's standards. A rarity. But still far from calm.

Pete continued to roam and say hello to everyone he saw. He loved running the restaurant. Loved not knowing who he was going to meet or what was going to happen. The place was always full of surprises.

And tonight was no exception.

While greeting patrons at one of the end tables, he caught a glimpse of movement in the property's backyard. He angled his head and glanced downward and let out a gasp as he saw a face he hadn't seen in years. It was brief. Illuminated by the moonlight one second, and gone the next.

Pete rubbed his eyes and stared again. But the face was gone.

Excusing himself, he headed back inside. Back downstairs and across the dining area. He left Tiko atop a coatrack that'd hardly ever been used and pushed out through a side door. He made it three steps across the backyard when a figure emerged from the shadows.

Pete froze a moment. Hovered his right hand over his holstered pistol instinctively.

Then he relaxed again as the figure crept back into the moonlight.

"Jeez, Red," he gasped. "What the heck you trying to do, give me a heart attack?"

Delaney remained silent. Just stood there ominously, then folded his arms and said, "What are you trying to do? That's the question."

Pete shook his head. "I haven't seen you in years, and this is how you show up?"

"Answer my question first."

"Why don't we go inside. Head up to my office. I could make some coffee."

Delaney took a step closer and glared. "I don't want to go inside. And I don't want to sit. The only thing I want from you is an explanation."

Pete raised his eyebrows, then held out open palms.

"If you got a problem with me, don't send some punk landlubber to do your dirty work. You got something to say or accuse me of, you man up and do it yourself."

Pete shook his head. "I never accused you of anything. And I never sent anyone to do my dirty work."

"Then why did that guy show up at my door?"

"I tried to call ahead. There was no answer."

"My landline's disconnected. Not all of us in the islands have had good fortunes like you."

Pete let out a long breath. "Logan's a good man. And he's fighting for justice here. He's trying to save people. Men, women, children. Can't you see that, Red? This goes beyond simple smuggling, and it certainly goes beyond you and me and our petty bullcrap history. This is about right and wrong. This has to stop."

Delaney snickered. "You do think I'm involved, don't you?"

Pete shook his head. "I never said that. All I said was that I thought you might know something. That no one knows the shrimp industry around here better than you. Which is true."

"Damn right it's true. But it doesn't mean I'm

involved. Maybe this Logan guy is involved. Ever think of that? I heard about what happened the other night. What was he doing out there beyond the Tortugas late at night anyway?"

"Logan's not involved, Red. Like I said, he's a good man. I can assure you of that."

"I've read some stuff about him. Heard more stuff. Well, the great, heroic man who discovered the Aztec treasure isn't as smart as the papers made him out to be." Delaney held up his left wrist. The orange Doxa clasped around it glimmered in the moonlight. "This was his, and I didn't steal it. The idiot lost it to me."

Pete glanced at the watch, then back up at his old friend. "Give him a chance. Talk to him. He's trying to help. I promise you that."

Both men turned as a sudden rustling in the nearby bushes startled them. They both hovered their hands over their sidearms and stared into the shadows. They gazed a moment, then an iguana came rushing out, scurrying across the edge of the yard and up into a coconut tree.

Both men sighed and relaxed a little. Turned back to face each other.

"He's not one of us," Delaney spat. "Dodge. He's not a conch."

"He wasn't born here, true. But that might be a good thing in this case. He's lived here a while now but grew up elsewhere. He can look at this whole mess with a different perspective than a local can."

"He's not a conch," Delaney repeated with a grumble.

"He's capable. Dodge. As capable as they come. Resourceful and good at getting to the bottom of criminal enterprises."

"I'm sick and tired of hearing all about how great this guy is. Everyone I've talked to and everything I've read makes him out to be some kind of superhero or something. He's just a man."

"Ever hear him boasting about anything he's done? No. He never does that. He blends in as best he can and treats people the same and he's humble. But make no mistake, he's trying to help. And he will get to the bottom of this. He used to be a privately contracted gun for hire. One of the best. And a Navy SEAL before that. He'll sneak up on whoever's running this thing and take them out before they even know what hit them. And then he'll head home to his family and crack open a beer and sit down for a hot fish dinner like nothing happened."

Delaney chuckled. "Sounds like you got a crush on the guy."

"Do you want to find these smugglers, Red? Do you want to put an end to this injustice?"

"Of course I do," Delaney spat. "Smuggling pot was one thing, but this... this is beyond inexcusable. And it puts a black stain on our line of work."

Pete nodded. "Then how about you leave our history where it belongs, shove your ego aside, and work with Dodge? You can help put an end to this. I know you can. And I know deep down you're still that good young man and boy who used to stand up alongside me for what was right. Who always had my back."

Delaney fell silent at that. Just stood there, speechless.

Pete bowed his head slightly, then said, "Good

night, Red."

The proprietor turned and headed back into his restaurant.

NINETEEN

Scarlett's heart was still thumping in her chest when Pete rounded the corner.

She and Cameron both kept perfectly still and silent behind the towering bougainvillea. Both of them watching Delaney intently. The man was a statue for a solid ten seconds, then grunted and turned and stomped around the opposite side of the restaurant.

When he was twenty yards away, Cameron let out a held breath.

"That was close," he whispered. "Too close."

Scarlett nodded. "I've never been more grateful for an iguana in my life."

The reptile had startled them and scurried across the edge of the property at the perfect time, taking all suspicions with it.

Cameron shook his head. "I didn't hear a word they said."

"I heard my last name. And they sounded heated. When was the last time you saw Pete acting like that? He's the friendliest guy in Monroe County."

Scarlett observed Delaney intently, angling her head and squinting for a better look as he reached the parking lot.

"Come on," she said, nudging Cameron's shoulder. "We're gonna lose him."

"No way," Cameron gasped, then held out his phone and pointed at the time. "You need to get home."

She shook her head. "Not happening."

"You're already past curfew."

She shrugged. "I guess the damage is already done then."

Without another word, she crept out from behind the bushes, skipped across the strip of grass, and stuck to the shadows of the restaurant on her way to the front. Cameron followed. Didn't have much of a choice.

He caught up with her and they both reached the edge of the gravel just as Delaney sauntered west along the sidewalk. They followed him for another four blocks. Two southwest to Elizabeth Street, then another two blocks southeast.

Just shy of the library, he stopped abruptly. He reached into his pocket and checked his phone. Hustled ahead and dipped into the library's dark narrow lot and held the device up to his ear and started talking.

They watched him from the sidewalk. Kept steady eyes on him as he strolled nearly to the end of the gravel, stopping beside a dumpster and a chain link fence choked with ivy. He was fifty yards from them. Too far to hear anything.

"I need to hear what he's saying," Scarlett said.

"There's no cover," Cameron said. "How do you suggest we get closer without him seeing us?"

Scarlett scanned the area. Thought a moment. Then tugged on his shirt.

She led him back to the intersection with Fleming, then down the whole front side of the library. Before Cameron could say anything, she cut right into a private residence. Hopped over a wooden fence.

"You're crazy," Cameron said.

But still he followed her across the small, manicured lawn. Past a swimming pool. Past a decorative fountain and a little koi pond. Then along a cobblestone path and another picket fence on the other side of the property. They landed on a short, overgrown path, cut right, then reached the opposite side of the chain link fence thirty seconds after Scarlett had gotten the spur of the moment idea.

"Trust your instincts," her parents always told her.

And at that moment, they were screaming at her.

There was a layer of dirt and tiny pebbles along the base of the fence that crunched under their shoes with every step, so they moved as lightly as possible. Knelt down right beside the base of it. The fence had vertical plastic strips about an inch wide running along it. The ribbons, combined with the ivy, created a nice barrier separating the public space from the nearby residences. Through the tiny breaks, they could just make out glimpses of Delaney on the other side.

He was barely five feet away. Still standing with

his phone to his ear. Still talking.

Only now they could hear him.

Scarlett and Cameron remained perfectly still. Listening.

"I told you I'm handling it," Delaney said.

He opened his mouth to say more, then closed it. Narrowed his gaze and breathed loudly in and out as he listened.

They could hear a voice through the tiny speaker. Just the faint mumble. Nothing distinct.

Delaney seemed to remain quiet forever. Just listening and shaking his head.

"I know," Delaney finally said, anger in his voice. "Yes, I know. There's—"

He went quiet another moment, then said, "It's a bad idea. Just trust me. I'll handle it."

He paced back and forth. Pressed the phone to his chest and sighed. Looked up and down. Side to side.

Then he froze.

Stared straight at the fence.

Squinted.

Hung up the phone and grunted and withdrew his pistol. Stepped toward the fence and took aim.

"I see you in there," he snarled.

"Crap," Scarlett whispered. Barely audible.

Cameron lowered himself and angled his body in front of hers. Before either of them could make a run for it, Delaney poked his revolver through the fence, the barrel aimed right at Cameron's back.

"I may be old, but my vision's as perfect as ever," Delaney said. "Tell me who you are right now or I'm pulling the trigger."

Scarlett gasped. Cameron looked at her, then

behind them. He was debating whether they should make a run for it. She was chastising herself—wishing she'd listened to him and just stayed out of it.

"Remain calm," she heard her parents' words in her head. "No matter what, remain calm."

They needed to run. It was the only way. Turn and dive and roll and then take off and not look back for at least a quarter mile.

They were about to jump for it when a vehicle rolled up. It turned off Elizabeth, pulling partway into the driveway. Slowed to a stop.

They watched through the cracks as Delaney turned and gazed at the vehicle. It was far off, but looked like a police cruiser. The driver's window was rolled down, and a familiar face poked his head out.

A brief moment of silence followed, then Delaney holstered his weapon. The police cruiser eased away from the driveway, pulling back onto the street.

Without another word to them, Delaney strolled away. Then the cop car drove away. Soon, they were both out of sight, and the teenagers were left there behind the fence. Speechless and dumbfounded.

"What the heck was that about?" Cameron said, staring at the empty lot where the strange interaction had taken place. "He was far away, but that looked like Officer O'Malley."

Scarlett shook her head. "I have no idea. But something's going on here. I don't trust either of them."

Her phone buzzed in her pocket.

She slid it out. Saw a message from her mom. She sighed, then gasped and placed a hand to her mouth.

"We need to go home, right now," she said, her

face pale.

"That's what I've been trying to tell you. We're way past your curfew."

"No, it's not that."

She held her phone out to Cameron. He read the short message, then his eyes widened. They scaled the fence, ran down Fleming until they reached her parked Bronco. Jumped in and Scarlett put the SUV in gear and mashed the gas pedal.

TWENTY

Our evening went smoothly until about eight o'clock. The trouble started when the young and innocent Olivier inquired about their mother. Esther was right beside him. She'd been eating Cheerios and perked up at the mention of her mommy. Her eyes wide. A smile on her face.

Then she looked around.
Then she stood up.
Then she looked around some more.
When she didn't find her, she started panting and then crying.

She'd called out for her mom before, but now she was having a full-on panic attack. Completely losing it. Shouting at the top of her little lungs over and over again.

And there was nothing we could do to console her.
She wanted her mommy. She needed her mommy. But she was gone. And she wasn't coming back.

Esther screamed for over an hour. Her face red. Tears streaking down her cheeks. Her little body shaking.

Her brother was crying too but allowed Ange to hug him and hold him close. Esther just pushed us away each time we drew near. Smacked her feet and fists into the floor.

It was hard to watch—hard to be a part of.

When Esther had finally relaxed, we gave her a bowl of sliced bananas and a bottle of milk. And she finally fell asleep alongside her brother just before ten.

Ange and I stood there, hovering over the kids. Both of our eyes had welled up with tears as well. They were dry now, but we were both still raw from the experience.

We stepped back out into the living room together. Even with both kids sleeping silently, it seemed like the walls were still shaking. Her cries still resounding. Her heartbreak still palpable.

I hugged my wife, then she went to the kitchen for some water and I stepped out and stood on the back porch and stared in silence at the dark sky.

The anger I felt at witnessing Esther's heart tearing apart in front of me was transforming into resolve. I decided that I was going to head out and start looking for answers in a more proactive way. Go looking for trouble, as they say. Maybe pay a visit to Delaney and smack him over the head with his grandfather's chess board until he told me everything he knew.

Either way, I was in an unusually sour mood where things like common sense and restraint are disregarded. And I was ready to go out and look for some trouble when the sliding door opened and Ange poked her head out.

"You should take a look at this," she said, then gestured toward her laptop cracked open on the dining table.

I followed her in. Slid the door shut behind us and she rotated the device around so I could see the screen.

I smiled. It was beautiful. I wasn't gonna have to go out and look for trouble. The heavy lifting had been done for me.

Trouble had found us.

We'd both been routinely looking over the footage from our property's security cameras all day. We had five of them. Two along the back of the house that were positioned to catch half of the backyard and sides, two more along the front of the house, and a fifth camera. That one was small and well camouflaged and attached to a palm tree at the edge of our front yard. Its line of sight was the whole front of the driveway and a long stretch of Palmetto Street.

We hadn't seen anything unusual recorded by any of them all day. But it was that fifth camera that'd caught something a couple hours earlier: a black Chevy Impala.

It was inconspicuous. Nothing strange about it, other than the fact that its windows were heavily tinted. Except that it'd cruised past our house three times in the last three hours. Each time slowly. The most recent instance barely thirty minutes earlier. And now it was parked maybe thirty yards to the right of our mailbox and across the street. Only the front half of the sedan visible at the edge of the frame.

"I guess your asking questions pissed somebody off," Ange said. "What's the play here?"

I thought a moment, then said, "Not here."

"Where, then?"

"I don't know. Somewhere quiet." I rubbed my chin. "Get ahold of Scarlett once I've lured them away from the house."

"Want me to call in for backup as well?"

I nodded. "Call Jane. Get her over here. But not to check out the Impala. I'll take care of them."

TWENTY-ONE

I stared out the kitchen window at the driveway. Thought for a moment. Ran through scenarios for about a minute, then picked the one I liked and turned and opened the fridge and grabbed a can of Sunset Clipper beer. Popped the top and drained its contents down the sink. A shame, but necessary.

Then I grabbed and pocketed a Rodriguez cigar from the cupboard, and shot my wife a look.

Ange could read my thoughts better than anyone I'd ever met, allowing us to communicate the basics of plans with subtle expressions and gestures.

She stepped closer and kissed me, then I headed out back, down the stairs, and into my makeshift gym. I grabbed my five-pound Indian club. Swung it a few times, then draped a small workout towel over my shoulder and went back upstairs, through the living room, and out the main door. I opened it fast and loud. Shut it even louder. Nearly a slam. Then I stomped down the stairs, slid into my truck, and slammed that door as well.

I set the Indian club and the towel and the empty beer can on the passenger seat, then fired up the engine, rolled down the windows, and cranked Pirate Radio. "Volcano" was playing. Buffet's iconic voice belting out right in the middle of the second verse. I sang along as I backed up, then cruised down the driveway. Not slow, not fast.

I was still singing as I hit Palmetto and shooting rapid glances in both directions before turning left. The Impala was still there. Still idling in the shadows across the street and just beyond the edge of my property. It faced me and remained still, but not for long.

A quick look at my rearview and I saw them start up and pull onto the road. They were thirty yards back. Textbook tailing distance.

I turned north for a block, then hit a stop sign at Flagler Avenue. There were cars heading both directions. I waited. The Impala pulled up right behind me. I grabbed the beer can and reared it back and hurled it out the passenger window. Made a real obvious show of it. The tin can collided with the corner of the curb with an audible clank, then tumbled into the tall grass.

I turned south on Bertha, then east onto A1A. Cruised passed the airport, then followed the natural bow of the road up and along the channel. Turned west over the bridge. I needed somewhere quiet. Somewhere with no one else around. And not a lot of places on Cayo Hueso fit that description.

I hit a red light on Stock Island and braked to a

stop. Grabbed the cigar as well as a Bic from the center console. Cut the tip with the edge of my dive knife and lit it up. Took a long drag, then exhaled out the window and held my hand out, the red ember glowing in the darkness.

I flicked on my signal. Casually. And when the light flashed green I turned right, and then right again, heading south on Fifth Street. I followed the road past shops and businesses. Past housing developments and parks. Drove the entire half-mile ribbon of concrete until it ended at a dirt-and-sand road on Cow Key.

I drove around a barrier, and onto the neglected pathway. The way was smooth at first but gradually got bouncier. Potholes and shrubs sprouting up everywhere and overgrown branches reaching out from the sides.

After another quarter mile, the dirt road ended, giving way to an even rougher route. The guys tailing me continued. Already committed. Eager to deal with me quickly and claim their cash and pats on the back or whatever it was they got from their boss.

I slowed a little as I reached a fork. The pathway east along the water wasn't terrible; the one heading west was barely noticeable at all in the roots and branches and jutting sections of rock.

I turned west.

My four-by-four seemed to like it. The offroad tires and suspension and chassis taking on the route like it was nothing.

The Impala behind me, not so much.

It was a city vehicle. Loved smooth paved roads and nothing else. But it made it farther than I'd expected. Maybe fifty yards before bottoming out with an audible crunch. The smack of the axles against the rock and ruts.

Then the tires screeched and fought for traction in the sand. The vehicle rumbled and shuddered.

The car stayed put and I continued on. Weaving around a couple of turns before reaching the end of the neglected track. My headlights cut through the tangles of mangroves ahead of me and shined upon a narrow shoreline and shallow waters.

I put the truck in park. Left the engine running. The windows down.

Took two deep puffs of the cigar. Eyed it a moment, then gazed through the rearview.

"Also a shame," I said.

I leaned forward and held the cigar at the front corner of the window, ember facing outside. Then I rolled up the window slowly until the cigar was held in place. Unbuckled my seat belt and cranked up the music and shimmied to the passenger door. Opened it and grabbed the towel and Indian club and slid out. Looked back, then shut the door and turned and disappeared into the thick foliage.

I rolled up and stuffed the towel into my back pocket and found a good spot in the mangroves about thirty feet on a diagonal line from the right corner of the tailgate. From that angle, I could see the entire truck. Its headlights on and beaming forward. Exhaust coughing from the tailpipe. The outline of the cigar, and the smoke rising up from it.

In the darkness, it looked like there could be a guy sitting there. Holding out his cigar. Staring out and pondering life or waiting for someone or who knows what. Either way, my pursuers bought it. At least long enough.

They appeared on the sandy track. Light footsteps at first, then silhouettes. Their details being revealed with every step they took closer in the evening moonlight.

They were both young, strong, and lean. Both wore nice clothes. Gray slacks and black dress shirts. Polished dress shoes. Getting all dirty in the mud as they tripped over roots and shoved aside branches.

They had short hair and were clean-shaven. Both moved pretty good. Clearly capable, but city boys. Far out of their element.

Judging by their builds and skin tones, I assumed they were Haitian. But there was no way to tell. Regardless, it didn't matter who they were or where they were from. What mattered was that they had answers. Something I desperately needed.

They were ten yards from the tailgate when they withdrew their weapons. Both medium-sized pistols. Both in their right hands. They spread apart a little and stuck to the shadows between the taillights. Not entirely amateurs. Held their weapons like they'd used them before.

They were barely ten feet in front of me. Backs facing me. Spread apart maybe five feet from each other and standing shoulder to shoulder. Eyes staring at the driver's side of my truck.

From that distance and with the element of surprise on my side, I had options.

I ran through them all like a secretary sifting through a Rolodex of contacts. Priorities were speed and silence. Minimum effort, maximum damage.

A bird splashed in the water across from us, briefly

startling the two men. With their backs still facing me, I sprang out from my hiding place. Was on them before they'd managed to rotate their heads thirty degrees in my direction.

I held the Indian club in my right hand and threw it across my body, the barrel pointing behind me. When it comes to blunt objects, the backhand is the way to go. With my body jolting forward, I planted on my left foot, shifted to my right and spun in a rapid exploitation of leverage that began at the hips and whipped up my body to a swift snap at my hand.

I'd aimed for his temple, but the club struck him square in the forehead as he turned. The barrel landed with a loud, violent thud and he was gone and collapsing before he'd known he'd been engaged.

I went with the momentum of the blow, then stepped forward with my right leg and bent my knees and whipped the club around. The guy on the right managed to turn his upper body all the way around before I hit him. Managed to catch a sudden, terrifying glimpse of me before the object blurred toward him and made painful contact with his knees.

The five-pound club bashed into his kneecaps. A savage, jarring collision. Devastating.

His legs bent in unnatural directions and gave out completely beneath him. He whipped forward and shrieked. I caught him just before he smacked into the sand. Turned him around and plucked the rolled-up towel from my back pocket and shoved it into his mouth to muffle his screams.

I crouched down and checked the first guy I'd struck for a pulse. Felt nothing. I grabbed a roll of duct tape from the back of my truck and wrapped it around the remaining guy's head until the towel was snug. Then I taped his wrists behind his back. There was no reason to waste tape on his ankles. They weren't going to be used again anytime soon.

With one man out cold and potentially dead and the other secured, I searched them. Both of their pockets were completely empty, aside from the still-conscious guy, who had a wad of cash and a cell phone in the front pocket of his dress pants.

I set everything in the truck's bed, then examined their handguns. They were both Kimber Classics. Nice weapons. Fancy and expensive and well taken care of. It was a shame the guys hadn't had a chance to use them.

I stowed them in the toolbox in the back of my truck and locked them up. Pocketed the cash and phone, then dragged and shoved the dead guy into the shadows. Reaching into the driver's seat of my truck, I killed the lights and rolled up the windows. Shut off the engine and closed the door.

Returning to the taped-up guy with mangled knees, I grabbed him by his fancy shirt collar and dragged him right into the thick of the mangroves. Pulled him through dense tangles of branches and roots. Through pockets of mud and loose sand. He was shaking. Letting out muffled wails and sobs and groans.

I dragged him thirty yards, nearly to the water's edge, then sat him down on his butt atop a natural seawall of mangrove roots, his back to the sea. I shoved his ankles aside and taped them to large branches one at a time. Wrapped the adhesive around again and again to make sure they were snug. Then I kicked his chest. He flailed backward, flipping around. His head splashing into the water. His body suspended upside down by his taped-up ankles.

He was forced to heave himself up, to use his ab muscles to keep his head above water. To keep from drowning.

His grunts intensified. His big eyes staring up at me. His face red. Fierce.

I stood there a moment in the darkness and silence. Just staring at him. Then I gestured to the sea.

"Tide is on its way in," I said. "Two-foot swing. That means it'll be up to your waist in a couple of hours. And it won't be down below your head until morning."

I knelt down. Looked the guy in the eyes. "I'm gonna take this gag out of your mouth. And when I do, you're not going to scream. If you do, I'll hit your kneecaps again with this." I held up the Indian club. Made sure he got a good look at it. "Nod that you understand."

The guy stared at me, then his head bobbed up and down.

With the club in my left hand, I withdrew my dive knife with my right. Slid the blade into the space between the tape and the towel in his mouth, then ripped up and sideways. The edge made easy work of the tape, slicing through the three layers.

I grabbed the towel and removed it, letting it hang there by the still-secure sections of tape.

The man groaned. Breathed heavily in and out. Winced and clenched his jaw and fought hard to keep his face up out of the water.

After a couple seconds, he stared at me and snarled, "What do you want?"

"Answers," I said. "Who sent you? Who's running the shrimp boat smuggling operation?"

The man raised his eyebrows. Winced and coughed. "You really have no idea, do you?"

I nodded. "That's why you're going to tell me. Everything."

He shook his head. "No... I mean you have no idea how fucked you are."

I held out my hands. "Go on."

"I wasn't sent by no damn shrimp boat smugglers."

"Who sent you, then?"

His intense and pained scowl turned to a gritty smile for a moment. Then he let out what nearly sounded like a chuckle.

"Barbossa," he said, uttering the name slowly and reverently.

I shrugged. "That name supposed to mean something to me?"

He laughed again, then winced and moaned. "Might as well be the devil himself to you, gringo."

I smiled. "If he's so scary, why'd he send you two rookies to kill me?"

The man scowled again. Stared long and hard and intensely.

"He will kill you. You and your wife. Just a matter of time and you'll both be dead. And he'll take back what's been stolen from him."

His words caught me off guard. I shook my head slightly.

"The kids," the man hissed. "They're his and he wants them back."

I stared the man in the eyes. Thought over his

words. Pictured Olivier and Esther.

"His kids?"

"His property."

"Why were they smuggled out of Haiti then?"

"They weren't supposed to be on that boat. It was a personnel error. Bad judgment. A mistake that's been rectified."

I thought back to the initial encounter. The man on the sailboat being shot as Ange and I approached. Rosalind and Leon must've paid the smuggler off or something. They must've hoped they'd flee far enough from Barbossa and disappear in the States before being discovered.

Clearing my throat, I said, "Who's running things here in the islands? I need names if you want to see the light of another day."

The guy snarled. Shook his head. "I don't know any names here. I'm not involved in this."

"You're just the clean up crew. Part of the kill squad."

The man smiled sadistically.

"Good thing you're not good at your job." I shifted closer. Withdrew my dive knife. "You complied, so you're free to go."

Reaching forward slowly, I ripped the tape securing his ankles. First his left, then his right. Then I helped him up onto the top of the groves.

Then I sheathed my knife.

Then I relaxed a little and turned away from the guy.

A test.

One he failed.

The moment I looked away from him, he reached

for an object strapped to his ankle. One just concealed under his pant leg.

He withdrew a subcompact pistol. Managed to rotate it about ten degrees toward me before I snapped back and caught his elbow with my left hand and his wrist with my right and whipped my upper body forward. The assassin's trigger finger flexed unconsciously as the barrel arched back a hundred and eighty degrees and a round exploded from the chamber and blasted through the top of his skull. Like his partner, the guy was gone before he hit the ground.

TWENTY-TWO

I retrieved the beer can I'd discarded, then turned back into my driveway thirty minutes after leaving the hitmen. Scarlett's Bronco was there, along with two police vehicles. One of them I recognized as Chief Verona's cruiser. The second was more generic looking, but I recognized the guy leaning against the passenger-side door.

He waved at me as I pulled up to a stop beside the Bronco. I killed the engine and slid out.

"Hey, Logan," Officer O'Malley said. "Everything all right?"

I nodded to him as I tossed the can into a recycle bin and made for the stairs. "Everything's fine."

Ange met me at the top step, and Jane was right behind her. Through the open side door, I could see Scarlett and Cameron in the living room. They were both wide-eyed and staring at me. Both appeared uneasy. Borderline shell-shocked.

"No issues?" Ange said, eyeing me up and down.

"No issues." Then I gestured toward our daughter. "What's wrong with them?"

Ange shook her head. "I don't know."

I strode into the living room. Approached the two teenagers, then looked them both over.

"You two all right?" I said.

They exchanged glances, then Scarlett said, "Something happened on our date."

"What kind of something?"

My daughter glanced over my shoulder at Chief Verona, then said, "It's not time sensitive. I can tell you later."

"You sure?"

"Yes, sir."

Whatever it was, it was clearly important. Scarlett hardly ever called me *sir*. But there were other important matters to attend to as well.

I turned and cut back across the room. Gestured to Jane, and said, "Can we talk out back?"

She nodded, and after the chief of police passed, I whispered into Ange's ear, asking her to begin packing overnight bags. She headed inside, and I followed Jane along the side of the house and around to the back balcony.

She turned around with her hands on her hips and said, "What happened?"

"What's he doing here?" I said, ignoring her question and pointing my head back toward the driveway.

"Sergeant O'Malley?" Jane said.

"Yes."

She paused a moment. Clearly unsure of how to

respond. Shook her head a little. "He's part of my team. He's here to help."

I folded my arms. Tightened my gaze.

"He's on my suspect list."

"You're kidding."

"Wish I was."

"You don't trust him?"

"I don't know him well enough to trust him." She went silent a beat, and I added, "Just send him away. And don't tell him where we're going."

She let out a breath. Gazed over the yard and channel. "You don't think that's being a little paranoid?"

"I mean it, Jane."

She nodded. Reached for her radio and ordered O'Malley to head back to the station. When the order was acknowledged, she eyed me skeptically.

"What happened?" she asked a second time. "Where'd you come from? Ange said there was someone here. Watching your house. Do you know who they are?"

"They *were* members of a Haitian crime ring."

She placed a hand to her forehead. Looked down. "Were?"

"That's right."

"They tried to kill you?"

I nodded. "Biggest mistake they ever made."

"And so, you killed them?"

"I gave them a chance," I said.

A half-truth. I'd given one of them a chance.

Jane rubbed her chin. "So, what are you going to do now, then? Go to Haiti and take on all of these dangerous criminals on foreign soil?"

"Not yet. There's business to be dealt with here first."

I listened as Officer O'Malley's vehicle started up, backed out, and drove off down our driveway. Once it was gone, I headed inside to help pack.

"Where are you going?" Jane said, following me.

"The fewer people who know, the better."

"You won't even tell me?"

"We'll be close by, Jane," I said. "Able to reach the mainland in under fifteen minutes if need be."

We packed overnight bags. Filled a cooler with food and drinks. Loaded everything into Scarlett's Bronco.

I drove my Tacoma first. And when it was clear there were no more tails, I messaged Ange and we all cruised over to Conch Harbor Marina. She took my usual spot just up from the waterfront. I parked in the garage half a block down. One level up in a dimly lit corner, then met them in the lot and heaved everything down the dock to the Baia.

"You sure this is a good idea?" Ange said, glancing at the two kids.

They were both fast asleep, Olivier in my arms and Esther in Ange's.

I knew right away where she was going with that. I'd been contemplating the same thing myself. These kids had just spent days at sea cramped aboard a tiny leaking vessel with a bunch of other people. And then they'd ended the voyage with a shoot-out and had been on a different boat as their mother had died. They were just beginning to get used to life on land again—just beginning to open up a little. Even smile at times. And now they were going to be waking up on another vessel.

But we both agreed that it was the best option and loaded everything aboard our boat. We set up the guest cabin for the kids. It had a bunk bed that could fold out, and we removed the mattress from the bottom one and set it on the deck. Then lined it with pillows and blanket to make the whole bottom their bed. Scarlett would sleep in the top bunk, her favorite spot, with her window cracked open, and would keep a close eye on them.

After setting the two kids down, Ange and I headed topside. We decided to bring our Robalo center-console with us, agreeing that having a smaller boat with a shallower draft could potentially come in handy given recent events. Tying it off to the stern, we cast the lines and I fired up the twin 600s and eased us out of the slip toward the opening into the bight. Kept our speed even slower than usual and my head on a swivel. Saw nothing unusual or suspicious. No one following us.

I kicked us up to fifteen knots and cruised west. The sea was calm, and the sky was dark with sporadic patches of clouds intermittently blotting out the moon.

I had options again.

There was no shortage of remote, quiet coves and tucked away bays in the Lower Keys. So, I ran through the many possibilities, then continued west. We wanted somewhere calm and quiet. With clear lines of sight. Multiple egress routes in case the next killers sent after us happened to have a boat or two with significant horsepower.

I wrapped around Fleming Key, then headed north

through Bluefish Channel. Three miles later, I cut east for just over a mile, then turned sharply south into a different channel that juts down into the Bay Keys. Ange pointed ahead and to the left, and I nodded.

I rotated the wheel and slid back on the throttle. Chugged us along until I found a good spot right between two of the little islands.

From there, the Baia was properly shielded from the wind. We were five miles from Key West, with a natural barrier of extreme shallows between us. The only way a vessel that wasn't a kayak could reach us was by wrapping all the way around and heading down the channel like we had. But we'd be able to spot anything approaching from miles away.

I dropped and set the anchor, then powered down the engines. The steady drone of the motors died off, and the world around us went silent. At the stern, I grabbed the rope secured to our Robalo and pulled it along the Baia's starboard side. Positioned a couple fenders and tied it off both forward and aft.

Once it was secure, I stepped below deck to check on the kids, and Scarlett met me on the bottom step.

"They're still asleep," she said.

I bobbed my chin. Then she followed me topside. Leaned against the back of the sunbed, facing Ange and me.

"What happened on your date?"

She leaned back and held up her hands. "Don't freak out. But I kind of, sort of, had a gun aimed at me. Twice."

"What?" I said, anger brewing. "How is that not time sensitive?"

"It's not what you think. It was Delaney." She

paused briefly, then added, "But he didn't know it was me."

Ange and I both raised our eyebrows at her. She sighed and explained herself, starting with how they'd seen Delaney in Old Town and followed him. How they'd watched his conversation with Pete.

"You spied on them?" Ange said.

"I didn't know he was going to talk to Pete. We just saw him strolling and thought it was suspicious. I wanted to help."

Then she continued to explain how they'd followed him again and nearly been shot before Officer O'Malley had cruised by and scared him off.

"Delaney was jumpy," she said. "Weary of being followed. He's hiding something. No doubt about it. Normal people with clean consciouses aren't that paranoid."

I shrugged. "Sometimes they are. He's reclusive now."

"He's hiding something," she said again. "I'm sure of it. Either he or Officer O'Malley are involved here. Or both are." She paused. Bit her lip. "But my money's on Delaney. He was so jumpy and defensive. And he was talking to someone on the phone angrily. Telling them he was going to handle everything." She let out a deep breath. "Delaney's in on this thing. And I think you both know it. I think Pete knew it before you and that's why he gave you the guy's name. Maybe Pete doesn't even know that he knows, but he does."

I eyed her quizzically, and she explained, "Like, maybe he's too close to see what's happening, you know? Or too biased because of their past friendship."

"How old are you again?" Ange said, amazed by our daughter's insight.

I was too. And I agreed with her.

"We believe you, Scar," I said. "You have great discernment. And we'll do everything we can to get to the bottom of this."

Ange hugged our daughter tight. Then I joined in.

"I'm glad you're both all right," I said. "We'll take care of this."

She relaxed a bit, then headed down to bed. I cracked open a beer. Took a sip, then handed it to Ange.

"What do you think?" she said after taking a long pull.

"I think she's right. But whether Delaney's in on this thing or not, we've got bigger problems on our hands."

"The one who sent those assassins tonight," she said.

"A crime boss named Barbossa apparently."

"Who is he?"

I pulled out my phone. Punched in Murph's number. "It's time to find out."

TWENTY-THREE

I awoke early the next morning. Kissed Ange on her forehead and slipped out of bed. Tiptoed out and across the saloon. Every movement gently rocked the vessel. It was a calm morning. Barely a breath of wind.

I peeked through the guest cabin door. Saw Esther and Olivier asleep on the cushioned deck. Saw Scarlett curled up above. I shut the door and turned for the steps. Atticus woke up. He eyed me and stretched. Kept quiet aside from his gently wagging tail hitting everything in its path as we headed topside.

The revitalizing fresh morning air greeted us. It was still dark, but the sun's glow was appearing to the east. Just about to blossom. Its brightness intensifying with every passing minute.

I took a look around. The lagoon was calm and tranquil, and quiet. No other boats within a mile of us.

Fish splashed up from the water, swiping bugs buzzing in circles and creating ripples on the surface.

The sea had that alluring turquoise tint that calls me like a siren. A sea that I have to jump into. A burning fire within me I can't control. An excitement to experience that deep, primal feeling of being alive and in the moment.

I took a full three-sixty survey before heading back into the galley. After downing a can of coconut water, I grabbed my mask, snorkel, and fins, then donned them on the swim platform and slid into the little cove. The water felt cool and refreshing. Taking a dip in the sea has always been one of my favorite ways to wake up in the morning.

I let the air out of my lungs and sank to the bottom and finned along the rock and coral. Visibility was perfect, allowing me to see all the way to the base of the two mangrove-covered islands. The place was teeming with life and color. Thousands of tiny fish. Scurrying crabs fleeing for turtle grass. Larger fish hanging out at the edges of the groves.

I performed a long sweep north all the way to the shallows, then back around toward the eastern island. Slow and steady at first, then working my way into a faster pace. Smooth kicks and pulls. Controlled breaths. Waking and warming up my muscles, then pushing them.

After thirty minutes of swimming, I reached the southern corner of the eastern island and kicked parallel with the groves, heading back toward the anchored Baia. The sun was up now, its rays shining through the translucent water and into the shadows of the submerged mangrove roots.

While finning, I thought over the events of the previous day. The two men sent to kill me, and to retrieve the two kids. Not only had we disrupted part of a very lucrative, very profitable, very illegal operation, but we were harboring two kids that the top dog wanted back. Things were spiraling out of hand. And fast.

I'd yet to hear back from Murph regarding his investigation into the Haitian crime boss named Barbossa. But a quick online search had given me a good idea of the kind of criminal I was dealing with. His name flooded Haitian and international news sites. He'd been suspected of everything from murder to smuggling and illegal arms dealing but had yet to face serious legal repercussions. A sign of the sad state of Haiti and its level of corruption.

As I kicked along the branches, I spotted no shortage of movement and life among the tangles. Mangroves are a godsend to coastal environments, vital to the land and marine life. Fish grow and flourish in the havens until they're big enough to take on open waters. They also serve as astoundingly efficient natural barriers to protect land from storms, reducing the impact of waves and surges.

When I was just thirty yards from the Baia, I spotted a unique, colorful fish hiding in a rocky alcove. One with venomous spines sticking out all over its body. As I swam closer, I saw two more hidden along the same ledge.

I kicked back to my boat. Slid off my fins and climbed up the ladder and retrieved my weight belt and speargun.

Thirty seconds later, I was back in the water,

finning back toward the ledge. This time armed.

I sucked in a breath and kicked to the bottom. Held onto the branches, took aim, and fired. The rubber tubing snapped, and the spear launched free and impaled a lionfish through its broadside.

I had a long list of reasons for loving the Florida Keys. One of them was the ability to wake up, rub your eyes, leap from your house and find a tasty fresh seafood meal right beneath your toes. And lionfish, being invasive and terrible for the native marine life, are always in season.

Ten minutes later, I had five of them in a bucket at the swim platform. The biggest was easily three pounds, massive for a lionfish.

After doing a final sweep to make sure I'd cleared out all of the colorful invaders, I kicked back toward the Baia and poked up from the sea right at the stern. Grabbed the swim platform and hauled myself up and came face-to-face with a young, curious pair of eyes.

Olivier was standing there. Right on the swim platform. Still and wide-eyed. Mouth partly agape.

I heaved myself out slowly, minimizing the sway of the boat, then turned and sat on the corner. Slid down my mask and eyed the boy.

"You caught those?" he said, staring at the dead fish in the bucket beside him. Then he gestured toward my speargun. "With that?"

"It's easier than it looks," I said. "And a whole lot of fun. You want to try?"

"I can't swim."

"Want to learn?"

He paused. Blinked and stared out over the water surrounding us. Shook his head.

"Well, if you change your mind, let me know."

I removed my fins and mask. Reached back for a towel and patted my face dry.

"Aren't you scared of sharks?" he said, staring down at the water.

"You're more likely to be struck by lightning twice than get attacked by a shark. But I take precautions regardless. Just in case."

I patted my dive knife strapped to the inside of my right calf. Regardless of the odds, I always liked to have it. And there tends to be an unfortunate amount of debris in the ocean. Discarded nets and other trash. Other than shallow water blackouts, the only thing I generally concern myself with is getting tangled with something. That's far more likely to threaten my life than a shark.

"Your dad hasn't taught you to swim?" I said.

He fell silent at that. Stared down at his toes.

"It may look scary," I said. "Heck, nearly everything is before you try it and get used to it. But it's a lot of fun, trust me. One of my favorite things to do on Earth." I smiled and pointed at the sea. "You can fly in the water. Soar and swoop and dive. Like a bird."

He blinked. Stared out at the water again, then said, "I guess I could learn. That sounds fun."

I don't remember learning how to swim. I can't recall a time when I ever gazed upon a body of water and thought anything resembling fear. Just a desire to jump right in and explore. Discover the whole new world that flourished beneath the surface.

Since I don't remember learning, I don't know how my dad did it. But knowing him, it'd likely been a somewhat hands-on approach that allowed me to go at my own pace. That'd been his style with most things. He'd teach me a few basics, then let me try whatever it was out on my own. Let me fail. Let me get back up and try again. Even if I'd been scared of the new thing.

Especially if I'd been scared of the new thing.

He liked to always say that he didn't know everything. That, in fact, I could very well know more than him. That maybe I'd discover a better way of doing something that he'd never thought of. That no one had ever thought of. I'd be five or six and he'd say things like that to me.

He was a great man.

So, I went with his approach. I taught the kid a few things. Swimming is about feeling. You don't learn by reading a book. You gotta jump in. Scarlett had known the basics when Ange and I had helped her the previous year. This was a clean slated five-year-old possessing both a wide-eyed allure and a terrifying dread of big water.

"The most important thing is to be relaxed," I said off the bat. "Humans were meant to swim. We're mostly water, after all. And when our hands and feet enter water, they turn wrinkly. Our skin literally adapts right in front of our eyes so we can grip things better underwater."

We started on the swim platform. Sitting cross legged shoulder to shoulder. Eyes closed and breathing in and out. Slow and deep.

"It's all about the breath," I said.

We sat there for five minutes. Just breathing in and out. Then I had him slide his legs into the water and kick, feeling the friction of the water against his foot. When he got that down, I had him turn around and slide a little deeper. With the water up to his waist, and me right behind him, he kicked and kicked.

"Your legs are much stronger than your arms," I said.

When he got tired, I let him relax a bit on the swim platform, then helped him slide all the way slowly in while supporting him. He was nervous at first, then calmed and floated on his back for a couple minutes, my hands on his back and upper leg. Just keeping him steady. He giggled as water kissed his ears.

Then I let go.

He floated there another ten seconds, then I told him that I wasn't doing anything. His heart rate picked up a bit and he jittered a little at first, then he breathed in and out and relaxed into the float.

"See," I said with a smile. "You can float just like that. You ever get tired. You ever get scared. Just flatten your body and breathe calmly."

Next, I grabbed a kickboard from below deck, and he kicked his way back and forth near the Baia's stern. Ange arrived, a big smile on her face as she stretched and watched Olivier.

"I'm swimming!" he exclaimed.

Ange held up her hands and gave a resounding applause.

I was amazed. I'd expected it to take a couple days at least for him to become comfortable in the water, but the kid caught on fast.

Esther and Scarlett awoke twenty minutes later, our daughter carrying the toddler topside. Even the two-year-old got in on the action, jumping in and kicking while I held onto her upper body. Wanting to be like her older brother.

We all had breakfast topside. Some eggs and toast and sliced up mango. After eating, it was right back into the water. Neither of them wanted to do anything but splash around and climb the ladder and jump back in, over and over.

It was a heck of a fun way to spend a morning, and a great way for all of us to take our mind off things. Especially the kids.

By the time noon rolled around, Olivier was asking to use a mask and snorkel. The kid who'd been scared of the water hours earlier was now obsessed with it. And we couldn't get him out if we tried.

He and his sister passed out just after lunch. We had grilled lionfish and potatoes. When they awoke, it was right back into the sea. Our own private swimming pool. One that we didn't have to buy, clean, or maintain. And one that featured a vast array of sea life for us to ogle.

I tired out Atticus by tossing a stick overboard so he could vault over the side, swim to fetch it, and bring it back. I'd once met a guy who lived in the Middle Keys and had trained his Lab to dive down and catch lobster. It was one of those things that had to be seen to be believed. I sure had to see it myself. His dog leapt over the side, dove down over ten feet, grabbed a lobster in its jaws, and brought it up to the surface.

It was utterly incredible. Not only had the guy's pooch provided many a delicacy, he'd also won a lot of bets for his owner.

Atticus wasn't quite there yet, but maybe one day.

But he could fetch a stick with the best of them.

In typical feline fashion, Boise spent most of the day in the prone position. She got up a couple times, but never traveled far and was content to observe our activities from a shaded perch.

As evening came, we settled in for a movie. Wanting to watch something we'd all enjoy, we snuggled up on the sunbed with blankets and pillows and played Treasure Planet on our laptop, connecting it to the Baia's topside speakers for surround sound. We enjoyed one of my favorite animated films while eating popcorn and ice cream sandwiches.

At one point, near the end of the movie, Olivier stared over at me wide-eyed. "Do you think places like that really exist? Hidden treasures and maps?"

I smiled. Shot a glance to Ange and Scarlett.

"I know they do," I said. Then I leaned forward, wrapped an arm around him then pointed my other hand toward the horizon. "And many of them are still out there. Just waiting to be discovered."

All day, I'd been expecting to get a call at any moment from Jane, inquiring about the two corpses that turned up on the southwest side of Cow Key.

Just before sunset, I got a call. But it wasn't Key West's chief of police. It wasn't anyone I'd expected.

I picked my phone off the dinette and stared at the screen. Blinked and let out a breath and answered before it could buzz a second time.

It was Dr. Patel, an ER doctor at Lower Keys Medical Center.

"I'm calling about the man who was airlifted here after your incident near the Tortugas," he said in his Indian accent. "The guy who was shot twice. He's awake."

He paused a moment, and I ran a hand through my hair. I'd completely forgotten about the guy. Figured he'd passed away midflight. He'd been in rough shape.

"Is he coherent?" I asked.

"Barely. But he's not looking good. I'm not sure how much longer he'll be able to hold on." I fell silent, and he added, "I thought you'd want to know."

"Police on site?"

"On their way. Along with CBP officers."

"I'll be right there."

TWENTY-FOUR

The Lower Keys Medical Center was just over four miles away as the pelican flies, on the northern side of Stock. Climbing aboard my Robalo, I tossed the lines and blasted north, then west, then south back through Bluefish Channel. Having to go around the shallows nearly doubled the distance, but I still reached Stock in roughly fifteen minutes.

I headed straight for the deep, dredged cove nestled against the College of the Florida Keys. The school's campus was situated right across the street from the hospital.

I'd been fortunate to meet and work with some amazing locals throughout my years in the Keys. Formed many strong friendships. One of those friendships was with Professor Frank Murchison, one of the most popular and qualified faculty members in the history of the college.

He'd taught at Harvard for years but had gotten

tired of the harsh winters and had done what Jack calls "trading deep pockets for sandy pockets."

I eased up to the college's docks, having kept the Robalo running near top speed for most of the transit. A student met me there. He was a member of the school's famous diving program that conducted much of its training right there in the deep bay. Murchison was revered on campus, so any friend of his was welcome.

I tied off and thanked the young man. Hustled across the campus, through the parking lot, then across College Road to the hospital. There were three police cruisers parked in the lot, as well as two CBP agent vehicles. I entered through the emergency room doors and headed straight for intensive care. Immediately spotted and approached a small group assembled down the hall just outside one of the rooms.

Jane was there, standing with her arms folded. So was Officer O'Malley. And so were Agent Briggs and his partner.

As I approached, I also spotted Red Delaney. He was wearing the same clothes he'd had on the previous day. His hair was a mess. He looked tired. And he wore my Doxa on his left wrist.

I wondered why Delaney was there, but didn't say anything to anyone. Just peered through the glass and saw the criminal who'd tried to kill me two days earlier. He was lying on the hospital bed, tubes sticking out from his tanned, tattooed arms.

His eyes were blinking subtly. His head bobbing and swaying side to side. Dr. Patel was in there, checking him over and speaking to the nurse beside him, who was staring at the vitals monitor.

A detective from the Key West Police Department was inside with them. He was wearing a suit, but his shirt had clearly been hastily tucked. The guy had probably just sat down to dinner when he'd received the urgent call.

The detective was standing at the foot of the bed. Arms folded like Jane's. Not really sure what to do. Unable to help, but sort of standing by and keeping an eye on the medical team, waiting for his opening to slip in a question for the smuggler.

But it seemed like that moment might never come. The man was in rough shape. Looked to be on the verge of death. And as Patel had said on the phone, it didn't look like he'd last much longer.

I reached for the door and entered. No asking for permission. No words uttered at all. And I shut it behind me before anyone could follow.

One of the nurses glared at me. She was about to speak when Dr. Patel tapped her shoulder and shot her a look over his glasses. She flattened her lips and looked away from me and went back to her work.

"He say anything yet?" I asked the detective. The guy squinted at me. We'd met and worked together a few times. But I was a civilian.

Angling his head, he peered through the glass at his chief, who gave him a quick bob of her head.

"You're still consulting for us?"

I nodded.

I wasn't sure whether I was or not. Earlier that year, Jane had brought me on as an official special consultant for the KWPD so I could help out with an investigation into a string of robberies and murders in the Keys.

"No," the detective said. He motioned to the injured criminal and added, "He can't talk."

Aside from his swaying head, he was motionless. Pale. His breathing fast. His heart rate fluctuating.

I stepped closer to the hospital bed.

"He can hear, right?" I said to Patel.

He nodded while keeping his eyes on his work—forced to help the man even though he was a murdering criminal. Part of the job. He was bound by the Hippocratic oath, a promise medical professionals made that dated back thousands of years.

I surveyed the room. Spotted a clipboard resting on a counter that wasn't being used. Grabbed it, then flipped over one of its pages and clamped the blank page on top. Dr. Patel grabbed a pen from his front pocket and handed it to me.

I moved closer to the head of the bed and the detective stepped back, giving the dying man a clear view of me.

Less than twenty-four hours earlier, I'd been a mile and a half south from that very spot. I'd had a dying criminal before me. But no eyes of the law around. No restrictions. I couldn't hang this guy upside down and wait for the incoming tide to convince him to start talking. I had to take a different approach.

I stared at the man a moment. Planted my hands on my hips and let out a breath.

"Time is precious," I said. Speaking loud and clear. Authoritative. "And you've only got a sliver of it left."

I held my gaze on him. He coughed and stared

back. Closed his eyes then scowled and eyed the far wall.

"Precious time to make peace with your creator," I continued. "To make things right." I paused again, watching the dying man. "Do the right thing and clear your conscience. Money can't help you now. Prestige and prosperity. Fancy houses and cars. None of it matters now."

I stopped again, letting my words sink in.

"But," I said, "you can save others. You can't right your wrongs, but you can make things right. Right here and now you can save thousands of innocent lives."

The man's eyes closed. He sealed them so tight his face shook. Then he turned his head from side to side. A tear streaked down his face. Then another. Then steady streams ran down both sides, down his jaw and then his neck.

I doubted he'd dreamed as a child that one day he would completely screw over his fellow man just to make a quick buck. That he'd make his living sending innocent men, women, and children to their doom. His state had no doubt manifested itself in increments. One compromise after another until it was too late.

Now here he was.

On his deathbed. The curtain closing and the darkness drawing near. Nothing but a mountain of mistakes and regrets. What-could-have-beens. What he'd originally wanted out of life. What never would be.

He'd made his choices. He was merely reaping what he'd sown.

"You don't have to go out with this stain on your existence," I said. "You can be the one. Right here and now. You can put a stop to the evil. The bloodshed and the slavery. With your last act on Earth, you can end it all." I leaned closer, looked him in the eyes, and added, "You can redeem yourself."

My heart rate picked up, emotion taking hold over me as well. I held out the pen. Stared into his watery eyes.

He glanced toward the window to his right. The one offering a view of the hallway. He was quick and subtle. But I followed his gaze and saw the group staring in at us through the glass. Chief Verona, Officer O'Malley, Agent Briggs and his partner, and Red Delaney.

I stomped around the hospital bed. Grabbed the edge of the curtain and yanked it, unfurling the fabric and covering half the window. I grabbed and did the same with the other side.

The same nurse turned and shot me the same look she had when I'd entered. And again Dr. Patel had my back and the curtain remained shut.

I returned to the foot of the bed. Shuffled in even closer to the dying criminal, then knelt down so our faces were barely two feet apart.

"You can save them," I said. "You can tell me who's running this thing in the islands and you can save thousands of innocents."

Tears continued to flow down the man's face. He closed his eyes again. Just as tight as before. Then he opened them and lifted his right hand ever so slightly. His hand was shaky, but fueled by conviction.

I handed him the pen, careful to make sure his

weakened extremity could keep it secure before I let go. He held it gently and I raised the clipboard and kept it steady just below the pen's inky tip.

He reached. Hands weak, eyes soaked, body giving out. He put the tip to the page. Drew a solid vertical line, then a small loop at the top of it. The letter P. Distinct and legible. He followed it up with a second letter. Clear as day. No space between them. Then he shook and sobbed and his hand fell. The pen slipped through his fingers and rattled to the floor. His mouth opened. His eyes bulged. He struggled and gasped, then his head fell back and his eyes closed, never to open again.

The last bit of air flowed out from his lungs. The life support monitor went from a fast-beeping rhythm to a solid drone.

Dr. Patel sighed. Checked the time.

"Time of death, eight fifty-six p.m."

Then the nurse spread a sheet over his face. And the room went silent.

I stared down at the clipboard. At the two letters, clear and distinct. Not what I'd expected, but an answer regardless.

The door opened and Jane entered first. She stopped in front of me. Glanced at the corpse, then at me, and then at the clipboard in my hands.

"He say anything?" she said.

I shook my head. "No. But he wrote this."

I turned the clipboard around and showed her the page. The two letters the criminal had written.

PD.

TWENTY-FIVE

Jane stared down at the two letters for a long moment. Like she was trying to process what she was looking at. Then she looked up at me with a blank expression, like she was trying to come to grips with what she'd just seen.

I slid the paper free. Folded it up and pocketed it and set the clipboard back on the counter. No one except Dr. Patel, myself, and Jane had seen the two letters. Not even the detective who'd been on the other side of the bed. He'd angled his head but had still only seen the back of the clipboard.

I stepped out. Got a good look at Officer O'Malley, the two agents, and Delaney, then turned down the hall toward the exit. I glanced back and saw them all watching me as Jane hustled to catch up. She fell right in step alongside me as I hit the sliding doors. Looked at me and wanted to ask a question. Clearly didn't know what to ask, so I asked one instead.

"Could it be true?" I said.

She sighed. Shook her head as we stepped out into the humid night air.

"I'd trust any in my department with my life," she replied. "I trust all of them. But at the end of the day, I'm human. And so are they. Yes, of course it could be true."

I stopped on the sidewalk. Observed the tough, competent police chief for a moment. She knew what was about to happen. Knew what needed to happen. And it was going to hurt. No way around that. It was going to be painful as hell, but necessary.

"What are you going to do now?" she asked.

A black BMW cruised into the lot as the words escaped her lips. The vehicle rumbled across the pavement and parked right in front of us. Homeland Security Agent Darius Maddox climbed out. The powerfully built, middle-aged black man just gazed back at us a moment.

"I won't be doing anything right away," I said to Jane. Then I motioned toward Agent Maddox. "But he probably will."

Over the course of the next forty-eight hours, a thorough joint-agency internal investigation was done into the Key West Police Department. Agent Maddox spearheaded Homeland's efforts, and a small contingent of FBI and detectives from the mainland were sent as well.

The note scribbled by the dying criminal wouldn't have brought on the storm by itself, but Jane was a great officer of the law. She believed in her men, of course. Believed in her people. But wanted to get to the bottom of everything. So, she called for the investigation herself. Reported that there was solid reason to believe that a member of her precinct was working with an illegal human smuggling operation that'd been flying under the radar in South Florida for who knew how long, potentially smuggling thousands into the United States for forced labor and prostitution.

It was a big mess. And a big, formidable nut to crack. So, the big guns were sent out.

Ange and I did our best to steer clear of the hurricane of suits and credentials and paperwork. Figured we'd just get in the way, and that if they started getting some traction, Maddox would keep us in the loop. Maddox and I had a strong relationship. Had saved each other's lives. Had earned each other's respect. And we'd both served and there was a bond there that went beyond everything else.

I heard nothing until the evening of the second day. We were anchored off Cayo Agua, roughly two miles east from where we we'd been the first night in the Bay Keys. It was Agent Maddox, asking if I could meet him downtown.

I cruised the Robalo to the waterfront and met him at Moondog Café, the same place where I'd first met him years earlier. I asked him how the investigation was going, and he went right into it.

Darius Maddox was good. Better than most. Better than me.

He'd spent thirty years in the Army's Special Forces. Green Berets. Like Rambo. Except Johnny the drifter had only spent a handful of years in the service. Maddox had spent half a lifetime. They were an impressive lot. I'd trained with them. I'd fought alongside them. And he'd spent the last couple years tracking down threats within the nation for Homeland Security. He'd been heavily recruited by every three-letter organization, and he'd had his pick of the litter. Had a solid position and was trusted to make decisions and conduct his own investigations. And he had some of the best agents working with him, a team of his choosing.

And in forty-eight hours the investigation had turned up nothing.

"What about Red Delaney?" I asked. "You guys check him out at all?"

"We searched his place," Maddox said. "Given your suspicions and given what happened with Scarlett."

"You got a warrant?"

"Didn't need one. He let us in. We went through all his books and personal effects. Doesn't have much. We searched every inch of the place and his dock and his old shrimp boat. He's clean." Maddox paused a moment, then said, "But something was found on Cow Key. Two things. A guy walking his dog stumbled upon a couple rotting corpses on the southwest side of the island. Deep in the groves beyond the dirt road. You know anything about that?"

I shot him a confident look. Didn't reply.

Maddox closed his eyes and pinched the bridge of his nose. "Jeez, Logan. Who are they?"

I shrugged. "I didn't catch their names. Pleasantries were never exchanged. But I know who they worked for."

Maddox held out his palms. "All right. Who did they work for?"

"Barbossa."

"Who the hell is that?"

Maddox was an expert. As good as agents get, but his focus was the United States. Domestic problems. And I imagined there wasn't a lot of excess time and energy and space in his mental arsenal to be learning about Caribbean crime bosses.

"I'd never heard of him either," I said, "Up until a few days ago. Apparently, he's a big-time Haitian crime boss. A mass murderer. Smuggler of drugs and illegal firearms and migrants and all-around despicable human. A real 'scum of the Earth' type."

Murph had gotten back to me but had yet to dig deep into the criminal's dealings. Just surface stuff, primarily. Many of the same things I'd read via simple online searches.

"And he wants you dead?" Maddox asked. "For what you and Ange did? If he's so big-time, why would one branch of his vast network be so important to him?"

"Because of the kids," I said. "Apparently, they belong to Barbossa. Whatever the hell that means."

"What?" he said, shaking his head. He leaned back and stared off a moment. "Then why were they on that smuggling boat?"

"One of the assassins said they snuck aboard. Bought off a smuggler. I don't know the whole story. Just bits and pieces. They're two and five. Don't exactly have much to say about it. But we'll know more when we find their father."

He paused. Looked away. His expression saying everything.

If we find their father.

It was a big fat if. And there was another one right along with it.

If their father was even still alive.

We both went quiet. Both in deep thought.

I eventually leaned forward and said, "What's your gut telling you here?"

"My gut's conflicted."

"You don't think local police officers are involved?"

"I mean, I'm just trying to think about it logistically. They have police boats and all that, sure, but the ones I'd have in my pocket if I were running an illegal operation like this are the Border Patrol agents. You know, the ones whose job description specifies keeping illegal aliens from our country."

"So, you're gonna check their office as well?"

"We already have," he said, slumping deeper into his chair. "It's been a busy couple of days."

"There really hasn't been anything discovered in the investigation? Nothing at all?"

Maddox took a bite of his sirloin, then downed a swig of coffee and wiped his chin with a napkin.

"Well, the *official* investigation has turned up zilch."

"Official?" I said, raising an eyebrow at him. "That mean there's an unofficial one?"

He nodded. "The main one is just a formality, really. Checking all of the boxes. Doing due diligence. You know how the government works." He looked around. Leaned forward and lowered his voice. "No effective criminal would have evidence just lying around, so the investigation is more just for show. The real work's being done by agents working behind the scenes. In the shadows."

"They're tailing officers?" I said.

He nodded. "And tapping their phones. And whatever else they can do. Going through their damn trash."

"Have they found anything yet?"

"This Sergeant O'Malley has got my vote."

"Why?" I said, wanting to hear his take before I gave him mine.

"Gut instinct at first. Just struck me as an odd character. He's got one of the biggest houses in Key West. If he needs money, why wouldn't he sell his place and get something more practical? And if he doesn't need it, why's he working as a low-ranking police officer? And he seems to be decent at his job, but he rarely gets promoted. Just sort of rides the line, you know? Not getting in trouble, not doing anything particularly stellar."

"I agree," I said. "He'd have my vote. He also has connections and family history with the shrimp industry here."

"You plan on sharing that with me at any point?"

"I didn't want you to be swayed by my opinion. I wanted you to treat this whole thing like a blank slate. Objectively." I paused a moment. Thought over everything Maddox had said. "You mentioned *at first*. Has something else convinced you of his involvement?"

He nodded. "We received an anonymous tip. A guy with a distorted voice telling us that O'Malley was involved. Then we recovered an old, deleted email on his work computer. It seemed like gibberish, but it was sent to an email created with a Haiti IP address. We think it could be some kind of code."

He checked his phone. Cleared his throat. "We're working to get a warrant to search his house. But we're trying to keep it on the down-low. Obviously, it's something you want to procure and execute without giving a heads-up first. Though, if these past two days aren't warning enough, I don't know what would be."

Maddox finished off the last of his steak and potatoes, then took another sip of coffee.

"You sure the dying criminal wasn't lying?" he said. "Trying to keep us off the real scent? Send us elsewhere? Maybe he was instructed to do that. If he ever got caught. Maybe he'd been instructed to lie and blame everything on local law enforcement."

"He was dying," I said. "His last breaths of life. Why would he lie on his deathbed? Isn't that where all the truths and revelations are supposed to come out?"

"I guess. But maybe he wasn't the only one threatened. Maybe he had a family. Even if no wife or children, maybe his parents were still alive. Or maybe he had siblings. They could've been threatened if he ever spoke up. It wouldn't exactly be unheard of. I've seen it again and again."

I fell silent. Thought about that. Pictured the guy lying there. All the equipment hooked up. Saw his face. The look in his eyes. Thick tears trailing down.

The expression of raw emotion.

"I believe he was being truthful," I said. "But I could be wrong." Maybe the emotion I'd witnessed had been inner conflict—the evil voice in his head waging strong until the end.

"I'll keep in touch," Maddox said, then pushed back his chair and stood. "Let you know once we've searched O'Malley's place."

TWENTY-SIX

Maddox offered me a ride, but I declined and took a stroll down Whitehead. Past the famous Green Parrot Bar. Past Mile Marker Zero, the end of the line or the beginning of it, depending on where you were heading.

I continued for another five blocks, turning inland on Green Street just after passing the Mel Fisher Museum. Downtown was alive, with people crowding both sidewalks. Heading this way and that. Spilling out of Captain Tony's Saloon and the Tiki House. Duval Street was its usual bustling spectacle, a different animal when the sun went down and all the characters came out.

While strolling, I thought about my talk with Maddox. And I thought about what I was going to do next. It looked like I was in for more waiting and staying and lying low. More hunkering down.

Or so I thought.

I was thirty yards past Sloppy Joe's when I felt like something was off. Like I was being followed or watched.

I picked up my pace a little. Then a little more. Cut across Anne Street diagonally and ducked into a public parking lot. It was dimly lit and surrounded by tall trees. I disappeared into the shadows, cut through an opening in a fence, then swerved around the base of a towering gumbo-limbo tree in the middle of the lot.

It was packed. A vehicle in every space.

I crouched in the darkness and peered around the base of the tree, right hand hovering over my Sig.

Thirty seconds passed. Then a minute. Then two minutes.

Nobody appeared. There were no sounds. No movement of any kind.

Then I turned to face Simonton Street, and a figure emerged from the darkness. The outline of a man walking around a parked SUV and coming into my view. He was marching straight toward me. Not saying anything. His shoes barely making a sound on the gravel.

I was just about to yell for him to put his hands up when he stepped into the dim glow of a streetlight.

"Little jumpy, aren't you, Dodge?" Red Delaney said.

I planted my hands on my hips. Stood tall and strode confidently toward him.

"When someone follows me for three blocks, I naturally get a little suspicious of them."

"I've been following you for five blocks," he said with a grin. Like that was some kind of victory for him or something.

"What do you want, Red?"

He shrugged. "Just to chat. Or maybe we could play another game of chess. I hear you got a gold medallion that's quite rare."

"You want to chat?" I said. "All right. How about you tell me what you were doing at the hospital?"

He glared at me. "I don't answer to you. You're nobody."

"All right."

I shrugged and walked onward casually, ambling right by him.

When I was three strides away, he said, "You want to know why I followed you tonight? The truth?"

I stopped. Sighed and turned around slowly.

"Delaney, at this point, I really don't care. But it would be in your best interest to tell me what you know."

"Why's that?"

"Because at the moment you're high up on my personal suspect list."

"You're not a cop. You're nobody."

I gave him a sarcastic nod. "All right. Good night."

"I don't know if I can trust you," he said.

I turned and strode right up to the guy. Barely five feet away from him. Stared him down.

"You know people involved, don't you?" I said.

He kept silent.

"Are you involved?"

"No," he spat. "I'm not involved."

"All right. Is Officer O'Malley involved?"

He hesitated. Just a second. Then said, "No. I don't think so."

"You don't think so. But he could be?"

"He's a friend of mine. We go way back."

I shrugged. "Sometimes friends break the law."

"I trust him."

"Sometimes people you trust break the law."

"By that logic, why isn't Pete being investigated?" Delaney snickered. "He's got more connections than I do in the islands. Has similar experience with shrimping and handling money and as good of an understanding of the geography of the Keys as anyone. He also has friends who are in the police and Border Patrol."

I didn't reply.

"Because he's a good friend of yours, right?" Delaney added. "Because you know him. That's Kevin O'Malley to me."

"Everyone's a friend of a friend. Someone's involved."

"Then investigate Pete," he said again. "His restaurant sure looks nice. Much nicer than it did just a few years ago. Seems like there's been a lot of renovations. A lot of money pouring into it."

I didn't reply. I knew the truth of how Pete had acquired the necessary funds to remodel his restaurant years ago. And it hadn't come from anything illegal. I'd also spent a great deal of time with Pete, both on land and out on his boat, over the years. And if he was involved in an illegal alien smuggling trade, he was one of the best liars, actors, and criminals the world had ever seen.

And he wasn't any of those things. I'd played poker with the guy. Pete Jameson was good at many things; deception wasn't one of them. The guy's poker face was easier to read than a children's book.

Feeling like the conversation was nothing but a big waste of my time, I turned away once more. This time I only made it two strides before Delaney piped up again.

"Truth is that young man was like a son to me. It tore me up seeing him dying in that hospital bed. I remember him as a kid. Getting him his first work on a shrimp boat. I had no idea he was involved in anything like this. And it's been eating me up." He coughed and cleared his throat and spat. Wiped his mouth and added, "You're not gonna stop, are you?"

"I'll stop. Once this whole operation's torn down and nothing but smoldering ash. But only then."

Delaney went quiet. Stared at me and then looked up at the night sky.

"I want to trust you, Dodge," he said. "I want to believe you're sincere."

"But?"

"You're not a conch."

"The hell does that have to do with anything?"

"The fact that you need to ask that means you don't understand."

"Are you an American?"

"What?"

"Are you an American?"

"Of course I am."

"Great. So am I. And our constitution is pretty clear about some things. Written in ink and everything so that all of us can understand who we are and what we stand for. That it doesn't matter where you're born. Doesn't matter how rich your parents were, or how much melatonin is in your skin, or what gender you are or how old you are or what color your eyes are. That stuff is frivolous. We're all equal. The same under God's eyes. We're all American."

I caught Delaney smile briefly. Then he promptly wiped it away.

"All right, Dodge," he said. "Let's see if what Pete says about you is true. There's something going down tonight."

I folded my arms. Eyed the guy suspiciously.

"I'm listening."

"In Safe Harbor. There's a shrimp trawler making an unexpected stop at my place to refuel and have some repairs done. They'll be at my dock tonight."

"What's the name of the boat?"

"*Miss Lucy*. It's based out of Brunswick, Georgia. It's got a familiar captain. A guy named Heinrich. But he's got a new crew apparently." He scratched his beard. "I've been suspicious of him for quite some time. Just too many things that don't add up."

"All right. Why are you telling me this?"

"Because, I can get the crew out and away from the boat. Have them help me with a nearby part. Some made-up thing. And you can search it while they're gone."

"Why are you telling me this? Why not go to the police?"

I already knew what he'd likely say, but I still wanted his answer.

"I've heard the rumors about the investigation. Everyone has. If there are Key West police officers working on this, or Border Protection, then they'll blow everything once they're alerted. They'd relay the tip to the smugglers and everything would be for nothing."

I thought a moment, then said, "When's the boat arriving?"

"One in the morning," Delaney said. "You'll have maybe thirty minutes." He held out a tiny pocket recording device. "I'll have this. And I'll have my backup security cameras up and running. And you'll search and find the hidden smuggling compartment and get footage of it. Then we'll call the police. Too much evidence will be stacked at that point. The smugglers will be arrested. Then they'll confess to everything. Bound to, eventually. And then we'll have the double-crossers." He brushed his hands together and added, "Case closed. Smuggling op dismantled. Crumbled and nothing but ash. Smoldering, right?"

I stared at the man. A long, hard look. He held my gaze. Appeared sincere.

He coughed and held out his right hand. "What do you say, Logan Dodge. Shall we put an end to this?"

TWENTY-SEVEN

"He's lying," Ange said as we sat at the Baia's topside dinette later that evening.

I nodded. "Most likely."

"So, what did you do?"

I thought back to the moment and said, "I shook his hand. Told him I'd meet him at his place on Stock at one in the morning."

Delaney had smiled again. Another rare and brief expression, then it'd vanished. And so had the man. He'd let go and turned around and trekked back into the shadows. Headed right on Simonton.

I'd stood there, watching him. Studying him. Trying to figure him out. My orange Doxa clasped around his left wrist and glistening in the moonlight.

I swung by a grocery store on the walk back to replenish our food supplies. Carried the bags to Conch Harbor, loaded them onto my Robalo, and motored away from the waterfront. Out of the bight and away from the bustling noise and bright lights and symphony of chatter from downtown, and into the sheer darkness and silence of the nearby uninhabited islands to the north.

I performed a couple turns and sweeps. Once I was certain no one was following me, I cruised north, then hooked back around to Cayo Agua, where the Baia was still anchored.

I'd tied off and headed aboard and down to the galley. Ange had whipped up a delicious lionfish stew with what remained of our rations. Everyone loved it. Olivier and Esther were both exhausted. Had spent the afternoon playing more games and swimming, and exploring a little nearby beach with Ange, Scarlett, Atticus, and Boise.

We'd played another game after dinner, then read them a couple books and put them to bed. Scarlett was in the galley doing homework, and Ange and I migrated topside and I eagerly told her everything about my surprise rendezvous with Delaney and his unexpected tip.

"He's lying," my wife said again.

Like it made her statement even more solidified. Going on record a second time and making sure her message was clear.

I nodded again. Took a long swig of coconut water. "Most likely."

"So, what are we going to do about it?"

It was an interesting situation. On one hand, if I called Jane and Maddox and everyone else and put the word out like a modern-day Paul Revere that the smugglers were coming, they'd descend. They'd stake out. Completely surround the place. And, if there was a mole within their ranks, the smugglers would be notified.

Even if only Jane and Maddox showed up, there was still a good chance word would get to the smugglers. People talked. People observed others. It was a small island. And when you live on a small island, no one's an island to themselves.

On the other hand, if Delaney was lying, which we were both confident the man was, I'd be walking right into a trap. I was also confident that a guy like Delaney wasn't capable of setting up a trap that would overwhelm me, but was that something I wanted to risk?

Delaney had his place pretty well covered. Cameras and strong vantage points and whatnot. Only one way in or out, that being a barren parking lot. Not much cover. Not many places for someone to sneak up and observe his dealings.

But, looking at his place from a different angle, there was all the cover in the world. He was right on the water.

"I'm gonna show up," I said. "Keep my word."

Ange shook her head. "A big risk. He's a wild card if there ever was one. And he's hiding things. And he's lying. He'll probably have half a dozen armed criminals hiding in his shack, ready to burst out and surround you with one gesture of his hand."

I shrugged. "If he's smart, he'd have a full dozen."

"And you're still gonna go?"

I nodded. "I'll be there at the agreed-upon time. But he won't see me."

Ange smiled. Sharper than the edge of my dive knife. Catching on and instantly moving on to the other variables that would need to be covered in order for an infiltration like this one to occur.

Two important and incredibly vulnerable variables were right at the top of the priority list. And in order to ensure Olivier and Esther were safe, I needed to call in a big favor.

Earlier that month, I'd been notified by Scott Cooper, a close friend and former brother in arms, that an old and dear friend had gone missing under mysterious circumstances. We eventually found and helped rescue retired Admiral James Harrington as well as his son.

The Admiral answered immediately when I called, and enthusiastically came to my aid. And thirty minutes later, we had the Baia's anchor raised and cruised north, then west, and then south back toward Key West. Instead of heading for Conch Harbor, we motored east around Fleming Key and into Sigsbee Marina at the northern tip of Dredgers Key.

The island was part of Naval Air Station Key West, and used primarily to house active-duty military personnel and their families. It also had a nice beach, parks, a commissary, schools, and a lodge.

We met the commanding officer, Captain Rinaldi, on the dock. She had a lieutenant with her as well as two masters-at-arms, who both had M16s slung across their chests.

I killed the engines and tossed fenders and we tied off.

"I can't thank you enough for this, ma'am," I said to Captain Rinaldi.

She waved me off as Ange and Scarlett climbed

over, helping Olivier and Esther.

"After everything you've done and for saving Admiral Harrington, the Navy will always be indebted to you," she said. "I'm glad to be of help."

The captain had agreed to house both the two kids and Scarlett for the evening. An act that was both unprecedented and appreciated. After driving us over to the lodge, we set them up in one of the larger rooms.

"In addition to the usual security, we'll have two MAs at the doors," Captain Rinaldi explained, "as well as more at the entrance. And additional squads patrolling out front and here at the marina. They'll be safe here."

"Thank you, ma'am."

"Please, there's no need to thank me. It's the least we can do."

We gave the two kids a hug, then gave last-minute instructions to Scarlett before hugging her as well.

"You're in charge of them, Scar," Ange said. "You can do this. We know they're in good hands."

We squeezed her tight, then were driven back to the Baia. I smiled with every armed sentry we passed. The only way any of Barbossa's men were going to get to the kids was if they felt like challenging the United States Navy. Something I'd highly discourage if they valued their lives.

TWENTY-EIGHT

Just before midnight, I stood at the bow of my Robalo center-console, keeping a watchful eye on the dark horizon. Jack was at the helm. Had the main engine shut off and was running a little electric outboard, the near-silent motor keeping us steady in the slight current as we waited three hundred yards from the mouth of Safe Harbor.

While I kept my eyes glued to the east, scanning for any sign of a shrimp trawler, Jack passed the time testing out a new fly rod.

Clouds rolled in. Big black ones that blotted out the moon. I held up my night vision monocular and surveyed the surrounding area. Saw no sign of a trawler.

"Looks like rain," I said.

With his fly floating barely five feet from the nearby mangroves, Jack tugged on the line gently. Tempting whatever swam beneath it.

"Nope," my old friend said without looking up. Then he glanced skyward for barely a second and added, "Well, maybe a drizzle."

I smiled. As a fourth-generation conch, Jack was as in tune with the islands as anyone I'd ever met.

"Thanks for coming," I said.

He waved me off. "No need to thank me. I'd say this wasn't what I had in mind when you asked if I wanted to go night fishing. But with you, it's kind of what I expect at this point."

I cracked another smile, then a fish burst from the shallows with a sudden splash, swiping the fly. Jack pulled back on the rod to give the line tension. A minute later, he had a good-sized bonefish in his net. He hauled his catch into the boat.

"Little too small," he said, holding it up.

He leaned over the side and set the fish back into the water, both of us watching as it flicked its tail fin and took off, vanishing back into the sea. Jack wiped his brow and took in a breath. Gazed to the east a moment.

"There it is," he said, pointing a finger.

He spoke in a nonchalant tone. Then grabbed his thermos and took a swig of coffee.

"Where?" I said, turning around and staring into the distance.

"Thirty degrees to port. Just over two miles out."

I used my monocular. Zoomed in and caught sight of the tiny dark silhouette of a vessel.

I lowered my optics and turned to Jack. "How do you do that?"

He grinned. "I may not be good at much, but I'm a waterman through and through."

I observed the trawler as it neared. It was slow and sluggish. A big, hulking mass of metal and booms and nets. We watched from the distant shadows as the vessel chugged closer, then nosed into Safe Harbor.

"Showtime," I said as I watched the boat round the corner and disappear from view.

I slid out my phone and shot Ange a quick text. Then I grabbed and donned my gear, starting with a drysuit. My Draeger rebreather came next, the closed-circuit diving apparatus strapped tight. Jack double-checked everything, then we did a mic check of the radio built into my dive mask.

Once ready, I grabbed a new gadget I'd gotten my hands on just a week earlier and had been itching to use in a tactical situation. Called Jetboots, the underwater propulsion device consisted of two lightweight propellers that strapped to my thighs to give me a powerful added boost through the water. Usually, I'd use my sea scooter for a task like that, but Jetboots were a gamechanger because they freed up my hands.

Once they were snug, I clipped a dry bag to my waist that contained my Sig 9mm, attached a dive light to my left wrist, then slid into my fins.

I gave Jack a thumbs-up, then flipped backward for an evening swim. Entering negatively buoyant, I sank to the bottom ten feet down. Hovering just above the seafloor, I streamlined my body and fired up the propellers and tore north through the water like a torpedo.

I've dipped below the waves many times. Both as a civilian, and in the military. Used the water to sneak up on unsuspecting targets so many times I've lost count. In SEAL training, we'd often train at night. Often in harsh currents and thrashing waves and near jagged, rocky shorelines. We'd learned to operate and think and act correctly when in a rip-roaring surf in sheer darkness while low on air with damaged and tangled gear. To remain calm and figure it out. Do or die scenarios.

That was how we'd trained. Always preparing for the worst possible situation.

And this was child's play by comparison.

A deep, calm channel. A straight line almost perfectly due north. And just a hair over a quarter mile. And all my gear was undamaged and regularly checked and updated and replaced as necessary. It was all top-of-the-line.

The motors propelled me through the dark channel. I had my dive light but kept it switched off. I could sense my depth based on the pressure, and the little moonlight bleeding through above me. And I had my compass to maintain my trajectory.

When I was halfway to my destination, Ange's voice came through the speaker.

"In position," she said. "Got a clear view of Delaney's place. Newly arrived trawler just docked. It's the one on the right. Nose in. Delaney's tying them off."

I triggered my mic and replied, "Copy that."

I ran the math in my head. Pictured a satellite image of Safe Harbor, and where I was in relation to the edges of the channel. Pictured myself entering the harbor, then passing the first dock reaching out from the Perry Hotel and Marina, and then the second. And the cove to the right where The Docks, the popular seafood restaurant, was located.

I was getting close.

I clicked my dive computer to illuminate the screen and tweaked my course slightly. A minute later, the solid black outline of a boat's hull came into view. A big V-hull, coated in grime and barnacles.

An old trawler.

I powered off the thrusters and finned the rest of the way. Passed right under the boat on the right, then curved and kicked for its stern.

I triggered my mic again and said, "What's our guy up to?"

"Still talking to the shrimpers," she said. A moment later, she added, "Wait, they're leaving."

"How many?"

"Four of them."

"What do they look like?"

"One gray-haired captain and three young, lean guys. Two black and one Hispanic." There was a short pause, then she added, "They're getting into Delaney's truck."

I mulled over her words. We'd expected a group to hide out in Delaney's shack and wait for me to show up. Then they'd try and hit me over the head with a hammer or something, motor my unconscious body out to sea, and deep-six my corpse.

But maybe I'd been wrong. Maybe his men would be in a vehicle nearby. Hiding and waiting elsewhere until I showed.

"Truck's heading north," Ange said. Then half a minute later, she added, "They're out of my sight. Heading inland."

I held still, listening carefully. Said, "Delaney?"

"Standing at the base of the dock. He's looking around. Checking his watch. Your watch."

"Roger that," I said. "Moving in."

The guy was away from his perch. And the shrimpers were gone. If I was going to make a move, this was the time.

TWENTY-NINE

An hour earlier, Angelina Dodge drove her daughter's baby-blue Ford Bronco south on Shrimp Road on the south side of Stock Island. She turned right into the parking lot for Bernstein Park. Slowed to a stop in a back space and killed the engine.

She sat there in the silence a moment, then rolled the windows up. Grabbed an oversized beach bag from the passenger seat and opened her door and slid her legs out.

She was wearing flip-flops and denim shorts. A black tank top. An old Florida Marlins ball cap.

She slung the bag over her shoulder and shut the door behind her. Skipped across Shrimp Road and headed south along the edge of the pavement. Her bag featured a Conch Republic flag on both of its sides. The conch shell with rays of sunshine beaming away from it. Stars at the flanks. All set against a dark blue backdrop. And it was plenty big enough to fit towels and toys and snacks for an entire day at the beach.

The darkness around her parted, and the bright lights of the Perry Hotel came into view. Between its buildings, she could see the marina on the other side, its two big docks reaching out into the harbor. Both were wide enough to provide a road, allowing boaters to drive right up to their vessels.

Ange entered the property and walked casually across the lot and then south along the promenade. The bustling establishment was winding down. Music drifted from Salty Oyster Dockside Bay and Grill, and boaters gathered at the restaurant as well as the two bars and swimming pool right along the water.

She headed down Ship Store Lane, the first of the hotel's two fifty-foot-wide piers that each extended three hundred yards into the harbor. Five docks extended off the pier's left side, each with fingers mooring everything from sparkling multimillion-dollar yachts to budget sailboats just passing through.

At the end of the pier was a group of buildings. She passed by a laundry room, reached a two-story structure with a store below and a lounge on the second level. Ange knew it well. She'd been inside it a couple times. A captains' club with books and couches and a nice upstairs balcony that was shaded and offered superb views of the harbor.

Just the views she required.

But not yet.

She waited in the shadows along the south side of the building. Grabbed a pair of binoculars from her bag and peeked around and saw Delaney perched up in his crow's nest at the top of his shack roughly two hundred yards away, at the other end of the harbor.

Ange turned and backtracked a short ways. Found a bench and settled in, her eyes trained toward the opening into the harbor, then scanned the area around her. There were a couple boaters relaxing on their vessels. Lazily smoking or nursing drinks. Reading, socializing, and listening to music.

Marina life. A congregation of a bunch of differences, and a bunch of the same. People of all backgrounds and walks of life drawn together by their love of the sea. Everyone relaxed and easygoing. Everyone friendly.

She reached into her bag and slid out a weathered copy of *The Sun Also Rises*. It was half past twelve and she was early. Might as well get some reading in.

She was just getting to the juicy nectar of the story when a boat entered the harbor. It was big, at least sixty feet. Tall and wide and slow moving. A commercial shrimp trawler. The stabilizers and outriggers and nets distinguishable from miles away.

She dog-eared a page.

She'd heard somewhere that some authors found it disrespectful in some way. Like it was degrading their work or something. She thought that was odd. Thought there could be no better prize for an author than for their books to be worn and dog-eared. It was evidence that they were read.

She put the book back into her bag. Stood and stretched. Watched in her peripherals as the shrimp boat chugged along, then eased right up to one of the three docks reaching out from Delaney's property.

The proprietor himself had vanished from his perch. Seconds later he appeared out the front door of his place, waddling toward the dock and reaching it just as the trawler slowed to a crawl. He helped them tie off, and the trawler's engines died off.

The man was now occupied. No longer observing the harbor.

Ange cut around to the east-facing wall of the store and captains' lounge. Stopped in the shadows under the second-level balcony. Thick beams supported it from below, but there were no outside stairs. The only way to get to it was from inside, and the place had been closed and locked for hours.

Ange hiked her bag higher up her shoulder, then jumped and grabbed hold of one of the vertical beams. Wrapped her thighs around tight and shimmied her way up like she was scaling a palm tree. Once high enough to reach the deck, she grabbed it with her left hand, slid the bag down off her right arm, then set it on the boards and slid it between the railings.

Another scoot and she was high enough to reach the balcony with both hands. She grabbed the rails and angled her body around. Got a foothold and three seconds later, she was up on the deck and into the shadows, her bag at her feet.

The porch was mostly taken up by two Adirondack chairs and a table. She shifted the furniture around. Pushed one of the chairs back against the wall, then turned it around to face a sliding glass door.

She sat with the table in front of her, facing away from the water as she brought up her bag and opened the main compartment. Pulled out the pieces of a collapsible sniper rifle. Attached the stock to the main body, then the barrel to the forestock. Tightened a scope in place. Then she grabbed a five-round magazine packed with .338 Lapua rounds and jammed it up into the spring follower.

She checked everything over, making small tweaks here and there to the alignment. Once ready, she spun around in the Adirondack, facing the back of the chair and sticking her feet between either side. Used the middle space between the cedar boards as a support for her rifle. Set it there, adjusted it forward and back a little until she found the sweet spot, then peered through her scope.

The trawler was tied off. Delaney was standing beside the dock. Men were climbing down from the shrimp boat to meet with him.

Ange put Delaney right in her crosshairs and watched the interaction. She kept Logan updated through her radio, letting him know everything she saw as he made his approach.

Blinking, she tilted her head back. Turned away from the scope and toward the flat expanse of water leading out to the south channel and then eventually the open ocean.

Her husband had covered the distance without making so much as a bubble. He was near the base of the trawler, down there somewhere. Ready to make his move.

And Ange was ready as well. She was just there to observe. That was the plan. Her instrument of observation just happened to be attached to a long-range rifle.

Just in case.

THIRTY

I removed my gear and tightened a strap around the base of a piling to keep it in place. Taking a final breath, I turned and kicked back toward the stern.

I surfaced, slowly and quietly. Just breaking free. The crown of my head, then the top of my face mask, then my eyes. I performed a quick scan, though it wasn't necessary. Just a habit. Ange was watching me, had my back from two hundred yards away. Which meant that I was about as safe as a human being can be in this life.

Looking up, I eyed the edge of the trawler's stern. It was floating high in the water. Empty. Like a freighter after it unloads. The deck's edge was maybe six feet above me, but there were two car tires secured over the side.

I kicked as hard as I could. Reached and grabbed the bottom of one of the tires. Held myself there in the shadows and the quiet. Let the water gently drip off me.

"I have eyes on you," Ange said. "You're clear from Delaney. Got the pilothouse and a veil of hanging nets covering you."

I removed my fins and pulled slowly, bringing my right leg up and hooking it on the tire. Then I stood tall and grabbed the edge of the deck. It was slick under my damp fingers. Chipped and rusted in places.

I pulled myself up and over. Rolled quietly, then came to a knee behind a winch.

The deck was clear and tidy. Plenty of cover and shadows between me and my destination. I couldn't even see Delaney from my vantage point.

I crept across the deck and quickly reached the pilothouse, pressing myself flat against the bulkhead. The boat looked familiar. It had the same color and layout. A door on the right. It looked just like the one I'd snuck aboard southwest of the Tortugas. Just like one of the boats I'd searched hours later.

I focused on the port side. The hawsehole looked identical to the one on the boat I'd climbed aboard and the one I'd searched.

Grabbing the handle, I slowly opened the door and stepped inside. I was ready and alert. It was very possible that the four men Ange had seen weren't the only ones there that night. There could be more lurking on the boat still. Waiting for the signal to burst out and help take down the local who'd been messing with their highly profitable operation.

But the interior appeared empty.

I shut the hatch behind me and looked around, then I froze, realizing it wasn't just similar to one of the trawlers I'd searched. It *was* one of the boats I'd searched. There was no doubt in my mind. Which also meant I'd spent nearly an hour scouring every inch of it and hadn't found anything.

It filled me with anger at the situation, and at myself. I was to blame. I'd slipped up.

I'd failed.

And now I was on a boat that I'd already searched extensively.

I headed straight for the cargo hold. The space looked like it had before, just without the shrimp. Before there'd been a mountain of the crustaceans. Piles of forty-pound bags stacked eight feet high in places and resting on a spread of pallets.

Now only the pallets remained. Twelve of them, fit snug into place, and most of them still fully intact.

I checked my watch. My old Seiko. It was five minutes to one.

I grabbed and triggered my handheld radio. "Update on Delaney?"

"Still standing there," she said. "Looking around. Looking antsy. He lit up a cigarette."

"Anyone come out of the woodwork?"

"Negative. He's still alone. No movement in or near his shack. Or his old shrimp boat."

I powered on my flashlight and searched the hold. Scanned the bulkheads with the beam. Piled all of the pallets into a single stack and crawled over every inch of the bottom of the space. Found nothing unusual. No sign of an entryway into a hidden compartment.

I spent ten minutes searching. I was sweating hard. It was hot and humid in there. No fans running. It would be cold later on. When it was full of frozen shrimp and ice. But now it was stuffy and hard to breathe. Making me dizzy.

I repositioned the pallets. Headed up a level to the crew space. It looked the same as before. Cramped and small. An efficient use of the minuscule amount of space. Three different alcoves with bunk beds just barely big enough for a grown man to crawl into. A little galley.

I searched everywhere and came up empty. There was still no sign of a hidden compartment.

"He's looking real antsy now," Ange said through the radio. "He's on his third cigarette and he's pacing. Talking to himself."

I checked my watch again. It was fifteen minutes past one. I was a quarter of an hour late.

"He's making a phone call," Ange added.

My cell phone buzzed a moment later. I opened the sealed waterproof bag. Retrieved the device.

"Hello?" I answered casually.

"What the hell, Dodge?" Delaney spat. "Where are you?"

"Something came up."

"What?"

"I guess you were right. I'm not a conch, so you shouldn't have trusted me."

"You're a damn piece of work, you know that? They're gonna be back any minute now. You lost your shot, Dodge. I thought you wanted to catch these bastards." He paused a beat, then added, "I trusted you."

"Another night, Red. Like I said, something came up."

"What the hell came up? What's bigger than this? If I'd known you were gonna flake on me, I'd have just gone to Chief Verona. At least she'd have—"

Delaney stopped midsentence. In the background, I heard the rumble of an approaching engine. The sounds of tires crunching across a gravel lot.

"Ah shit," Delaney said, "now they're back. You idiot. We had one chance to—"

I hung up.

Triggered my mic and said, "Still nothing, Ange?"

"Negative," she replied, "no sign of any kind of trap. I think he might've actually been telling the truth."

It was good to learn that our instincts had likely been wrong. That the guy was just a hermit, rough around the edges, and rubbed people the wrong way. But that he evidently wasn't involved—that he wanted the criminals dealt with just as we did.

That was the good news.

The bad news was that I was still on the trawler and I hadn't found any sign of a secret cargo hold. And the supposed smugglers were returning.

I pocketed my phone and held up my radio.

"What's the verdict, Ange?" I said.

"If it's a trap, these guys are better than any stakeout experts I've ever encountered before."

"So, Delaney's cleared."

"Looks that way. Find anything?"

"Nothing."

"You heading back?"

I looked around the interior of the trawler. Heard the sounds of the approaching vehicle in the distance.

My heart thumped in my chest. A clock ticking down. I glanced right toward the steps. The route up and across and up again. Back across the entirety of the aft section of the vessel. Back over the side. Back into the water.

It would take me a solid fifteen seconds, and that was if I booked it and threw stealth to the wind.

But there were other options. Riskier, from a personal life-and-limb standpoint. But potentially much more beneficial to the cause.

"No," I said. "I think I'm gonna need to improvise."

"Why do I get the sense that improvise is code for 'you're about to do something incredibly dangerous'?"

"It'll only be dangerous if I slip up."

She paused briefly, then stated, "Then you'd better not slip up, Dodge."

I grabbed my fins and mask then turned left. Pulled a hatch from the deck and climbed a ladder deeper into the bowels of the vessel. I shut the hatch behind me and landed in the engine room. The boat was equipped with an enormous pair of diesels. Both of them well maintained. Pipes and hoses ran in every direction. There were two generators, a primary and a smaller backup. And there was a small workstation.

Like every space aboard the boat aside from the cargo hold, it was cramped. A working boat. Things like comfort and ease of movement were far down on the priority list.

Hiding places were sparse.

The vehicle engine sounds died off, replaced by distant chatter. Then footsteps, first on the dock, and then on the trawler itself. They'd be below deck soon. At least one of them would likely be sent down there to check things before they headed back out to sea.

With the clock ticking, I searched around and down. Discovered a hatch leading to the bilge at the aft end of the space. I pulled up the metal grate and climbed down into a tight crawl space. Shut the grate down over me and shimmied forward and nestled into a spot just above the shaft with my back against an arched section of the hull.

I looked around and considered the hiding place. The only way for one of the crew members to find me would be if they pried up the hatch and angled themselves down into the space like I had. They'd likely poke their head in first. Look around with a flashlight. Maybe check the bilge level, if they didn't have remote indicators.

I pictured it. A shrimper peering down. Seeing me. Surprise on his face, and then disbelief.

Hesitation.

Enough time for me to make the first move—to grab them and yank them down. Headfirst toward nothing but a spread of various unforgiving solid metal components.

I listened and waited in the silence. Ready. But no one ever came down. The engines groaned and fired up. The shaft rotated, and we began to move.

THIRTY-ONE

Ange watched from her perch as the trawler grumbled backward away from the dock, turned around, and crawled out of the harbor. The four crew members who'd left had all climbed back aboard. But they had a visitor now—a stowaway hiding out somewhere in the bowels of the vessel.

She shot a text to Jack, letting him know the shrimp boat was on the move, then turned her attention back to Delaney. The local stood at the end of his dock and watched the trawler for a minute. He sighed. Shook his head. Checked his watch. Checked his phone. Looked up at the night sky and then around the harbor and shook his head again.

He flicked what remained of his cigarette and turned and headed toward his shack. Ange glanced back toward the trawler. It was nearly out of the channel, making a wide turn before heading into the open waters of the Strait.

She turned back to Delaney. Watched as he lumbered toward his front door. He reached for the knob. Nearly grabbed it when two vehicles pulled into his driveway.

One was a Key West police cruiser, the other a black BMW. They both moved slowly. Casually. Not a raid or an arrest. Just two sedans crunching over the spread of gravel, nosing in right beside Delaney's beat-up truck.

Delaney froze in his tracks and stared at the four high beams. Squinted. Then the lights shut off and the engines turned off and both driver's-side doors opened in unison.

Chief Jane Verona exited the cruiser, and Agent Maddox the Beamer. Logan and Ange had contacted the two law enforcement officers, letting them know what was happening that evening so they could act as backup in case things went south.

With Delaney staring at the two officers of the law, Ange grabbed her bag. Her rifle had already been disassembled and stowed. She'd been using her binos. She climbed out of the Adirondack and arranged the furniture where it'd been. Set the bag on the floorboards between the same railings they'd squeezed through before.

Then she performed the same acrobatic feat in reverse. Legs over the railing. Crouch and grab onto the support beam. Thighs squeezing tight to hold her snug she grabbed the bag, then inched her way along before dropping five feet to the ground.

She shouldered the bag, put on her hat, and sauntered back to shore.

Chief Jane Verona and Agent Maddox spent half an hour searching Delaney's place. He'd welcomed them openly when they'd arrived. Opened the door himself and ushered them in. He'd been his usual sarcastic, borderline irritating hermit self, but he'd been compliant every step of the way.

And again, nothing incriminating was found. Nothing at all connecting Delaney to criminal activity of any kind.

While searching, Jane got a message from Ange.

"Looks like Delaney might be clean."

As she read the words, Maddox received a message as well. He stared at his phone, pressed a number on the device, then stepped outside. Jane heard nothing but his muffled voice, and he returned just thirty seconds later.

He gestured for her to meet with him outside, and they shut the door behind them and strode twenty paces away from Delaney's place.

"That was Judge Mathis from the Monroe County Court," he said. "We have the search warrant."

Jane nodded. Then silence a beat.

"Where's Officer O'Malley now?" he added.

"On duty. Six hours into his shift. Likely back at the station now, but possibly still on patrol."

"No one lives with him?"

Jane shook her head. "No. As far as I know."

"You ready for this?"

Jane took in a deep breath. Collected herself. He'd been a trusted colleague for years, and a friend for much of her life.

It wasn't personal. It was protocol. Following procedure. It wouldn't affect their friendship.

She told herself that. But she knew it was crap. Things would change.

Jane swallowed hard and said, "All right. Let's go."

They drove up to US-1. Turned west and cruised four miles to Old Town. Officer O'Malley's house was on the Atlantic side of Duval, just a couple blocks from the beach and the Ponce de Leon Fishing Pier. It was one of the biggest residences on the famous street. A wide three-story house painted rich maroon.

There were two unmarked Homeland vehicles already parked along the street. Members of Maddox's team. Jane and Maddox pulled right into Officer O'Malley's driveway. It was empty aside from a restored green 1966 Austin-Healey convertible. A multimillion-dollar house and a seventy-thousand-dollar vehicle. Owned by a police sergeant.

Jane believed each and every member of her team. She believed O'Malley when he said he'd inherited everything. Everyone knew his family's history. Everyone knew they'd always had money. But so had Delaney's family. And they'd lost it all. And sometimes people lie and sometimes people will do anything to keep their lifestyles intact.

Jane and Agent Maddox climbed out and headed for the door. Broke it open and stormed inside alongside other agents. They broke off, ready to search every inch of the place.

Barely fifteen minutes into the search, Jane discovered a pile of evidence that blew the entire investigation wide open, and nearly caused her to stumble to the floor in astonishment.

THIRTY-TWO

I'd been waiting for hours. After the trawler chugged out of Safe Harbor and headed south by southwest into the Strait, I bunched up my drysuit and lay back and closed my eyes. Whatever happened, one thing was certain: I was in for a long night. Might as well get some sleep.

I awoke a couple times. Once when the engines slowed and a man whistled and nets were moved into position. I checked my watch. It was a quarter to three. Clearly, the trawler's unusually powerful engines had swiftly pushed it to a sufficient starting point.

Shrimping, like all commercial fishing, is a slow, methodical process. And whether they were really just after shrimp or not, I had no doubt they'd drop a net and trawl for what remained of the night. They'd need to at least partially fill their cargo hold, in case of inspection. A shrimp boat returning empty-handed would be suspicious, I imagined.

The second time I awoke was when the nets were hauled in. Even over the engine, I could hear the sound of boots on the topside deck. Nets being muscled over, and shrimp dropped and sorted. They likely wouldn't have an impressive haul by any means, but they'd probably have enough to create a convincing charade.

The third time I awoke was when the engines stopped altogether. It was just after four in the morning. The big machines grumbled and died, and the shaft wound down and rattled a little from the residual centripetal force. Then the space went silent. Quieter than silent. The empty void of nothingness that follows hours of powerful white noise.

Then the generator powered on and hummed steadily. Beyond the drone, I heard footsteps and voices. A yell. Then the rattling of ropes. No nets.

Time to move.

They'd be quick. I knew that much. There were weak points to their operation. The very weak point Ange and I had witnessed. The one that'd started the whole thing. Kinks in the armor.

The hand-off periods.

Loading migrants from their boat onto the trawler would be the weakest. Out on the open sea. Exposed.

They'd do it as quickly as possible.

Time to move.

I pulled out my radio to try and get ahold of Ange but got nothing but static.

Odd.

I tried again. Then I turned off the device and powered it back on. Still nothing.

I let out a breath and looked around. Figured that

the smugglers must've had some kind of jammer aboard. Something with range, maybe, to ensure no boats in their immediate vicinity could call them in for suspicious activity.

I pocketed my radio. Rotated my body. It was stiff. My right leg asleep. I stretched and crawled to the hatch. Pressed my fingers to the bottom of the metal grating and pushed gently. When the weight lifted, I eased it up slowly just enough to get a view of the engine room. It was empty, which I already knew. I'd have heard anyone shuffling about.

I pushed the hatch up the rest of the way. Climbed out and closed it behind me. Opened a drawer in the nearby workstation and rummaged through it. Found and pocketed a crowfoot wrench then moved to the ladder and listened again. The bulkhead ahead of me separated the engine room from the cargo hold. I heard nothing on the other side, but voices emanated from the galley and crews' quarters above.

I reached the base of the ladder, then froze. Heard footsteps. Two people shuffling about and heading for the same old stairs I'd used. Heading topside.

I climbed the ladder. One rung, then two. Hit the third and angled my head for a view into the passageway. Lifted the hatch an inch. Froze as I saw a pair of legs standing five feet in front of me. Heels, not toes. The man's back facing me. Voices called out. The man grabbed something from a gear locker and shuffled topside.

I let out a held breath. Pushed the hatch up the rest of the way and climbed out and shut it silently behind me. Crept along the passageway and into the cabin closest to the stairs.

No one would be sleeping. Not now. This was work time. So I held my position in the cabin and tucked the edge of the curtain around to conceal me. Poked my head out and could only see three-quarters of the way up the steps to the main deck.

I heard voices. Lines cast. Orders given. Everything swift and efficient.

Less than a minute later, I heard a group shuffling about. Heading toward me.

A smuggler appeared first. A young, wiry guy with black boots and jeans. Heavy, confident steps. Like he'd escorted victims of human trafficking thousands of times. He probably had. Behind him came a group of wide-eyed migrants in a zombie-like state. They all had tattered clothes. The stench from long hot days bunched together on a small boat with no showers filling the space.

I cut back into the curtain and shadows as the lead shrimper reached the bottom step.

He said something in Haitian Creole I didn't understand, then in English he added, "You smelly filth."

There were four of them in the first group. All of them women. All of them young. Teens to early twenties. Stumbling as they fought to keep up with the smuggler. Exhausted and malnourished from their desperate voyage.

The man led them around the corner and down into the cargo hold.

I made my move—emerged from the cabin and strode across the narrow passageway. The moment I stepped out, a second smuggler appeared. His steps were loud as well, but faster. Hammering down and racing right toward me.

I backtracked and threw the curtain in front of me once more, but I wasn't fast enough.

The guy froze when he reached the bottom step and stared toward the curtain. Tiny holes in the old, cheap fabric allowed me to make out his faint, dark outline.

He took a step closer and said, "Randal, what the hell are you—"

The guy was inches behind the curtain when I struck him. Hurled a row of knuckles into the fabric and onward into his throat.

He wheezed, and I slid the curtain aside. Wrapped an arm around his neck and clamped a palm over his mouth and dragged him into the shadows of the cabin. Forced him all the way to the bed, then knelt down and squeezed with everything I had.

He barely put up a fight. The first blow had been devastating, and he was soon unconscious in my arms.

Once out, I stuffed him into the bottom bunk, then slid that curtain over. Gathered myself and headed back toward the main passageway. Heard the sounds of the other smuggler and the four women in the cargo hold as well as activity above.

Heading forward, I crept down the narrow steps to the cargo hold. Reached the bottom and peered into the space.

The smuggler had moved the forward port pallet aside, resting it against a stack of bags stuffed with shrimp. He was on his hands and knees, a little cleaning brush in one hand and a water bottle in the other. He brushed aside the dirt, then began squirting liquid through the bottle's nozzle.

Ten seconds later, he located a tiny latch that looked to be barely the size of a dime. He hooked a screwdriver under the loop, pried a hatch up enough to get his hands under, then heaved it up the rest of the way.

It was no wonder we hadn't found it. Hidden under pallets and mountains of shrimp. Then a minuscule latch on a floor that covered a hundred square feet and was coated in dirt and grime. Even the smuggler needed time and proper tools to locate it efficiently.

The guy had his back to me, and from my angle I could barely see a sliver of the pitch-black space beneath the hatch that was barely the size of a manhole.

I emerged from the stairwell as the smuggler gazed down into the opening. One of the women noticed me immediately. I practically had to push her out of the way. But she barely made a sound. I wasn't part of the crew, but they didn't know that.

"All right, ladies," the man said, waving a hand to beckon their newly loaded cargo. "In you go."

Keeping his eyes locked on the hidden space, his knees slightly bent, and his body sideways, he reached without looking for the nearest woman with his right hand.

Instead of grabbing a thin, feminine wrist, his own arm was snatched. I'd lunged forward and caught him right at the end of his reach, my left hand clamping tight around his forearm. I squeezed as hard as I could while shifting all my weight to my left leg and snapping my right forward, anchoring him in place with my hand for the fraction of a second it took for my front kick to extend.

My foot struck him in the face. Nearly dead on. He'd barely been able to flinch and jerk his head sideways an inch at most from the path of destruction as my heel pummeled squarely. There was an intense mashing of cartilage and bone. A crunch, and a violent snap backward of his head.

I released his wrist on impact and he flailed backward, folding into the dark space and striking the bottom with a jarring thud. His head smacked into the edge and his limbs folded awkwardly.

I peered down into the hiding place. The man was motionless, his chin tucked unnaturally into the top of his sternum. His body shoved into the tight corner. Blood cascading from his battered nose.

I switched on my flashlight and shined it all around. The hidden space was much bigger than I'd expected. I estimated that roughly forty adults could be packed into it. Maybe more if there was no effort to be humane, which I guessed wasn't something high on these guys' priority list.

With the smuggler gone, I turned to the four women. They were staring at me. Wide-eyed and slack-jawed. Breathing fast.

I stabbed a finger at the motionless smuggler. "He's a bad man. They all are. They're trying to sell all of you. As slaves. You understand?"

None of them replied. They all just stood there frozen in shock.

I was about to say more, when a loud, rough voice barked from above. "What's the holdup down there?"

The sounds of heavy footsteps followed. A man stomped down the stairs, then across the passageway, then to the second set of steps leading to the cargo hold. I cut across the space while removing the wrench from my pocket. Held it with my left hand and swung it in a wide arc, timing my movements with the pace of the steps. The wrench made contact as the guy dropped into view, striking his leading left leg just as it planted. The devastating blow bashed into the guy's knee, caving it in completely. He fell forward, grunting and moaning as he tumbled the rest of the way down. He landed on his back, hands over his mangled joint.

I kicked him in the side of the head, knocking him out. Then I grabbed under his shoulders and dragged him across the space. The four women stepped out of my way, and I positioned the smuggler at the edge of the opening, then folded him up and shoved him through the hatch. His motionless body fell the four feet, and he collided into the first guy.

I stood tall, still gripping the wrench.

Three out of four down.

Seventy-five percent attrition in under five minutes.

I hustled up both sets of stairs and poked my head outside. Caught a view of the main deck. Saw well over a dozen migrants in the middle. Assembled in a tight bunch. Mostly young women and children.

Ange had provided descriptions of the smugglers. Three young, and one middle-aged with a gray beard. The captain.

The one still alive.

And it wouldn't take long for him to realize that he was now a crew of one.

As if the thought itself had conjured reality, I

caught sight of the captain four steps before reaching the deck.

He was standing near the base of the starboard stabilizer. He was twenty feet away. The deck was dark, but the little moonlight allowed me to make out his short, stocky frame. His thick, long beard. His big T-shirt and torn-up ball cap.

And the shotgun gripped in his hands, its barrel aimed right at me.

THIRTY-THREE

I took a silent half step back. Dropped from the guy's line of sight and withdrew my Sig. Raised it shoulder height.

The migrants were gathered right between us. One pull of the captain's trigger and a storm of pellets would explode from the barrel. Burst free and spread and charge forward at a thousand feet per second, mauling everything in their path.

At least half of the migrants would likely get hit, and I'd receive the brunt of it.

"Come on out where I can see you," the captain barked.

His voice was rough. He was clearly experienced. A career mariner. Probably had spent over thirty years out at sea, in one capacity or another.

"Drop your gun," I ordered.

"You can forget that."

"This is your last chance."

"Get up here where I can see you," he said again, yelling this time.

"Drop the gun first."

"Like hell. You got five seconds or I'm gonna pull this trigger and splatter these people all over the deck."

He began counting down.

Made it to four, then was interrupted by a powerful, blaring horn and a sudden burst of intense light shining into his face.

I sprang up the final steps. Saw the captain standing with his shotgun still aimed my way. His head snapped to starboard, hunting the source of the blinding glow.

His shoulders followed.

Then his hips.

The moment the shotgun angled away from me, I took aim with my Sig and pulled the trigger in a rapid, fluid series of movements that took all of three tenths of a second. The muzzle flashed and the 9mm round burst free. Another two hundredths of a second and the bullet caught the guy at an angle, striking into his right shoulder blade. The projectile punched him into a spin and he lost his footing and slipped, landing hard onto his back. Somehow the guy held on to his weapon, like a quarterback getting sacked but maintaining control of the football.

The bullet had punched through the front of his right shoulder, rendering the arm useless. He rolled onto his chest, making his only retaliatory option to turn all the way around and take aim at me one-handed, all while ignoring what was very likely the worst pain he'd ever felt.

I bet the house on my agility. Rushed up the remaining steps and darted toward the captain. Reached him before he gathered himself and kicked the shotgun free. It rattled and slid into the port gunwale. I kicked him again, this time striking the man in the side and whacking the air from his lungs. He wheezed and coughed and cried out as I grabbed his fallen weapon.

I searched the wailing captain. He had nothing on his person but his wallet and some loose change and a cell phone. I grabbed and pocketed the phone but left the rest. As his face caught the moonlight, I realized that I recognized the guy. I'd seen him before around town. At Sloppy Joe's or Smokin' Tuna. He ran with the old sea dogs crowd. I'd even seen him around Pete's now and then. We'd never been introduced, but I knew that he was respected in the community.

To the west, the blinding spotlight shut off, followed by the siren immediately after. Then I heard the Baia's familiar engines grumble to life, propelling my boat toward the trawler.

As expected, my wife had played her part to perfection, following the trawler all night but keeping her distance. Then creeping in as they rendezvoused with the captives and blasting the remaining smuggler with a spotlight to distract him. It'd all been a loose, fluid plan. And she'd made her move at the perfect time.

With the captain cursing on the deck, I turned to the group.

"Any of you speak English?" I said. When no one replied, I asked the same question in Spanish. Two of them spoke it, and I asked them to translate for me.

"You're safe now," I said in Spanish. "These were bad men. Criminals. They were going to kill some of you and make slaves of others."

One of the men relayed what I'd said. They all stared at me blankly. Fear and confusion and disbelief in their eyes.

"It's true," a woman's voice said in Spanish from the stairwell. One of the first migrants taken below deck appeared, followed by the three other girls. "They were going to imprison us."

The Haitians were still terrified and eyeing me suspiciously. But at least I had some of them on the right page.

Turning my attention back to the captain, I grabbed a fistful of his shirt and heaved him off the deck. Plopped him down beside a winch.

"You're lucky," I said to him

He fought to catch his breath. Spat, "The hell you talking about?"

"If you'd been standing about five feet to the right, my wife would've shot you. And you'd be left with a missing limb instead of just a mangled shoulder. So, count your blessings."

Ange brought the Baia up along the trawler's port side. I threw tires over the gunwale and she positioned fenders on the Baia, then I tied her off. After shutting off the engine, she climbed up onto the shrimp boat and looked around.

"The three others are below deck," I said. "One in the crews' quarters, two in the smuggling hold."

Ange folded her arms. Surveyed the deck and the migrants and the captain. She slid off her backpack and removed a first aid kit. We performed a rough patch job on the guy. Quick and minimal. Just enough to stop the bleeding. We needed him conscious and cognizant.

"Ouch," he snarled as my wife finished stitching him up.

"Shut up," she replied. Then she motioned to the captives. "Your guests look hungry. And thirsty."

We forced the captain to haul up bottles of water and juice from the galley. After distributing them, we prodded him into the wheelhouse. Forced him to his knees and taped his ankles and wrists and left him right beside the helm.

Ange and I stepped back to the door and observed the migrants downing bottle after bottle of fluids.

"I couldn't get ahold of you," Ange said.

"They've got a jammer on board somewhere."

She nodded. "I figured." My wife paused a beat, then added, "Maddox called a couple hours ago. They finished their search of O'Malley's place."

"And?"

"And he said they found communications between O'Malley and Barbossa's guys. And Captain Heinrich here. As well as evidence of bribery and an offshore bank account in O'Malley's name."

"You're kidding."

"No. And that's just part of it. They found a plan of his to take you out and reclaim Olivier and Esther. It would have gone down early this morning."

I let out a sigh. Leaned against the corner of the pilothouse. Thought over all the interactions I'd had with the man. Pictured the black-and-white photograph of the two kids and the toddler hanging on the wall at Pete's place.

"He's in custody?" I asked.

Ange nodded. "He was out on patrol. They surrounded him at the Popeye's drive-through."

I folded my arms. Eyed the Haitians, and then the injured, taped-up captain on the floor. Progress was being made, but it was time to drop the hammer.

I strode over to the captain. Stared down at him with my hands on my hips.

"Your smuggling days are over."

He gasped. "You gonna kill me?"

"That depends."

"On what?"

"The choices you make going forward."

I knelt down to meet his eyeline. "You're going to do what we tell you to do. If you can manage that, we won't kill you."

"How can I trust you?" he hissed.

"Simple. Because I'm not like you. I keep my word and hold myself to a standard. The word for that is integrity. If you do what you're told and survive the night, I suggest you look up the definition. Burn it into your psyche and maybe become something resembling a decent human being."

He glanced back and forth between Ange and me. Shook his head. "You'd let me off the hook?"

I nodded. "If you play ball."

I'd let him off the hook. But that didn't mean that others would. Others with guns and handcuffs and keys to barred concrete rooms.

He stared back at me. Mouth hung open. Face red and coated in sweat.

Letting out a long breath, he said, "What do you want me to do?"

THIRTY-FOUR

We reached Edward B. Knight Pier on the south side of Key West two hours later, just as the first glimmers of sun were appearing. I was at the helm, the captain curled up on the deck. Ange was back aboard the Baia, piloting alongside us and keeping an eye on the migrants huddled on the trawler's deck.

I glanced down at our speed and blinked in disbelief for what felt like the tenth time since I'd manned the helm. The trawler could hit twenty knots. I'd never heard of a shrimp boat being able to move that fast.

I dialed our speed back to an idle by the time we were a hundred yards from the shore. The trawler's emergency life raft was already inflated and ready. I lowered it into the water, then helped the Haitians one at a time down into the vessel. Then I pointed to shore, where Chief Verona was standing with her flashlight shining. Two of the men nodded, then paddled the boat toward the beach. A couple of them thanked Ange and me, and I put my hand to my heart and bowed slightly to them.

We'd called ahead to Jack as well, and my best friend was waiting nearby aboard our Robalo. He motored up and tied off to the Baia, then Ange jumped back over to the trawler. I threw him a wave and he saluted back, ready to stick beside us for the rest of our upcoming journey.

Once Ange was aboard, we headed back into the wheelhouse.

"All right," Captain Heinrich grumbled. "Now you let me go. We had a deal."

"The deal was that you do as I say."

He shook his head. Looked around. "What do you want me to do now?"

"Now we cruise north," I said, helping him to his feet. "To where you were supposed to drop them off."

His mouth hung open. His eyes widened.

He shook his head again, but before he could utter a sound, I added, "You take me to the drop-off site. You introduce me to whoever's running the show there. Then you get to walk."

"And if I don't?" he said. "You can't make me do anything."

I took out my Sig and folded my arms. Thought about all the people the man before me had helped kill and those he'd sentenced to a life of horrifying servitude.

"If you don't I'm gonna rip open your stitches," I said. "Then I'm gonna hang you over the side and go for a little cruise." I shrugged and added, "See if the sharks can make you do something."

He went quiet. Stared at both of us a moment, then down at the floor.

"All right," he sighed.

I slid out my dive knife. Held the blade right over his shoulder a moment, then lowered it and slashed his wrists free.

"Helm's all yours," I said.

He rubbed his wrists, then stepped to the wheel. Grabbed it with his left hand only, then turned and reversed the throttles, turning us around before taking us on a northeasterly course up the island chain.

It took just over six hours to reach the Upper Keys, then we cut across Biscayne Bay at a forty-five-degree angle. The sun was up and hot. The waters alive, buzzing with boat activity. We fit right in. There were other shrimp boats out on the water. This was the end of May, like Delaney had said. Busy time, and we fit right in as we chugged the homestretch to our destination.

"That's it," he said, pointing toward an unassuming gray warehouse building right along the shore.

There were fences topped with spirals of razor wire on both sides. A commercial fishing dock to the north, a small shipping facility to the south. A cove in front of the warehouse with piles of rocks on both sides. Like they were marking the property line out to sea. As we approached, I saw that the warehouse had a big overhead door right over the water.

"Okay," I said, eyeing Heinrich, "how does this usually go down?"

He hesitated. Let out a deep breath and wiped the sweat from his brow.

"I call them," he said. "Tell them I'm here. Let them know everything's good."

"You use a code?"

He shook his head. "Just old-fashioned English."

"You'd better not be lying to me."

"I'm not."

"You know what we'll do if you are lying, right?"

He nodded. "I know what you'll do. I'm not lying."

"Okay. So, go ahead."

He pulled out his phone and punched in a number. The call was picked up on the first ring.

"All good," he said. "Coast is clear."

He hung up right after, and I smiled. "You weren't kidding."

He said nothing. We were fifty yards from the warehouse door when it opened. Just lifted into the ceiling like a curtain at a play, revealing a dark, open space behind it.

"How many people will be in there?" Ange said.

He shrugged. "Usually just two. Until the buyer shows up. He'll be standing by."

"Tell us what happens," I said.

He wiped the sweat off his forehead again. Closed his eyes and fought to control his breathing.

"Distributors check the products," he said. "Check to make sure everything's good. Then they message the buyer and they back a box truck through a door on the opposite side."

I rubbed my chin, thinking everything over. "A real well-oiled machine you guys are running here. Too bad there's a cog in the gears this morning."

I opened Ange's bag and pulled out a twenty-two along with a suppressor. Dropped to a knee and screwed it onto the end of the barrel.

"Tell me what you see, Heinrich."

"A big room. Three walls. A roof fifty feet up."

"How many people?"

"Two. One on a dock off the port side. One dead ahead at the water's edge."

"Armed?"

"Always."

"Okay," I said. "Throw them a wave. No reason not to be courteous."

He did as I ordered. A shaky but casual greeting with the only good arm he had. A quick departure from the helm, then back to it, easing us into a position at a low speed, then dialing back on the throttle, then idling, then shutting it down.

"They look confused," he said. "There's usually men topside to help with the lines."

"All right," I said. "I should go and help them, then. On your stomach."

Heinrich did as ordered again, and Ange zip-tied his wrists.

Staying in a crouch, I shuffled aft, then out the door. Pistol concealed. Ready.

Ange stayed in the wheelhouse, watching over the guy with his shotgun.

The overhead door reached the top, then rattled right back down. Smooth, but noisy enough to cover my movements.

"Anybody home?" the guy on the dock said, irritation in his voice.

I crawled to the port gunwale and popped up, weapon raised, muzzle aimed at the guy's chest from barely ten feet away.

"Hands up!" I barked.

The guy's hands didn't go up.

Instead, he narrowed his gaze. Bent his knees a little and reached for his sidearm like a cowboy in the Wild West. He was fast. Knew what he was doing. But no way able to compete with the time it took for me to flex my right index finger an eighth of an inch.

I fired. A muffled, subsonic whisp. Like an air gun. The low-caliber bullet punching him in the chest. I fired again, hitting his right arm, and he shook, relinquishing his pistol and letting it bounce and fall into the water off the other side of the dock. He spun and fell to the floor, landing into an awkward fetal position.

I sprang toward the bow and took aim at the second guy. Ordered him to freeze as well.

He did freeze. Like a statue. Completely stunned by the rapid turn of events.

I wagered he'd probably gone through the motions dozens of times. Stood right where he was with his hands on his hips and observed while his partner threw the lines and tied off the boat and escorted a group of terrified migrants out of the bowels of the trawler. Probably made them sit on the floor for a head count. Probably confirmed all the details, verifying who was being sent where and for what.

Now things were different.

Now the tables had turned. He was the one stunned

and then terrified. I could feel the dread emitting off him like steam from an ice cube dropped on a hot plate. It was palpable.

I kept my sights locked onto him. My eyes on his face and his hands.

He was thinking about it. Was about to make a very bad decision, then Ange poked her head up, the barrel of her twelve-gauge locked onto the guy, and the idea vanished when he realized it was a two-on-one game.

His hands snapped to the sky without another word from either of us.

"Drop your gun," I said.

He hesitated a moment, then said, "I don't have one."

"Great. But if you're lying, I'm gonna use whatever I find on your kneecaps."

The man turned rigid. Swallowed hard and gasped. Used his left index finger and thumb to grab a concealed black Colt XSE with a walnut grip. A big, intimidating handgun. Over the top. Just to send a message. The guy probably hadn't fired it in ages. Just used it for show. To scare innocent victims and nothing more.

He held it out, then dropped it to his feet.

With Ange holding the guy with her shotgun, I leapt over to the dock. Ignored the dying criminal I'd shot twice and stomped right toward the second one. The guy who hadn't been on the dock to help tie us off.

The obvious leader of the pair.

He was a couple inches taller than me. Had a shaved head and a tattoo around his right eye. Wore sunglasses, even though he was inside.

I kicked his Colt into the water, then forced him to his knees and patted him down.

"I'm gonna give you the same offer I gave Captain Heinrich," I said, gesturing to the trawler.

I kicked him onto his chest. Shoved my heel into his back. Nearly put all my weight onto it.

"You do what I say, and I won't kill you."

I didn't want to shoot him. Not that I cared about his life or his limbs, but I needed him breathing and able to talk normally and be mentally cognizant for at least a few more minutes.

I looked back at Ange. Gave her a knowing look, which she returned.

"What do you want?" he snarled.

I held out the guy's phone right in front of his terrified face.

"I want you to make a call or send a message," I said. "Whatever you usually do right about now."

He hesitated again. Facing a dilemma. The devil he knew versus the devil he didn't. It was tough for him to make up his mind because he didn't know Ange and me. Didn't know what we were capable of. If he did know us, he'd be grabbing the phone and punching in numbers or letters as quickly as his fingers would move.

He bowed his head. "I can't do that."

"Sure you can. Because if you don't, you die right here and now. It's that simple."

The man paused again. The war waging in his mind. I was getting tired of looking at him. Was about to send my message a little louder and clearer with a round through his kneecap when he began to plead for his life.

"He's rich," the guy said. "My boss. We could work something out."

"Like what?"

"Cut you in. Make you head of security or something. Make you rich."

"I'm already rich."

He eyed me up and down. "You don't look rich."

"I've got everything I need and then some."

"I'm serious. I'm talking millions here."

I shrugged. "Make it billions. I don't care. My soul isn't for sale." I forced his head back down. Pressed the barrel of my pistol into the back of his right knee. "How do you feel about your legs?"

He raised his eyebrows in utter confusion.

"Is walking something that's important to you? Something you'd like to keep doing?"

I pressed the muzzle of my Sig hard against his right kneecap. "'Cause if I flex my trigger finger, you'll never take another step for the rest of your life."

"We can work something out here," he pleaded again, his body shaking.

"Time to stop begging and lying." I held out his phone again. "Time to call the buyer. Last chance."

He stared at the phone a couple seconds. Swallowed hard. Then grabbed it and began typing. A message. I was glad for it. Hard to read someone's tone in a message. Hard to sense trouble in someone's voice.

He held the message out to me.

"That's the one you always send?" I asked.

He nodded.

"You promise?"

"Yes."

"It better be. 'Cause I've got nine more rounds in here and don't need any more incentive to set them free."

He sent the message. I grabbed his phone and waited. Watched as the message status went from sent to read. There was no reply.

I raised an eyebrow at the guy.

"He doesn't reply," he said.

"All right. What happens now?"

"Now we wait. For him to drive here."

"How long?"

The guy shrugged. "Couple minutes. He'll be close by."

Just under two minutes later, a light across the room illuminated, and an overhead door on the eastern-facing wall opened.

THIRTY-FIVE

"Stand up," I said to the guy. I helped him to his feet, then said, "Stay right here. Stand tall. Hands on your hips."

Once he had the right posture, I disappeared into the shadows to the left, and waited.

A box truck backed right up to him. Stopped and the driver put the vehicle in park and stared through the rearview. He said something to the guy in the passenger seat. Something was off, and he knew it. There was usually a group of captives huddled on the floor.

The driver looked around, a little frantic. He reached for the shifter out of instinct.

Before he could put the truck back in drive, my suppressed twenty-two was aimed at the side of his head from three feet away.

"Out of the truck," I ordered.

He froze. Stared at me. Was hardheaded and

wasn't going to comply. I could see that from about a mile away.

He turned and reached for something just out of view. I angled my aim downward a couple degrees and pulled the trigger, blasting a round into his rotator cuff. The bullet entered from the front and burst out through his shoulder blade. Like a reversal of the shot I'd hit the captain with.

I grabbed the handle and threw the door open. Snagged the driver by the arm and yanked him out. The second guy reacted quickly. Far quicker than I'd expected. He ducked out the passenger door and fell into a crouch and scrambled toward the tailgate. I had the driver tight in my arm, all my attention on him. Because the second guy wasn't a concern. Because the moment he reached the back of the truck he came to a troubling realization, just a fraction of a second too late.

Ange was right there.

Fifteen feet from him.

Ready.

He made it a foot into an upward arc with his weapon before she fired. She used the other twenty-two, the muffled round pounding into the guy's chest. She pulled the trigger a second time, hitting him in the same place and he flew to the ground and his weapon fell and bounced away.

With the captain tied up, Ange jumped down from the bow and closed in, suppressed pistol raised. Her target wasn't dead, but he was down for the count. Not getting up and putting up any kind of fight anytime soon.

We rounded them up and taped their wrists. Shut

the overhead door and stood in front of them, observing as they winced and groaned. Their blood spilling out and pooling around them.

"That bullet bored right through your glenoid cavity," I said to the driver. "No doubt splintered and took some of your scapula and humerus with it. Must hurt like hell."

His face was red and all scrunched up. He was sweating and tearing up and heaving from side to side.

I knelt down beside him and said, "Isn't much fun when people fight back, is it, tough guy?"

He glared at me. "You... have no idea who we are."

I shrugged. "Sure I do. You're the buyers."

"No," he snarled. "You don't know *who* we are. How powerful we are. How powerful our connections are. You should be very afraid of Barbossa."

I held out my pistol, aiming it at the ceiling. "You know, that's not the first time I've heard that in the past couple of days. And yet, here I am, standing over four more of Barbossa's men. I think he should be afraid of me."

I dug a hand into my back pocket. Pulled out the picture Rosalind had given me just before she died. Unfolding it, I held it right in front of the criminal.

"I want to know where this man is," I said, pointing at the guy in the photograph.

The criminal examined it through slits. His eyes were watery and red.

He shook his head. "We deal with a lot of faces. I don't remember—"

"Try harder. He came in just a few days ago.

Probably around eight o'clock, after being held up in the islands by the unexpected searches. And he had a fresh wound to his head."

The guy still looked blank, and I added, "He's young. Maybe mid-twenties. Lean and strong."

The man closed his eyes. Grunted. Opened them and said, "He was sent to a worksite."

"Where?"

He closed his eyes again. Turned his head away. So I encouraged him to answer by stepping on the entry wound to his shoulder. He cried out and grabbed my leg. But he was weak and in pain. I leaned forward, putting more weight onto it. He pounded the floor with his left fist and threw his head back.

"I can stand here all night," I said. "You're bleeding out, but it's a slow trickle. You'll probably survive for a couple of hours. Then I can patch it up and keep at it."

"Dakota," he said. "North Dakota."

I leaned back, taking most of my weight off him.

"What city?"

"I don't know."

"You got contact info for them?"

He slid his shaking left hand into his front pocket and came out with a cell phone. Stared at the screen and punched some keys, then held it out to me.

There was the name of a company and a phone number.

"Guy named Josiah Clark runs the place," he said. "You'd better not tell him I gave you his info."

I stared at the screen a moment, then pocketed the guy's phone. "That's the least of your worries. Trust me."

I slid out my phone. Shot a quick message. Then Ange pressed a button along the right wall and the big overhead door behind us opened, slowly revealing the waters of Biscayne Bay. Two boats thundered into view. The first was a Homeland Security patrol boat, and the second was a CBP boat. Agent Maddox stood on the bow of the lead one, an M4 rifle in his hands. I'd messaged him moments after leaving Key West, sending him my phone's location and giving him ample time to follow us and organize a raid.

As Ange and I watched the arriving agents, the left-side door of the warehouse flew open. I turned and caught a brief glimpse of a man stumbling outside, and then vanishing.

It was Captain Heinrich. Making a daring attempt at an escape.

With Ange keeping the other criminals pinned, I darted across the warehouse and slipped through the door ten seconds behind the captain. Saw him twenty yards ahead, frantically climbing into a parked Mazda Miata.

I strode closer and raised my weapon but didn't fire. Homeland and CBP weren't the only law enforcement descending on the compound. Local police were on their way as well. I could hear the distant sirens.

I watched as Heinrich fired up the little sports car's engine and blasted out of the dark lot. He accelerated at a rapid clip down the short drive, rocketing away from me. He stuck his head out through his window. Held out his hand, middle finger protruding. He cursed me out and hollered like a madman.

He brought himself back into the vehicle just as he blurred past a stop sign, tore into the intersection, and was immediately struck by a southbound semi. The collision was destructive, the massive truck pummeling into the side of the Miata at over fifty miles per hour. Absolutely demolishing the little vehicle and crushing and thundering right over it. An earsplitting, catastrophic smash.

And Captain Heinrich was gone.

By the time I returned into the warehouse, Maddox and the other agents had taken over the scene. He was in charge. The senior man of the group. He'd handle everything from there.

As I approached my good friend, another vessel entered through the overhead door. Our Baia Flash, with Jack standing at the helm.

As agents bound the still-breathing criminals and searched the trawler, Maddox gave me a pat on the back. "With Officer O'Malley in custody and this smuggling hub located, I'd say this is one of the most productive days of my career."

"That's saying a lot," I replied.

He eyed Ange and me as the sirens got louder. "Time for you two to get out of here. I got this."

He knew that neither of us wanted money or recognition for what we'd done. We both just wanted one thing: anonymity.

We wanted no mention of our involvement. And Maddox would handle it.

"You guys figure out where you're going next?" he asked.

I nodded.

"Where?"

"You'll find out soon enough."

He placed a hand on my shoulder.

None of us said another word. We just gave each other knowing nods.

I retrieved my gear from the bowels of the trawler's engine room, then Ange and I headed for the dock and climbed aboard the Baia. The moment our feet hit the fiberglass, Jack reversed the throttles, motoring us out of the warehouse before turning around and blasting back across the bay.

THIRTY-SIX

Scarlett stood on a dock at Sigsbee Marina on Dredger's Key. She held Esther in her arms while Lauren stood beside her and Olivier played at their feet. He had a tiny fishing pole in his hands and was dangling a lure into the water while gazing over the edge with wide eyes.

The four of them watched as a boat rounded the opening into the cove. It was a Sea Ray 45. Jack's fishing boat. Pete Jameson was at the helm, piloting the vessel toward them.

He snugged the boat up to the dock and tied off. Then the seventy-year-old restaurant owner held up bags of boxed food.

"Hope you're all hungry," he said. "Oz whipped up some of his best."

They ate lunch up in the flybridge. Grilled grouper on beds of Spanish rice. Shrimp rolls. And of course, Scarlett's favorite, a pile of conch fritters.

While digging in, Pete said, "You heard from your folks?"

Scarlett nodded. "They located the smuggler's distribution depot near Miami. Now they're on their way back."

Pete grinned. "Of course, they did."

Captain Rinaldi arrived, pulling into the nearby lot and greeting two masters-at-arms with M16s draped across their chests, before heading down the dock. She was wearing her Navy service uniform, the khaki garments clean and pressed as usual.

"Thanks again for letting us stay here," Scarlett said after the CO of the base settled in. "I'm sure this kind of thing is unusual. And hopefully we won't have to be here much longer."

"You'll stay as long as you like," she said. "We have the capacity to help, so we're helping. But given what I know about your parents, I'm betting it won't be long before any threats against you or the children's lives will be neutralized."

Scarlett smiled. Ate some more.

The conversation turned to Pete and his upcoming election. The previous mayor, Ezra Nix, was currently serving time in jail and awaiting trial for charges of criminal activity. And there were government and law enforcement personnel who believed Pete would make a good fit.

He laughed when they asked about his campaign.

"No, I won't be doing any of that," he said. "I'll debate. I'll give a speech when I have to. And I'll put my name on the ballot." He shrugged and added, "If people want to vote for me, they can. If not, that's fine as well."

"You'd do a great job," Captain Rinaldi said.

Then everyone at the table nodded in agreement.

"You guys heard anything about O'Malley?" Scarlett asked.

Everyone shook their head.

"Far as I know, he's still in custody," Pete said. He shook his head. "Hard to believe he was involved. I never would've guessed that one."

Scarlett swallowed a bite. Then washed it down with key limeade and thought a moment before saying, "I still think Delaney's involved too."

Pete nodded. "Logan told me about you and Cameron the other night. I gotta say, I'm impressed. Either you're both part ninja or I'm really getting old, but I never noticed you."

"Sorry about that, Pete," Scarlett said. "It wasn't you I was concerned about. And it wasn't until we followed him after that my suspicions about him peaked."

Pete waved her off. "It's all right. You're curious by nature. Don't lose that." He took a swig of beer, then added, "I just hope you're wrong. Old Parker just tends to rub people the wrong way. I think that's it."

"Who?" Scarlett said, raising her eyebrows.

"Delaney," Pete said, clearing his throat. "His name's not really Red. It's just his nickname. Though he doesn't go by Parker very often anymore."

Scarlett fell quiet. Stared off into space.

Then her mouth fell open.

Parker Delaney, she thought. *PD.*

I received a call from Scarlett just as we were cruising through the Middle Keys. She was breathing fast. Words rushing from her mouth in such a frenzy I couldn't understand her.

I climbed down into the saloon to escape the howling wind and said, "Start over, Scar. I didn't catch a word—"

"PD!" she exclaimed.

I squinted. "How did you find out about that?"

"I overheard you and mom... that's not important. What is important is that Delaney's first name isn't Red. That's just his nickname." She paused. Let out a gasp, then said, "His first name Parker. Parker Delaney. PD."

I blinked. Stared off into space. Wondered how in the hell we'd missed that. Then I wondered if it could be a coincidence, or an intentional move on the dying smuggler's part. The guy had been in a tough spot. He'd been conflicted. He'd wanted to do the right thing, seemed like. To somehow try and rectify all the evil he'd been involved in.

But he was also weary. He couldn't just come out and spill all the beans. No, he was afraid. Not for his life. He could tell he was dying. He'd been afraid for someone else. Or multiple people. Family members or friends. People he cared about. People he felt the need to protect.

I thanked Scarlett and we ended the call. After mulling over her words, I returned to Ange in the cockpit and relayed Scarlett's revelation.

My wife's only reaction was to give a proud smile

and stare off toward the sea ahead of us. She was quiet a long moment. Eventually said, "Sounds like we've got a stop to make before heading to Sigsbee."

I rubbed my chin. "It's a pretty huge stretch." She stayed silent, and I added, "What are we going to do? We've already talked to him. So has Maddox. So has Jane. He's been questioned and his place has been searched."

"So, we can talk to him again," Ange said. "This time we'll bring up the PD thing. See how he reacts." She shrugged. "I don't see the harm in it. Not like Safe Harbor's far out of the way or something."

I sighed. Relented. She was right. There was no harm in stopping by and confronting the guy about it. It probably wouldn't lead anywhere, but there was still a chance.

The only downside was I didn't relish the idea. We were both tired. Running on caffeine from mug after mug of coffee. Taking power naps, but needing a full sleep.

I didn't feel like talking to Delaney. Didn't feel like seeing him. But our daughter was insightful. We'd known that from the start. And she had good instincts. Another facet of her character that we'd have to be inept to have missed after all we'd already been through together.

So, we cruised along and forty-five minutes later, we passed Boca Chica Key, then slowed and turned back into the opening into Safe Harbor. Chugged north along the same line I'd swam less than twelve hours earlier. Passed the Perry Hotel and its docks off the port bow. Spotted Delaney's little crow's nest up ahead off the starboard bow.

But we didn't talk to him because he wasn't there.

His house was dark. He was nowhere in sight. And his old, decrepit shrimp boat wasn't tied off to his dock.

After knocking on his door and peering into his place, Ange and I returned to the Baia. I splashed into the harbor. Retrieved my rebreather, along with the rest of my dive gear, then returned to her side. We both stood there, staring off into the distance.

Then my wife shot me a look that said it all.

We'd find Delaney. We'd confront him and bring him to justice if need be. But not yet. There were other matters to attend to first.

THIRTY-SEVEN

Florida Strait
Earlier that Day

Parker "Red" Delaney was a man with a plan.

Things may have been expedited due to unexpected recent events, but he'd always had a strong, fleshed out exit strategy.

He stood at the helm of his old shrimping boat. Felt the worn, teak under his fingers. The vessel that'd been in his family for three generations. His grandfather's first commercial boat. The one that'd started it all.

His great-grandfather had been a bold, ambitious young man. He'd ventured north for the Alaskan gold rush. Allured by tales of prospectors acquiring riches beyond the wildest of imaginations. But all he acquired was bankruptcy and frostbite.

Doctors told him he should find somewhere

warmer to heal and recover, so he settled in Key West. Married and had a son and taught him about frenzies and opportunities. How to best capitalize on a craze. Then a new rush happened. The pink rush. And this time, the family was ready. Knew how to best profit from it all. Knew how to grow a fortune.

But they didn't know how to hold onto one. Didn't know how to build an empire that would last generations.

Delaney flashed back to the present. Felt the worn hardwood beneath his fingers once again. The vessel that'd started it all.

Ironic, he thought. *Now it will end it all.*

He was steaming south. Full speed. The past at his back. The future before him. Leaving everything he'd known. Trading it for something better. Starting new.

Two men entered the pilothouse, snapping him from his thoughts. Both were middle-aged. One was short and wore round-framed glasses. The other was average height and bald.

"We're twenty miles out," the short one said.

Delaney coughed. Blinked and looked around. Checked his watch. The orange Doxa. It indicated a quarter past five in the morning.

Quarter past five. Twenty miles out. Time to execute.

He turned to the short guy with glasses. Ned Anatoli. His accountant. And then to the bald guy, Craig Gentry. Craig was a former shrimper and old friend. He'd been the recruiter. The one who'd identified potential shrimpers around the Gulf who would be good fits with the operation. Both men had worked mostly behind the scenes and had kept their hands particularly clean. But they both knew the ins and outs of the operation.

"It's time," Delaney said. "You boys ready to reap the fruits of our labors?"

The men smiled back. Gentry said, "Hell yeah. First round of hookers are on me. Soon as we jump through these hoops."

Delaney smiled. Patted them both on the shoulder. "It's been a long time coming, boys. Let's do this."

The three of them headed below deck to the cargo hold. Ned dropped down, found a secret latch in the deck, and opened a hidden hatch. It was the original smuggling space—the hidden compartment Delaney's grandfather had installed sixty years earlier.

Then Ned and Craig smiled and climbed down into the space.

It was another ironic twist.

They'd utilize one of the very shrimping boats that had been used for smuggling to smuggle themselves into a different country. Delaney had already taken care of everything. Bought off the right people. Forged the right documents. The plan was for him to motor into Havana Harbor, deal with customs officials on his own, then the others would be given their documents the following day.

Then they'd all be scot-free to do as they pleased and live out the rest of their days in wealth and prosperity, and free from America's reach.

That was the plan.

Delaney pulled out a bottle of champagne. Handed it down to his two co-conspirators.

"Feel free to start the party early, fellas," he said. "I'll see you on the other side."

They grabbed the bottle, then helped Delaney ease the hatch back into position. Once it was flush, Delaney repositioned the metal loop, then quietly slid the locking mechanism back into place and twisted it snug.

Then he stood and stared down at the deck.

In order for his plan to work, he had no choice but to clean up—to leave no stone unturned. There couldn't be any evidence leading back to him. There couldn't be any witnesses.

Ned and Craig were old friends. Key players in his criminal enterprise. But they were also something else...

Loose ends.

And in order for the exit strategy to be successful, there could be none of those.

He returned topside. Shut off the engines. Strode to the stern and lowered a dinghy with a 15-horsepower Evinrude clamped to its transom. Kept it tied off as the trawler slowed to a drift. Headed back down to the engine room. Could hear faint pounding coming from the adjacent cargo hold. Shutting off the engines hadn't been part of the plan.

Delaney smiled.

He grabbed a spare fuel can that'd been positioned beside a workbench. He twisted open the cap, then grabbed a rag and shoved it into the nozzle. Positioned the can against the aft bulkhead and lit the end of the rag with a lighter.

A minute later he was back in the dinghy, untying the lines and powering up the little outboard and chugging south.

The explosion came thirty seconds later.

A sudden, muffled boom and the jarring and rupturing of metal.

The explosion wasn't big enough to engulf the vessel. Just enough to blast a door-sized hole through the stern.

Delaney turned back and watched over his shoulder as water flowed into the trawler, quickly overtaking the old vessel. The bow angled up, then sank rapidly, the Caribbean bubbling its way into each compartment. Less than a minute after the explosion, the trawler was gone.

Delaney pictured Ned and Craig. Imagined the two men realizing what'd happened. Pounding against the hatch and bulkheads. Locked inside. Water slowly seeping in as the foundered boat sank four-hundred-feet to the bottom of the Strait.

There was no remorse there. Whatever moral foundation Delaney possessed had been utterly demolished years ago. He was out for himself, and that was that. Nothing else mattered.

And he was on the verge of victory.

He could see it. His destiny. His earned paradise. All glowing in the distance in the form of Havana Harbor.

THIRTY-EIGHT

McKenzie County, North Dakota
The Following Day

Two thousand miles from Key West, Leon Baptiste rubbed his red, callused hands. Breathed in cool evening air and gazed up at the enormous star-studded sky. He looked around. The supervisors were out of sight, and he took advantage of the brief moment of respite. Closed his eyes and let his mind drift.

He thought back to his grueling sail from Haiti. The violent scuffle in the Florida Strait. Waking up in the trawler's cargo hold and eventually being forced out and into the dark warehouse. Then passing out again before the long journey to the worksite. He'd awoken the second time tied up and locked in the back of a cramped dark truck with two other young guys.

They didn't see daylight for a day and a half. Stopped occasionally, but only briefly. The first one had been the only eventful stop. One of the two other guys had begun shouting and pounding his fists on the truck's metal panel walls. Then the other had joined in. Both making a ruckus, trying to make as much noise as humanly possible.

The truck's rear doors slammed open. The wall of refrigerators slid aside. Leon saw a brief glimpse of darkness and an open pasture and trees in the distance, and nothing more. Both men had been grabbed and beaten. Struck with clubs again and again right in front of him.

"Any of you makes another sound, and I'll do the same," a shadowy figure had said. "And I can hear perfectly through this front wall."

No one spoke again after that. Not another sound for thirty-seven hours. The temperature dropped. Ears popped occasionally with altitude changes. Leon tried his best to guess where he was, but he didn't know the geography of the United States very well. Just general knowledge. New York and Miami in the east, Los Angeles in the west. A bunch of places in the middle.

The back of the truck was silent. The two other men beaten raw. Leon deep in his thoughts and reflections. Pondering how he'd ended up there. Pondering where *there* was and where they were going.

It was late on the second day when they arrived. After half an hour of rough travel over bumpy, rocky covered roads, and after countless turns, they stopped. They were ordered out of the truck at gunpoint. Leon blinked and looked around and saw nothing but hills and grassland and trees in all directions. They were standing beside the only man-made structures in sight.

Portable buildings lined one side of the flat fenced-in property. There were rows of big metal cylinders. Stacks of oil drums. Parked vehicles and heavy industrial equipment. In the middle of the property was a hive of pipes and machinery surrounding a narrow tower of crisscrossing metal that rose over a hundred feet into the air.

Leon took in deep breaths. It'd been stuffy in the back of the truck, but here the air was fresh and cool. The smell of pine carried in the breeze. There were no sounds other than the grinding and groaning of industry. They were surrounded by nothing but the natural world. Nothing but emptiness.

The rest of his first night was a blur.

Clothes and work boots were divvied up, and they were prodded into a big tent with metal bunk beds. Then they were given a quick orientation. Told what to say if someone happened to talk to them. Given fake IDs and other paperwork.

They'd be working at a satellite oil drilling operation. They'd get paid, that part was made clear. Paid more than any of them had ever been paid in their lives. But there was a catch.

As of that moment, they were all in serious debt. Though they'd paid for their passage to the United States, they'd been smuggled thousands of miles into the mainland of the country and given jobs. And they'd been given fake new IDs and paperwork. Clothes, shelter, and food. All of which came at a hefty price. All bought and paid for, and they'd need to repay the debt. And the interest was absurd.

Leon spoke to the older migrants. Some of them had been working for the company for over ten years and had barely made a dent in what they owed. And they'd had no communication during that time with anyone back home. They weren't allowed to use the internet. Or a phone. Or write letters.

No one knew who they were. It was like they'd skipped off the face of the Earth. Alive and well and working their tails off from before sunrise to after sunset, but no one knew about it.

And their supervisor's firearms ensured obedience. Punishments for not doing what you were told were painful, but not debilitating. Intended to invoke as much pain as possible without impairing their ability to work. Things like burns with hot iron rods.

The older guys said they always worked remote jobs. Usually in the mountains. Far away from curious eyes and ears. Far away from everything.

On his first morning, Leon was given a hard hat and thick leather gloves. He was tasked with grunt work. Didn't know enough to operate anything or help with the drilling. That would come later on. So, he moved things around and cleaned up and performed the tasks no one else wanted to. The hardest, most backbreaking work. A newbie working his way up from the bottom.

Leon had been at the worksite for four days when he spotted a small, low-flying aircraft on the horizon. It appeared from the south and performed a quick flyover maybe a quarter mile to the east. Then it looped back and performed a second flyover, passing just to the west.

It was an amphibious plane. He could see the floats attached to its underside. He figured it was a common sight, this far out in the middle of nowhere. Figured there were probably people who lived so far off the grid that their essentials needed to be flown in and that lakes would prove a convenient flat place to land and take off amid the hilly landscape.

Leon didn't think anything of the plane. He'd been told over and over again by the old-timers that hope was a dangerous thing out there. That he should abandon it all and accept his new fate and forget his old life. That it was the only way to survive out there.

Some hadn't made it. Some hadn't been able to adjust and had been dealt with accordingly. Inhumanely and unceremoniously. Shot and dropped into pits that were bulldozed and covered. Buried thirty feet down in the remote wilderness.

The managers had a pit right beside their main office. One that'd been dug as a warning—a reminder of what could happen to any of them if they didn't do as they were told.

Six hours after the low-flying aircraft completed its two passes, a big, loud pickup truck rumbled up the dirt road. It was far off, but Leon watched as it stopped only briefly at the main gate, then thundered through the opening into the property and pulled right up to the main office.

THIRTY-NINE

"What's the play here?" Ange said, gazing through the windshield at the temporary work structure ahead of us.

It looked like a portable office. Maybe ten by twenty feet. Tiny. Able to be hauled up onto a flatbed and driven anywhere with ease, even up dirt roads and switchbacks. Its walls were metal panels. Just sturdy enough to remain intact against normal weather patterns.

I sat in the driver's seat of the Ford F-250 Super Duty. It was a nice rig. Big and bulky and powerful. Four-wheel drive with substantial offroad tires. I felt like I could gun it and blaze north all the way to Canada on any road I hit. Probably clear across Saskatchewan. Probably all the way to the northern tundras, and nothing would stand in its way.

The diesel grumbled ahead of me. Exhaust coughed out the back and steamed in the cool air.

I glanced down at the key ring hanging from the ignition. There was a steel tag hanging from the loop with the words "Big Dog" engraved into it. We'd met the vehicle's owner about an hour and a half earlier, at a crossroads northwest of there. He was the contact from the guy in Miami's phone. Josiah Clark.

After taking off from Tarpon Cove in Key West the previous day, we'd flown northwest. Refueled at Clarksville Regional Airport, right at the border between Tennessee and Kentucky, and then took off for the second, even longer leg. We performed a flyover of the worksite. Surveyed it from afar. A quick evaluation and a head count. Then we landed in Watford City and met up with the buyer's contact. He'd proven an easy man to manipulate. After a quick chat, we knocked him out and borrowed his ride. He'd be found eventually. Dazed and delirious, and tied up in his dingy hotel room.

We were now idling at the end of a dirt road seven miles south of Johnson's Corner, scanning a drilling site that was tucked away in the hills along the Little Missouri River. We'd counted thirty workers from the air. Maybe half a dozen armed men. They weren't even trying to be discreet with their rifles. Not out there in the middle of nowhere.

"I'm gonna go talk to whoever's in charge," I said. "See if I can learn something."

I opened the door and slid out. Headed inside.

Five minutes later, I returned to the truck. Opened the door and leaned inside and waited. It didn't take long. We watched through the windshield as men appeared, some hustling into view from corners of the site, some rumbling up on ATVs. They all approached from the back side of the office, and they all shot curious glances my way before entering through its back door.

I threw waves to all of them. None of which were returned.

"What did you say to them?" Ange asked.

"Him," I said. "There was just one guy in there. A slob with a big gut and a bigger ego. And I told him I knew what they were up to and that I wanted payment in exchange for silence. Threatened to go to the police and tear his operation to shreds if he didn't do what I asked."

Ange laughed. "You tried to blackmail him? What did he say?"

"He agreed," I said with a smile. "I told him I'd wait out here and for him to wave me in when he was ready to hand over the payment."

As if my words had summoned the guy, the front door opened and he appeared, taking up most of the empty space. He stared toward me, then beckoned me in. I waved back and he backstepped and shut the door again.

With one simple request, he'd done all the hard work for us.

He'd rounded up a group of his supervisors and they were all standing in there with their weapons drawn, waiting for me to return. They'd riddle me with bullets and probably toss me into the hole behind the structure.

I climbed back into the truck. Shut the door and buckled my seat belt. Shoved the shifter into drive and mashed the gas pedal, spitting rocks and dirt behind us. The V-8 roared and the chassis jerked, and we rocketed forward.

We covered the fifty feet to the office door in seconds. Pummeled into it at thirty miles per hour. The thin walls smashed and caved, offering no resistance to the three tons of metal. A loud crash, and a jolt, and then a screech as we continued through the interior. Then cries and shouts as we struck one guard and then another. Bodies bouncing off the grille and hood and flailing over the roof.

We drove clear through to the other side, smashing a massive cavity straight through the heart of the structure.

I braked and turned a sharp left, skidding to a stop while gazing out my rolled down window. Scattered pieces of debris were still falling, and dust hung in the air. Four men were down and motionless, knocked unconscious by the truck. Including the big guy I'd spoken to. Two were crawling and wailing, struggling to recover.

I aimed my Sig at them and climbed out. Ange and I both scanned the area. When no backup arrived, we grabbed the two conscious criminals and dragged them down to the dirt. Removed and tossed aside their weapons. One had a broken leg. The other had a hyperextended elbow and was bleeding from his forehead.

I held out Leon's picture.

"First one who tells me where this man is doesn't get shot," I said.

They both stared at the photograph.

But before either of them could reply, a man approached us from the northwest. I turned and squinted and took aim. Then smiled and lowered my weapon.

The man held his hands up as he hustled toward us. He was forty yards off, but I knew immediately that I'd seen him before. A week earlier, lying unconscious on the deck of the shrimp trawler near the Tortugas. The same man from the photograph his wife had given me during her final moments.

FORTY

We splashed down just north of Dredgers Key twenty hours later. It'd been a long two-thousand-mile journey back to the islands. All following a long week of dangers and unknowns. What felt like a nonstop escapade ever since I'd first spotted that foundering sailboat off Monte Cristo.

Maddox and his team had taken things over back in North Dakota. Cleaned up and shut down the operation just like they had near Miami. Then we'd been given a ride back to Watford City Municipal Airport.

We stopped in Cape Girardeau, Missouri, to refuel and eat, downing plates of brisket and St. Louis–style ribs. Leon was dealing with emotional blows I couldn't imagine. After the whirlwind of being knocked unconscious, taken two-thousand miles to an alien world and spending four days in a modern-day labor camp, he'd been liberated, only to be informed moments after that his wife had perished.

He'd asked what'd happened and we'd told him immediately. As much as it hurt for us to say it. And after getting over the initial anger, he'd wanted to burn the entire drilling site to rubble.

He hadn't spoken much initially. But over the course of the long flights, he relaxed and opened up about his life and the circumstances that'd led to his family's fleeing from Haiti. He'd been well off, far better than most. Educated and comfortable in the upper class. But eight months earlier, his wife and children had caught the attention of the deranged criminal Barbossa.

Rosalind was a stunning woman. And their children were both beautiful. And Barbossa had wanted them for his own. One night, six months earlier, his men had swept in and abducted Rosalind and the two children from their home. They'd left Leon for dead.

But he hadn't died.

He'd survived and eventually recovered his strength enough to formulate a plan to get his family back.

It was risky. Bold. There was a high probability of failure. But there was also a chance that they'd be able to start a new life.

Childhood friends with a smuggler who'd been caught up in Barbossa's dealings, Leon had convinced his friend to sneak them aboard on his next departure. He'd thrown in a bag of cash to sweeten the deal. But somehow, Barbossa had caught wind of what'd happened. They'd shot the smuggler and tried to take Rosalind, Olivier, and Esther back to

Barbossa.

And that's when Ange and I had arrived.

After telling his story, Leon went quiet again. He was torn up. His heart shattered. The woman he loved and had tried with everything he had to save, was gone.

Ange and I did our best to console him—to help him see that there were still good, bright things ahead. Things worth living for. But it wasn't until he laid eyes on those things that a surge of life entered his body.

Ange motored us along the cove and right into Sigsbee Marina. There was a small group gathered at the end of the nearest dock. Scarlett, Jack, and Lauren, along with Captain Rinaldi. And Esther and Olivier standing in front. Both watching intently.

Leon couldn't contain his excitement. He was out the passenger door and climbing to the float the moment he laid eyes on the kids. Leapt to the planks and dropped and threw his arms around them. They stayed like that for a couple minutes, lost in the moment and the emotional embrace.

Jack helped tie us off, and Ange killed the engine, and we climbed out. I shook his hand, then Ange and I hugged Scarlett as well. A long, strong hug.

We shared a meal at the nearby Sunset Lounge with Captain Rinaldi, and I took her aside and thanked her again for everything.

"They're gonna be moved now," I told the captain. "To the CBP station in Marathon."

"They'd be safer here," Rinaldi said without a moment's thought. "For the time being. Just until Barbossa is dealt with."

"I can't impose on your hospitality any longer. You've already done so much. Much more than your duty required of you, that's for sure."

She took one look at the kids and their father, then said, "Well, I'm the commanding officer here. That means I make the decisions. And the family stays here until your mission's done."

I smiled and conceded, then returned to the meal.

While enjoying burgers and fish sandwiches, Jack said, "Still no sign of Delaney. The old seadog just disappeared."

I nodded. Hadn't expected there to be any sign of him. Not anymore. He was gone. Forever. After many generations, his family had left the islands for good.

He could hide all he wanted. Karma would find him.

But not yet.

There were more important matters to deal with than a vile, corrupt shrimper with his tail between his legs.

My phone buzzed in my pocket. A call from Murph.

I stepped away from the group and answered.

"I've been digging more into this Barbossa guy," the notorious hacker started. "And the more I look, the worse things get."

"What have you found, Murph?" I said, stopping right along the rocky shore and staring out over the water.

"The drugs, illegal arms, and human smuggling are just a part of this guy's operation. His biggest moneymakers are online businesses."

"Pornography sites?" I said. Just a wild guess,

given what I'd learned about the vile criminal so far.

Murph cleared his throat. "He's produced thousands of hours of content. Tens of thousands. And most of the victims are underage." He paused, clearly having a hard time getting the words out. "I live much of my life online, Logan. I've seen some messed-up shit. But this... this is as bad as it gets." He went quiet again, then came back with firm, strong resolution in his voice. "So, are we gonna get this asshole or what?"

Murph was a detached, analytical man. In all the interactions we'd had over the years, he'd rarely displayed more than minimal emotion. He was stoic. Able to look at life and situations the same way he looked at code and intersecting networks to find a pattern. To reason things out logically. But he was showing emotion now. I could hear it in his voice. Felt like it was transmitting right through the phone.

"Yes, Murph," I said. "We're gonna get him."

"Damn straight. This is top priority, Logan. I'm focusing all my energy on this one."

That was a first as well. He was an exceptional multitasker—a sought-after talent who often tackled multiple important projects at once. To have his undivided attention was priceless.

He told me he was working on gathering intel on Barbossa. His whereabouts and the places he frequented. Told me he'd get back to me with everything he discovered.

We ended the call and I stood there a moment. Gazed out over the water, feeling the ocean breeze against my face. A tear streaked down my cheek as I thought over Murph's words. Then a second streaked down as I turned and observed Olivier and Esther over at the restaurant.

They were Barbossa's kids.

That's what the guy sent to kill me had said. And now I knew what he'd meant by that, and it sent a powerful, disturbing chill up my spine.

Once back at the Navy Lodge, Leon asked me, "What will happen now?"

"I don't know," I said, answering truthfully. "But you're alive and well. There's hope."

I didn't know the answer to his question. Couldn't know the answer to it. Regardless of what happened next, they had a long road ahead of them. And whether they were able to stay, or they were sent back to Haiti, one thing was certain: they weren't safe anywhere so long as Barbossa was still breathing.

We hugged and said goodbye to him and the kids. Just for now.

On the short drive home, Scarlett leaned forward over the center console and brought up Delaney.

"We're gonna let him go?" she said.

"His time will come," I replied.

But not yet.

I'd made a promise to Rosalind. One I hadn't broken yet and didn't plan on breaking.

FORTY-ONE

Ange and I were both exhausted. Mentally and physically.

We'd spent the past week involved in one trying whirlwind after another. But the job wasn't done. In the field of battle, you let up an iota, and your enemy defeats you. They take that sliver of an opportunity and they pry it wide open and they capitalize on it. We weren't about to give Barbossa any more time. We weren't about to let our guards down and declare victory just yet. The most challenging battle was still to come.

Ange was on the same page. With one look, I knew it.

All roads led back to Haiti.

All roads led back to Barbossa.

Not only did his very existence pose a grave threat that lingered over Leon, Esther, and Olivier's lives like a black cloud, but he was also the leader of a vast, cruel, pure evil criminal network. We'd disrupted parts of his smuggling operation's distribution chain and taken down many of his cronies, but he'd find new ones. He'd recruit and build everything back up in no time. And so he needed to be stopped.

We were back in the Cessna. Main and auxiliary fuel tanks topped off. Flying just south of east over the Strait. Skirting around Cuba on a trajectory that would take us over the lower corners of the Bahamas, through the Greater Antilles, and straight on to Haiti.

Barely an hour into the eight-hundred-mile flight, Ange voiced her concerns regarding the upcoming conflict we'd be barging into.

"Tracking down and neutralizing a small illegal mining operation in the Dakotas is one thing," she said, "but we're talking about a major crime boss here. He probably has hundreds of men at his disposal. Not to mention government leaders and law enforcement officers in his pocket. The place has been especially economically unstable since the earthquake. Lot of desperate people looking for work."

I rubbed my chin while staring through the windshield at the sea ahead of us. "We've hunted and dealt with more powerful men before."

"Just the two of us?"

"We just need to get close to him. Or far away with a clear line of sight for you. It just takes one bullet."

Ange leaned back. Sighed and shook her head. "We can't fight an army, Logan. If we try to, we'll never leave that place. We'll never see home again."

She went silent a beat, then added, "You should try calling Scott again."

I'd contacted my old friend and brother in arms twice over the past few days. He was in the thick of it—fully engaged in eradicating his own list of adversaries.

"He's busy, remember? And if Scott says he's busy, it means he's up to something big."

"I'm sure he can spare a day."

I relented. Pulled out my phone and tried his number. The rhythmic drone went on and on with no reply. It was his emergency line. The one he always answered, which meant that he was still fully occupied elsewhere. The man had a knack for routing out evil and squashing it. Unlike me, he sought it out. Searched for vile men doing vile things around the world.

I tried the number a second time, just in case. Same outcome.

Pocketing my phone, I glanced at Ange and she said, "You're not worried?"

"About Scott Cooper? No. Especially given the new circle of operatives he's assembled."

"Isn't Wake still off the grid?"

I went quiet at that. Let out a deep breath. "We need to plan this as if we're going at it alone, Ange. 'Cause that's the reality. But if any two people can do it, it's us."

I took over the controls while Ange slept. Thought over what we were about to get ourselves into. Relished the quiet and the steady drone of the engine as the waters reeled in beneath us.

After four hours, Ange awoke and I slept. I passed

out right away. There was a lot on my mind, but if there's one thing that all soldiers have learned quickly throughout history, it's the ability to sleep whenever and wherever you can. Back in the Navy, I'd even taken many power naps while standing up.

We were flying over land when I woke up. The sprawling lights of Port-au-Prince were far to the east. We were just twenty miles from our destination of Jacmel, a port town southwest of the nation's capital city. Barbossa's mansion was apparently just down the coast from the port, perched high on the cliffs above the water.

In addition to discovering the location of Barbossa's mansion, Murph had used the contacts from the phone of the hitman who'd tried to kill me in Key West to discover other locations where the criminal's men hid out, calling them "hot spots."

"There a plan here?" Ange said.

I nodded, then gave her the one I'd come up with while she'd slept. "We'll start with one of the smaller hot spots. Scope out where these criminals are congregating in small numbers. Then we'll try speaking their language at first with bribes. If that doesn't work, we'll speak ours. That will put the message out real quick that we're there."

"Barbossa will mobilize his forces and be on the alert."

"Or he'll be spooked."

"I think he'd call in reinforcements and hole up in his mansion. Making things even worse for us. Making it even harder for us to get to him."

I sighed. "You've got a better idea?"

She usually did. She was the smart one and I was

used to it.

"I say we go right for the heart," she said. "Strike fast and strike hard. Don't give him any time to increase defenses. Take him down in his mansion before he even knows what's happening."

"We'd need more than just the two of us for that strategy to work." I shook my head. "We need to lure him out somehow."

Ange nodded. "I agree. We would need more than just the two of us for it to work."

She had a confident look on her face as Haiti's southern coast came into view below. Before I could say anything more, she said, "Scott called while you were asleep."

"Why didn't you wake me up?"

"You needed rest. We have another long night ahead. Besides, he was brief. Just a quick message."

"What was it?"

She gestured to the right window. I leaned forward and peered through the glass. Saw a long stretch of mostly untamed rocky shoreline. Intermittent beaches and mountains infested with trees. A string of coves and cuts and jutting rockfaces. In one of the coves was a large vessel. Looked to be around two hundred feet long.

I didn't need to see its name to identify it almost immediately.

I knew the ship.

I'd been aboard it before.

I glanced back at Ange, and she smiled. "Scott just said two words: saddle up."

FORTY-TWO

We splashed down a hundred yards off the vessel's port side. The R/V *Valiant* wasn't much to look at. Its paint was chipped and faded. Rust gathered at its corners and on its deck cranes and A-frames. But the generic design and apparent years of wear were a facade.

The ship was barely a year old. Everything brand-new. Everything top-of-the-line from its keel to its radar. No expense had been spared. The *Valiant* was one of the most advanced vessels ever to float, but its appearance ensured it would rarely garner more than a second glance.

Which was exactly what its designers wanted.

As we motored up along its port side, I spotted Scott Cooper leaning against the gunwale. I climbed out and threw a wave as Ange brought us closer and shut off the engine.

"Want to toss a line so we can tie off?" I said.

Scott waved a hand. "I've got a better idea." He gestured behind him and added, "Well, Finn did, actually."

Kelvin "Finn" Castro, the group's lead engineer, showed up and gave a quick salute.

"Sit tight, Logan," the sprightly Venezuelan said.

The vessel's five-ton deck crane rotated around, its boom stopping right over us, and a sheave with two nylon straps dangling from it lowered at the end of a thick cable.

I climbed up onto the wings. Unhooked the straps one at a time, then looped them around the Cessna's fuselage. One strap forward of the wings, the other behind them. Then I climbed back on top of the cockpit, gave the guys above a thumbs-up, and held on.

The machine rumbled and the cable tightened. The Cessna's frame groaned a little as we were pulled right out of the Caribbean. Lifted free of the sea, water dripping off as we were brought twenty feet into the air.

Once clear of the railing, the crane swiveled back clockwise, bringing us over the side and to the main deck. It stopped as we suspended over the center, then eased us down slowly, gently letting the floats touch the deck. Once we'd settled, I slid off the wings and jumped down.

Ange climbed out from her door as I landed and met up with Scott.

"Welcome aboard," he said, shaking my hand.

The former SEAL commander, senator, and current head of the covert organization was barely an inch shorter than me but possessed the confident presence of a giant.

I threw an arm around him. "I can't tell you how great it is to see you guys."

"You think we'd miss an opportunity to take down a notorious criminal scumbag?" Finn said.

Scott glanced back and forth between Ange and me. "You two were going to take this guy on all by yourselves?"

Ange chuckled. "That's what I said."

"Bold," Scott said, "even for you guys."

"How was Puerto Rico?" I asked.

Scott shot Finn a knowing look. "Different than expected. But nothing we couldn't handle. We just managed to wrap the operation up, and we just so happened to be three hundred miles away when I got your message. We got here an hour ago."

The four of us headed inside. The *Valiant* may not have looked like much from the outside, but below deck was a vastly different story. Everything was new and modern. Sleek and functional. The bridge and its control panels looked like the bridge of the starship *Enterprise*. Touchscreens and big flat-screen monitors. An expert, professional crew hard at work.

We headed straight for the control room. A small space with a table and chairs and a wall with three monitors. One of the screens displayed a head shot of Barbossa, one that I recognized from my earlier searches. The thirty-six-year-old Haitian had short black hair and intense eyes. A menacing scowl on his face.

Alejandra Fuentes met us there, the former Bolivarian Intelligence agent tapping one of the monitors.

"Where's Wake?" I said after we greeted Alejandra.

Scott shrugged. "We don't know. Jason has a tendency to jump off the grid. Remind you of anyone?"

I smiled. Though I was still never one to back down when danger presented itself, Jason had a proclivity to leap without looking, a mentality that I'd had in my early twenties.

"But we sent word out to him," Scott said. "He said he'd come, but heads or tails if he'll make it here in time."

"Here's what we have so far," Finn said. "I just completed a high-altitude flyover of the compound with our drone."

He brought up footage of the mansion on the monitor. Pointed to various sections of the compound and the winding road leading up to it.

"Can we confirm that he's home?" Ange said.

"That's easy," Finn stated. "'Cause apparently, he hardly ever leaves. It's his kingdom. His sanctuary. A hundred-acre, fifty-million-dollar estate. Money like that can buy you a palace anywhere in the world. In Haiti, it buys you an absurd display of wealth. Extravagant and beyond over the top in every way."

"And it's got impressive security," Alejandra added.

Finn nodded. "That's right. He's safe in there. Has everything he needs. Everything is brought to him. Outside those tall, razor-wire-covered walls, he's vulnerable. Even with security surrounding him at all times. There are a lot of people in Haiti. Many of them are about as poor as you can imagine someone being. Little more to their names than the clothes on their backs. Desperate. Willing to do just about anything to change their lot. And Barbossa has friends, yes, but he also has enemies. A long list of them. A lot of people who wouldn't hesitate to pull the trigger or detonate a homemade explosive device or slip some arsenic into his coffee if given the chance. So, he stays in there. Surrounded by people too terrified of him to dare hurt him in any way."

I eyed Finn with amazement. "I thought you guys have only been here an hour."

"We work fast," he said. "And Murph's been feeding us vital intel."

Scott said, "It helps being private and independent. No bureaucracy. No red tape to deal with."

"The drone still airborne?" I asked.

Finn nodded. "Flying circles at five thousand feet. It'll be up there all night. Its powerful night optics allowing us to distinguish a person's face from up there. If Barbossa leaves, we'll know it. But he won't leave. The only activity in the driveway since we arrived was a metallic gray Lamborghini that left maybe twenty minutes ago. But Barbossa wasn't inside it. Like I said, he never goes anywhere without a big posse. He's got over a dozen high-end luxury sports cars supposedly. But he only drives them with an armada protecting him."

We ran through infiltration options. Parachuting into the compound was out of the question. All the lights seemed to be on, the place lit up like a cruise ship at night on the open water. And it was situated on a promontory with cliffs on three of its sides. We'd be forced to land on or near the house, and our chutes would be spotted long before we reached the ground.

Their group had a prototype extraction drone capable of carrying up to three adults out of a dicey situation. Scott and I had utilized it as a deployment method months earlier in Panama, soaring low over the Gatún River on a clandestine approach to Gatún Dam, the heart and one of the most vulnerable parts of the Panama Canal.

But that wasn't an option either, not given the layout of the property. In order for the drone to work, we'd need a dark, stealth route of approach and landing. The compound didn't offer either of those.

A frontal assault was quickly ruled out as well. The fourth side of the property was protected by a ten-foot-tall, three-foot-thick concrete wall with three spirals of razor wire at its top. And the only gate into the compound was a serious metal number flanked by well-armed guards. It was the kind of security you generally see protecting military installations or nuclear silos. I'd never seen anything like it protecting a personal residence.

We turned our attention to the water, but the challenges there were evident as well.

"Those swells are problematic," I said.

The place was situated on the south side of the island on a jutting rockface. Right where two powerful currents met. It created a constant struggle of combating waves that pounded into each other and the towering cliffs. The rock faces were over a hundred feet high. Jagged and sheer. And there was a colossal pillar of rock just off the coast that protected the spot like a natural guard tower.

As we ran through the water approach, Finn got an idea.

"I think we should take a lesson from pirates of old," he said. "How would they board and take over their enemies?"

"You suggesting we swing over on ropes?" I said.

He smiled. "Well, not swing, but the same basic idea." He tapped his fingers against the touchscreen table and brought up a blueprint for a device on one of the monitors. "I think this will give us the perfect opportunity to use a gadget I've been itching to bust out since I joined the group. It's been in storage for some time, waiting for the opportune moment. Waiting for this."

He described what we were looking at—a cable launcher system with a rapid insertion device. The hook would be launched by a powerful air cannon. It would burst through Barbossa's front wall, then its arms would extend and lock it into place.

"Then, you just hold on for the ride," Finn said.

"Can the *Valiant* operate that close to the cliffs with these swells?" Ange asked.

"She'll be all right," Scott said. "Our captain assures us we can get within twenty yards of the rocks. Our computer-controlled buoyancy system and hull sensors will work with the triple-water-jet engines to make sure we're stationary and not bouncing around."

The room went silent a moment, then Ange said, "All right, so we can get boots on the ground. Then what? Do we have any idea what sort of force we're going up against in there?"

No one had any way of knowing exactly how

many men Barbossa would have, but we all agreed it would be a substantial force, if the walls and position of his mansion were any indication of his level of paranoia.

"We need a way to take down a large number of them before we ever set foot in the compound," I said. "But humanely. There are going to be civilians in there as well. No doubt about it."

"I think we can manage that," Scott said. "Some more toys we haven't utilized yet should do the trick."

We worked out the rest of the plan, ironing out all the details as best we could given the situation. Less than an hour later, we were all in position and Scott gave the order.

FORTY-THREE

We observed the compound from the air and from about a quarter mile off on the *Valiant*'s deck, then made our first move just after three in the morning. There was still some activity. Guards around the perimeters. Some roving, some stationary. Everyone we'd seen earlier at the outdoor pools had migrated inside, so the place was mostly quiet.

I triggered my mic and said, "Anything, Ange?"

She was posted in the crow's nest, a narrow platform thirty feet above me at the top of the bridge. And she'd been sweeping the exterior of the mansion with a high-powered scope for the past half hour.

"Nothing but the sentries," she said. "No sign of Barbossa all night. But you can't see anything through the windows."

They were all tinted to extreme levels. Just solid black and reflecting the sky and turbulent sea.

"But my view will improve soon," she added.

I glanced up at her and gave a knowing nod. Before climbing to her perch, I'd kissed her on the cheek, then she'd turned and pressed her lips to mine. No words had been said between us. But everything was said with our eyes and expressions. Her telling me to be safe. Me telling her I always was.

We were about to embark upon as dangerous an endeavor as ever, but some things were worth the risk.

I pictured Olivier and Esther in my mind. Pictured their mother Rosalind, and father Leon. Imagined the thousands of others whose lives had been ruined by the men inside that mansion.

Some things were worth jeopardizing life and limb for.

When everyone was ready and in position, Scott gave the order through his earpiece radio.

The first priority was proximity.

The moment Scott gave the order, the engines fired up and propelled us toward the shore. The *Valiant* was maneuvered expertly around the jutting crag and into the swirling currents. All the while the deck remained stable enough to keep a marble in place, the smart ballast system working to perfection.

We observed the compound as the cliffs drew nearer. By the time the vessel was in position and holding steady barely twenty feet from the cliffs and breakers, a handful of the guards had noticed our arrival.

Scott wasted no time giving the second order.

Speed was key. Barbossa would have no shortage of men inside the mansion, but he had even more nearby. Reinforcements in surrounding areas that could be called in and descend upon the mansion. We needed to get inside, take him down, and get out of there before that happened.

"All right," Scott said. "Send this place to the stone age in three... two... one... execute."

A moment later, an abrupt zapping noise filled the air and every single light in the compound went out, casting the place into sheer darkness faster than a blink.

Scott triggered his mic again a second after the lights shut off and said, "Shattered. Execute."

He and I bent down and donned noise reducing earmuffs. A sudden and powerful blast filled the air next. Not an explosion of fire and heat, but an invisible attack. An isolated, focused beam of sound. A high-powered ultrasonic wave that ripped toward the compound. The pulse struck the mansion, and every sea-facing window shattered at once, shards bursting inward and raining down upon the floor.

"You're up, Al," Scott said, gazing upon the palace that was now pitch black and windowless. "Smokescreen. Execute."

Alejandra was on the roof of the bridge just forward of us. She and three other members of the crew were crouching along the base of the gunwale and wielding compact, shoulder-mounted rocket launchers. The four of them rose and opened fire at once, blasting four small rockets toward the mansion. The projectiles hissed and produced thick trails of smoke as they blasted toward different levels of the structure.

We could see people now. Distant, dark figures inside. Scrambling and yelling out. Guards closing in from the outskirts of the property to see what was happening. The rockets soared through the shattered windows then exploded with muffled booms, emitting thick white clouds that rapidly spread throughout the interior and spilled outside like lazy waterfalls.

The rockets had been armed with smoke grenades that'd blasted away from the main shell and exploded in various corners of the interior. The last thing we wanted was to seriously injure any potential civilians. But the clouds of smoke were more than potent enough to cause everyone inside to rush for an exit and fresh air as quickly as possible.

As armed combatants flooded out from the interior, powerful spotlights switched on, washing bright light over the entire back side of the mansion. The gunmen covered their eyes and mouths due to the smoke, then couldn't see a thing with the beams shining into them. The result was a mass of easy targets.

Alejandra and the three men beside her had already set their rocket launchers aside. They were now holding strange rifles that looked like something out of a science fiction movie. The moment my attention returned to the four of them, they all opened fire in unison, then let loose at will with sporadic discharges. Releases of high-pressure air unleashing a barrage of rubber balls into the gunmen.

The advanced, smart weapons featured built-in range finders that dictated the amount of pressure released, and therefore the velocity of their projectiles. This ensured the rubber balls hit their targets with enough force to incapacitate, but not kill.

The weapons worked like a charm.

In a matter of seconds, the first wave of criminals to pour out from the mansion were all on the ground. Still alive but writhing in pain. Subdued and unable to fight back.

"Visual on the mark, Ange?" Scott said.

"Negative," my wife replied.

She was still above us. Still sweeping the area with her high-powered rifle scope.

Scott turned and gave me a look.

"We're going in," he said.

I did a quick, last-minute adjustment of my gas mask, then gave Scott a confident nod in reply.

We both stepped forward to a harpoon gun mounted to the rail. It was pre-calibrated and lined up with its target, but Scott checked the aim a final time, tweaking it a couple of inches. Then he opened fire, blasting the titanium harpoon from the device. It tore across the gap, cable zipping and paying out freely behind it, then struck the mansion on the second floor. Driving into the concrete wall, the pointed projectile burrowed right through, then its arms sprang out and held the harpoon secure.

With the projectile having finished its rapid flight, the automated spool beside us clicked, then whirred in the opposite direction, reeling the loose section of cable until it was taut and then locking it into place.

Scott and I attached an electric pulley rig to the cable. We clipped into the device, then he said, "Hold on tight."

We both grabbed onto its handholds and angled our bodies in preparation. A second later, Scott flicked up a plastic cover and pressed a button. The device burst free of the harpoon gun, jolting us over the gunwale and nothing but sixty feet of open air.

Wind howled by us and the white capped sea crashed into the cliffs below. I kept my eyes forward as we zipped toward the compound. The place looked like a luxury haunted mansion, smoke billowing out from its shattered windows.

In a flash, we traversed the gap and soared right up to the impressive façade. Scott maintained control of our speed, slowing us just before we reached the white, concrete wall. On his signal, we unclipped and let go, dropping five feet to the main pool deck. We both landed with a roll and caught ourselves against the base of a slate water feature. Withdrew our sidearms and looked around.

There were close to a dozen men strung about, most on the nearby grass or main pool deck beside us. All of them were on the ground. Some unconscious and others groaning in pain. The few who did see us paid us no attention as we made our way for the nearest shattered glass door. The smoke was already dissipating along the high, blustery coastline, giving us a relatively clear view of the inside as we poked around the corner.

The destroyed entryway led to a spacious living room filled with rich, comfortable furniture. Everything was marble or granite or heavy hardwood. Soft colors with gold accents. More water features and plants at the corners and a multi-tiered, dazzling chandelier overhead. And the walls were covered with opulent artwork.

We scanned the space. Spotted movement in the left corner. Three slender bodies huddled between the wall and a lush bonsai tree.

Scott and I approached. Realized they were girls through our night optics.

Young girls.

Barely in their teens, we guessed. But they were dressed like grown women, with skintight dresses and jewelry.

Scott covered me, and I lowered my weapon and knelt down beside them. Removed my gas mask.

"It's okay," I told them in Spanish, hoping they understood. "You're safe now. But you need to get outside. Get outside and stay near the pool. You'll be safe."

One of them at least appeared to understand me. She helped me lift the others to their feet and they hurried toward the shattered egress.

With Ange perched in the *Valiant*'s crow's nest, they'd be safer than they'd ever been in their lives. If any armed criminal so much as looked at the innocent girls the wrong way, my wife would ensure they never looked at anything ever again.

Scott and I turned and worked our way toward the opposite side of the living room, knowing that the deeper we went, the more likely we were to find people who hadn't been affected by the smoke.

We crossed into a dining area. Crossed another lounge.

Reached a short, wide hallway, then we heard movement up ahead. Then voices. The noises were coming from upstairs, high up and echoing down a grand circular staircase near the main entrance.

We reached the base of the steps and hid behind the thick, densely packed balusters.

Waited a couple seconds, observing everything

through the light green tint of our optics.

The footsteps grew louder, rushing down toward us.

Two men, sounded like.

We waited there in the darkness until they were nearly on us, then jumped around the corner and surprised them. Scott took down the first guy with a left backhand to the side of his head. As he spun, the second guy cut right and raised his weapon. But I was on him before he could pull the trigger, landing a sweeping kick to his knees that sent him cartwheeling over the bottom stairs and smacking hard into the floor near the front door.

Scott knocked out the first guy and we checked them both over. Neither was Barbossa.

Then we heard more sounds coming from the top floor, high above. Angered whispers and heavy footsteps. We glanced skyward and spotted three more men rushing down toward us and a fourth figure vanishing from view, making a run for it while he sent others to fight.

We cut to the wall, hugging it as we rushed up the steps. We could hear the three above us, shouting and grunting. Stomping. Their weapons rattling with every jerky movement.

We made it up one flight with near-silent steps, then cut to the rail. Leaned over and took aim skyward. Both of us fired two shots just as the men spotted us. I struck a guy in the shoulder as he rounded a corner, the force of the bullet throwing him into a spin. He slid and his waist hit the rail, and he flailed over the side, screaming as he free fell thirty feet to the entryway below, colliding with a violent thud.

The guy Scott hit fell the opposite way, tumbling out of sight. And the third was just out of view and managed to be spared.

After the quick double taps, we sprang back to the wall for the next flight. We cut into a hallway before the two men reached us. I went right, dipping into the shadows of an alcove behind a towering white marble statue of a woman draped in a thin veil. Scott continued deeper down the hall, then swerved left into an open bedroom.

The first guy blew right past me down the hall. Breathing heavily. His weapon raised. As the second stumbled around the corner, I sprang forward and threw my shoulder into the base of the statue. It teetered, then toppled over completely, falling right toward the guy. The hundreds of pounds of marble smashed into him, invoking a sudden grunt and breaking bones and pinning his motionless body to the floor.

When I turned back toward Scott, I watched as my old friend hurled the first guy headfirst into a mirror, spiderwebbing the glass and making his forehead bleed. He reared the guy back and struck him a second time, battering more shards free. Then he let go, and the limp criminal collapsed and curled up on the carpet of glass.

We both turned as the sound of a distant, crashing window tore across the air. It came from upstairs, and the moment the noise reached our ears, we rushed back to the stairwell and took on the final flight to the third floor of the mansion.

We raced down a hallway, following the sounds of

crackling glass. Burst into a lavish bedroom with vaulted ceilings, a Persian carpet, and an enormous bed. The far window was shattered at the bottom, and we sprinted over and poked our heads out. Saw the flat concrete roof just as a barefoot man wearing a robe reached the edge.

He turned his body and swung his legs over the side, allowing us to catch a brief glimpse of his face in the moonlight. He was twenty yards off, but it was clearly Barbossa. He looked scared out of his mind. Completely terror struck and overcome with disbelief.

The criminal leader was gone as quickly as he'd appeared, vanishing over the edge of the roof.

I stepped onto the sill, ducked, and jumped out. Tore across the roof and reached the end and saw Barbossa climbing down the trunk of a coconut tree. He slipped and fell fifteen feet from the ground. Landed awkwardly on his side in a spread of bushes. Groaned and wailed and heaved.

Scott and I both took aim and opened fire.

Before he could reach any form of cover, one of our rounds buried into his upper back, jolting and knocking him forward. He shrieked and barely caught himself in the dirt. Continued his desperate charge between the trees and then across a lush, manicured lawn and onto his stone driveway. He stumbled and staggered his way around a huge fountain with gold figures being doused in the spray.

"First rule of mansion raids," Scott said, removing a coil of nylon rope from his bag, "always bring a rope."

We looped one end around the raised base of a nearby skylight, then tied it off and threw ourselves over. Used our holsters to protect our hands as we slid forty feet down and landed between the coconut tree and rows of bushes.

Sprinting across the front lawn, we caught sight of Barbossa again just as he rounded the fountain. The towering metal gate was twenty yards ahead of him. Two sentries closed in from his flanks. He yelled at them and pointed at the gate, but it just stayed where it was, blocking off the crime boss's escape.

He smacked one of the guards across the face, then stabbed a finger toward us, yelling at them to take Scott and me down. We had our weapons raised as we emerged from the shadows of the fountain, eyeing the guards and our fleeing target who had nowhere to run.

FORTY-FOUR

Barbossa's heart pounded relentlessly against his rib cage. He'd nearly died before, countless times. He'd been high out of his mind on every powerful drug he could get his hands on. But this was a new, foreign, and disturbing sensation unlike any other. The rapid shift from complete and utter security to death bashing into his sanctuary was overwhelming.

But now the terror was being overtaken by the extreme pain surging across his body. The bullet had caught him in the right shoulder blade. It hurt like hell. Felt like he'd been brutally punched and stabbed and burned all at the same time. But he willed himself forward. Gazed ahead as two of his guards descended upon him from the gate.

"Get this thing open!" he barked, stabbing a finger at the barrier.

The two men's jaws hung open as they stared at their boss blankly.

"It won't budge," one of them said. "It's locked down."

"Override it!" Barbossa screamed.

"We can't," the other said, shaking his head.

Barbossa smacked the nearest guard across the face. Then the criminal leader turned and saw movement near the right side of the house. Two shadowy apparitions appearing from the darkness.

He grabbed the man he'd struck and shoved him toward his attackers.

"They're right there," he snapped. "Shoot them. Shoot them now!"

Barbossa turned and took off as fast as he could along the wall. Past the edge of the gate, over the corner of the driveway, and into another spread of grass. He glanced back only once—just long enough to see both of his sentries go down in rapid succession. Two quick pops, then they fell to the smooth stone.

Barbossa snarled. Winced and grunted. He was bleeding heavily. Shaking. Doing everything in his power to ride the wave of adrenaline toward some mad hope of deliverance.

He staggered under the shadows of tall trees. Soon reached a part of the fence right beside a line of barberry bushes. They were thorny and taller than he was. Looking back, Barbossa saw his two attackers once more. They were on the driveway now, making their way around the fountain with their weapons trained forward. They'd be on him in seconds.

He turned back to face the thick, thorn-riddled bushes. Snarled as he grabbed the branches and heaved himself skyward. Every movement hurt. The sharp spikes digging into his hands and scraping his chest. His robe ripped and tore. He cried and moaned, but kept moving. Managed to reach the top of the dense hedge. Wobbled his way across its width to the wall. Looked up.

Only three feet remained to its top, but above the concrete were three coils of razor wire, the sharp edges glistening menacingly in the moonlight.

He remembered the orders he'd given to the designer of the wall years earlier. Making it clear that no one would be able to enter, unless they had a death wish. Unless they wanted to bleed to death before they'd made it ten meters onto his property.

But Barbossa wasn't about to stop. He wasn't going to give his attackers the satisfaction of taking him down. He'd fight to the last breath and he'd bleed to death from his own defenses before perishing at the hands of his enemies.

He reached and wrapped his hands over the concrete edge. Pressed his palms to the top and heaved himself up. Came to a shaky knee, his body inches from the tangles of wire. He stood. The two bottom spirals extended to his waist, the third to the top of his head. And the wall was three feet thick. There was no right way to go about it—no way that didn't involve an extreme degree of pain.

Barbossa looked back one more time. Saw his attackers closing in on the grass and tree line. They were a hundred yards away at most. Marching confidently. Not hustling. They knew as much as he did that he was stuck.

He turned and faced the concertina wires. Shifted his weight and shielded his face with his arms and jumped. He launched off with everything he had, hurling himself skyward like a high-jumper and then angling his upper body over, trying to whip himself over the top. But he was injured and the wall was too wide. His upper body somehow cleared the highest wires, and then gravity kicked in, throwing the crime boss's hips into the top of the menacing tower.

Barbossa squealed as hundreds of jagged razors tore at his flesh, digging right through his robe and slicing across his hips and legs. His lower body caught in the tangle, and his upper body hinged forward, and he slammed face first into the outer bottom spiral. He resisted the urge to catch himself, keeping his arms tight over his face.

The coils warped and clanked into each other, and the blades cut deeper across his arms and chest as he slowed to a painful stop. He shifted to his right side, every movement an agonizing struggle. The spirals grabbed at his body and hooked into his flesh, absorbing his movements and holding him in place, just as they were designed to.

Barbossa wiggled with everything he had, squirming through the sea of knives and managed to get his head free, dangling over the other side of the wall. Hearing the two men approach, he writhed and screamed and forced his body through. Slipping off his robe and squirming until his body tore free of the menacing beast.

He fell the ten feet, spinning a full one-eighty and landing on his back with his head at the base of the wall.

He couldn't feel anything but pain. Everywhere hurt. He was mutilated, his body torn to shreds. But he'd made it.

The enraged man willed himself to a knee, then to his feet. He eyed the long driveway ahead of him, then headed toward it. First stumbles, then a fast walk, then a slow, desperate jog.

He was fifty yards from the wall when he saw headlights winding up the driveway. Then a hundred yards from the wall when the headlights washed over him. A metallic gray Lamborghini rumbled up fast. It braked and turned sharply, tires screeching and smoking. The passenger door flew open right in front of the criminal leader.

Barbossa smiled as best he could. Pushed through the pain to traverse the final distance and then caught himself on the roof of the luxury sports car.

I always come out on top. I always find a way.

He groaned as he folded down through the open door and slid onto the low leather seat. The grumble of the eight-hundred horsepower, twelve-cylinder engine shook the frame. Barbossa's blood splattered all over the seat and door as he slammed it shut and pointed away from his compound and shouted, "Drive! Drive! Drive!"

FORTY-FIVE

Scott and I had just reached the wall when Barbossa somehow managed to scramble free of the razor wire and plummet to the earth on the other side. We observed the desperate act in utter astonishment. I'd never tussled with the stuff myself, but I knew what it was capable of. Had read into the effectiveness of its design. The way it worked. The way its barbs don't just mutilate flesh, but latch onto it and secure victims in place.

Barbossa landed on the other side with a lifeless thud.

Not only had he been shot, but he'd fought through three coils of concertina wire. He'd be on the brink of death. Bleeding out profusely, and if he didn't get expert medical care soon, he'd be gone.

Scott and I stood there, listening for movement. Hearing only muffled grunts and groans at first, then the sounds of heavy, shuffling footsteps.

"He's still on his feet?" Scott said, shaking his head in disbelief.

"Not for long," I said.

I turned and headed back for the gate. Reached for my earpiece and triggered my mic.

"Finn, he just climbed over the front wall. Just north of the gate. You got eyes on him?"

"Affirmative," Finn said. "He's stumbling down the drive. He'll be dead in under five minutes I'd wager."

I reached the gate and looked around for a way of getting over the wall without diving through razor wire like Barbossa had, when the sounds of a roaring engine cut across the air. They got louder, the thunderous grumbles oscillating like a vehicle slowing into sharp turns and accelerating out of them.

I was about to hail Finn again, when the Venezuelan's voice came through the earpiece.

"You've got to be kidding me," he gasped.

"What is it?" Scott said.

"The Lamborghini," he said. "The one that left earlier. It's back."

I glanced at my watch. It'd been seven minutes since we'd activated the EMP and made our move. What were the chances it was returning now?

"You need to stop it, Finn," Scott said. "Use the drone. Deploy the net and crash into it. Whatever you have to."

The Lamborghini's driver mashed the gas pedal,

screeching rubber against the pavement and spewing smoke and jolting them forward.

"Get me to a fucking hospital, Omar!" Barbossa cried.

He was overtaken with pain and delirious. Going into shock. His heart jackhammering. His eyes glazed over and making everything blurry. So much so that he hadn't realized who was in the driver's seat.

"I'm not Omar," the driver said, uttering his first words since Barbossa had entered.

Barbossa gasped. Rubbed his eyes and gazed across the interior. Saw a white, dark haired young man. He gripped the wheel with his right hand and held a Glock 21 pistol across with his left, the muzzle aimed at the crime boss.

"Who the hell are you?" Barbossa said.

"Jason Wake," the man replied. "It's time to buckle your seat belt. We're going for a little drive."

Barbossa shook his head and spat, "I'll be dead in minutes if I don't—"

"Don't worry about that," Jason interrupted. "Just buckle your seatbelt."

Barbossa scowled. Reached a shaky right hand back and grabbed the buckle. Brought it across his bloodied body and clicked it into place.

"I'm bleeding to death you idiot," Barbossa said. "If you're gonna make demands, you'd better get me to a doctor."

"Don't worry about that," Jason said again.

He accelerated to the end of the first straightaway. Just before hitting the turn, he eased his foot off the gas and onto the brake. Angled right instead of left, blazing off the shoulder and through a thin row of shrubs.

The sports car bounced and rattled on the rocky, uneven terrain.

"Where the hell are we going?" Barbossa snarled.

Jason ignored him. Kept his foot heavy on the gas and rode right along the ridgeline toward a promontory that jutted out to sea up ahead. A hundred yards from the cliff, he let off the gas and slammed the brake and skidded them to a stop.

Jason grabbed the handle and pushed open his door. Without a word, he bent down and reached for the gas pedal. Took one more look at Barbossa, then said, "Have a nice flight."

The moment the words escaped his lips, he released an object in the footwell and the engine whined and the tires spun like mad, kicking back rocks and dirt. Jason jumped back as the tires caught traction and the vehicle shot forward like a rocket, heading up the steady grade toward the cliff up ahead.

Barbossa flew backward, his body shoved hard into the seat back as the engine's power let loose and burst at once. The pedal planted and stuck on the footwell, releasing an extreme amount of torque that could accelerate the car from zero to sixty in under three seconds.

As the sports car raced toward the edge, Barbossa reached for the seat belt. His shaky hands frantically grabbed hold of the buckle and it seemed to take forever to click it free. He could see the rising cliff up ahead, growing bigger and bigger. Then everything went black in the windshield. A cloud covered sky and moon.

Barbossa shifted his body and reached for the

handle to try and throw open his door and jump out in a last ditched effort to escape an impending death. But the handle wasn't there. Nothing was there. It'd been broken clean off the mechanism, leaving behind just a hollow indent where it'd once been.

Enraged, he threw his shoulder against the door. Screamed from the pain. No budge. He scrambled toward the driver's seat. Made it halfway across the center console when the Lamborghini reached the end of the line, bouncing and bucking and soaring over the edge at over a hundred miles per hour.

The vehicle took off, its wheels whining like mad. It angled upward and then rotated down nose first due to the weight of the engine. Barbossa stared wide-eyed through the windshield at the whitecapped surf a hundred feet below.

FORTY-SIX

Jason Wake watched as the Lamborghini screamed over the cliff, sailing out over the coast, spinning forward, and then smashing into the sea with a violent crash.

He stood there in the darkness. Stoic. His eyes forward.

As the wreckage settled, he slid his left hand into his front pocket. It wasn't empty. He pulled it out and held a small lever. The Lamborghini's passenger door handle. He twirled it a couple times while watching the final bubbles gurgle up from the fiery wreck and the white haze subside, then flung it over as well, a slow underhand lob. It picked up speed, splashed in the last of the haze and sank to catch up with the rest of the luxury car.

Jason stood there a moment longer. Heard distant sirens. Police and ambulances, making the long winding approach toward the mansion. Then a different sound filled the air. A low, buzzing noise like a giant insect.

Jason peered skyward as a drone appeared from the darkness. It was about the size of a golf cart with a large net hanging from it, and the craft descended rapidly before sweeping in and stabilizing to a hover right in front of him. He stared at the camera mounted to its base, then the craft weaved and bobbed a little. An invitation for a ride.

To the south, the *Valiant* was just appearing around the corner, its bow poking out, followed by the rest of its exterior. Jason took another look down at the water, then eyed the drone's main camera and shook his head.

He smiled, took two steps back, then took off forward, driving over the rocks and hurling himself over the edge. He soared feet first, cutting through the blackness, and splashed into the turbulent surf. Sank deep and eased to a stop, then kicked for the surface. Breaking free, he side-stroked toward the *Valiant*.

As the drone buzzed toward the vessel, one of the deck cranes swiveled over and lowered its cargo hook. The cable lowered right in front of Jason. He grabbed hold of the mechanism, threw a thumbs up, and held on as it hoisted him out of the water.

Scott and I couldn't see a thing over the wall, but we heard everything. Heard the Lamborghini's engine roar, heard its tires chew up earth in the distance, and heard it bounce and then whine like hell as it went from land to air. Seconds later, we heard the resounding crash of machinery striking the surf.

"What happened, Finn?" Scott said into his radio. "You have eyes on Barbossa?"

"Negative," Finn said. He paused a moment, then added, "He was in the Lamborghini. He's gone."

"What happened?" Scott asked again.

Another pause.

"Wake happened."

Scott and I exchanged smiles. Turned and hustled back across the driveway, through the mansion, and out the back. We grabbed hold of the pulley rig and were back aboard the *Valiant* less than a minute after Barbossa's Lamborghini had run out of road.

The cable was released, and the *Valiant*'s engines fired up and nosed us between the end of the cliffs and the nearby island, then around the corner to the promontory. I hugged Ange, then the three of us headed up to the bow and watched as Jason came into view. He stood right at the edge of the cliff, and moments after we laid eyes on him, he stepped back and then threw himself over the side, soaring through the sky and splashing into the sea ahead of us.

"Sometimes his flare for the dramatic borders on insanity," Scott said, shaking his head.

I smiled. Patted him on the shoulder and said, "You can't argue with results."

We headed down to the main deck, meeting up with Alejandra just as Finn landed the drone and Jason poked up over the gunwale, holding onto the end of the cable.

"You guys engaged without me?" Jason said.

Scott chuckled. Folded his arms. "And you still

managed to find a way to steal the thunder."

The crane swiveled and lowered Jason over the middle. He leapt down five feet above the deck and landed right beside our Cessna.

"Nice of you to drop by," Alejandra said, as he approached the group.

He smiled. "You know I never miss an opportunity to take a Lambo for a joyride."

"Good thing you stopped and climbed out when you did," Finn said. "I was about to crash the drone into your ride."

Jason and I shook hands, then he gave Ange a hug.

"Good to see you both again," he said.

"You too," I replied. Then I motioned to the water at the base of the nearby cliffs, and added, "Thanks for dealing with him."

"I've never seen a guy so cut up in my life," he said. "What did you guys do to him?"

"Not us," Scott said. "His own wall and razor wire did that."

Jason shook his head. "You two must've really scared him."

We all headed inside as the *Valiant*'s engines maneuvered us away from the cliffs and then rocketed us out to sea at over forty knots.

We were just stepping into the control room when Scott got a phone call. He spoke for barely a minute, then hung up and addressed the group.

"Local authorities are seizing the compound," he said. "Now that Barbossa's gone, they should have no fear in dismantling the operation."

"Ideally," Alejandra said. "But I've seen this play out before. He could just as easily be replaced with the next guy in line."

Scott rubbed his chin. "We need to hope for the best. But we can work with aid groups and members of their law enforcement that I trust to try and ensure that doesn't happen."

My old friend turned to me, and I nodded, "We did what we came to do. The rest is out of our hands."

Once again, I thought about all the innocent lives that'd been ruined at Barbossa's hands. I thought about Olivier and Esther. I thought about Leon. And I thought about Rosalind dying in my arms.

Her children were safe now. I'd done all I could to ensure it.

"You guys heading back to Key West?" Jason said.

"Not yet," I replied, then eyed my wife. "We have one more matter to attend to."

FORTY-SEVEN

Red Delaney had been smiling for two days straight.

Sometimes plans work out to perfection. Sometimes all the intricate details fit together like a puzzle, and the cogs of the world mesh into place, and you come out on top.

And he'd never felt more on top in his life.

He sat in a padded recliner on the deck of a private villa. Held a cigar in his right hand and a glass of rum in his left. Wore nothing but swim trunks.

A pool steamed beside him. A trickling waterfall flowed in the distance. He was surrounded by the dark, towering, tree-covered hills in a remote region of the Sierra Maestra mountains in southeast Cuba.

He took a deep drag from his cigar and admired his oasis, and the beautiful women around him. Half a dozen of them. All young. All naked. And all of them there for him.

He bobbed his head in shear satisfaction. Smiled even broader. Taking it all in. Basking in the glory of his sweet victory.

He was so relaxed, so lethargic, and so inebriated, that he barely heard the distinct metal click six inches behind his head.

Sometimes plans work out to perfection.

And sometimes everything goes to hell at the last second.

I emerged from the shadows, my Sig trained on the back of Delaney's skull. My finger on the trigger.

The lounging criminal sucked in a deep breath, then let it out. With my target in my sights, I scanned the villa yet again. None of the nearby women seemed to notice me. They appeared too drunk and high to notice anything.

"I told you this is what I'd do, Delaney," I said. "That this was how it would end."

"I have security," he stated, confidence in this tone. "Armed men on this property tasked with keeping me safe."

"I know."

"They're all well trained."

"Not well trained enough. I'm afraid they're all asleep on the job tonight."

Delaney let out another frustrated sigh. Shook his head.

"I'm a hundred damn miles off the grid. How the hell did you find me?"

With my right hand firmly gripping my pistol, I stepped closer and reached over his shoulder with my left. "Give me my watch."

He held up his left wrist, my orange dialed Doxa still strapped around it. "I won the game," he scoffed. "Fair and square. No need to still be sore about it."

"No... you didn't." I held out my hand. Pressed the barrel of my Sig to the back of his head. He unclasped it. Slid it off his wrist. Held it over his shoulder to me.

I grabbed it and held it up. Inspected it. Was glad to see it had no new scratches.

Ange had given me the watch as a Christmas present. She knew my lifelong interest in Cussler and his famous hero Dirk Pitt. I've never been big on material things, but it's my favorite piece of jewelry I've ever owned.

Under normal circumstances, I'd have never wagered it in a game of chess. Especially against someone who clearly spent a solid chunk of his time in front of a chess board. But they hadn't been normal circumstances.

And my timepiece wasn't a normal wristwatch.

It was a gift from my wife. My formidable, intuitive wife.

My protective wife.

And she'd made a customization to the watch.

I flipped the timepiece around. Ran my thumb over the silver case back. Felt a tiny, circular appendage. It was smaller than a button battery and secured nearly flush. Barely noticeable, even upon close examination.

I held the watch out in front of Delaney.

"You see," I said, tapping the tiny tracking device with my thumb. "I won the game. Checkmate, Delaney."

The man grunted. Shook his head in bewilderment. "You cheated. I figured as much. A man like you. I'd expect nothing less."

Then he went silent. Took a long drag of his cigar and said, "You know, my grandfather was a self-made man. Started from nothing. Worked and saved and hustled all his life. Worked tirelessly. Built an empire and became one of the richest men in Florida. Owned hundreds of shrimp boats. And by the time I was in my twenties, everything was gone. It was all swindled from our family by vile, corrupt, relentless businessmen who swept in like vultures and attacked. My inheritance. My family legacy. My livelihood. All gone."

"Boohoo."

He glared at me. "Don't you see? I've only reclaimed wealth that was rightfully mine."

"At the expense of thousands of innocent lives."

He chuckled. "Key West was built on the backs of smugglers. It's in our blood. I would never expect you to understand."

I scanned the villa again, then said, "Where are the others? The rest of your team."

"You'll never find them."

"I found you."

"You think I'd split my profits with anyone? They're gone."

I nodded. "I figured as much. A man like you. I'd expect nothing less."

Delaney took another puff from his cigar. Wiped

his lips with the back of his hand and said, "So, how does this go down?"

I reached into my pocket. Grabbed a tiny capsule. Reached forward and dropped it into his drink. It splashed and fizzled and dissolved before our eyes.

"What's that?" he asked.

"Mercy."

He nodded. Took a final drag of his cigar then flicked it into the pool and reached for his drink with his left hand. But my eyes stayed on his right. Watched as he crept his fingers to his hip. Watched as he removed a tiny, concealed switchblade. Pressed a button and the knife poked out.

He turned to engage me, arcing his knife toward me. I caught his wrist. Sprang forward and rotated. Cracked his shoulder free and wrapped my opposite arm around his neck. Squeezed tight, crunching his trachea. He shook and grunted and kicked. Thrashed desperately, hopelessly, for thirty seconds.

Then he was gone.

I looked around. Some of the women were looking my way. None of them seemed to register, or care, what had just happened.

I left Delaney slumped in his chair. He looked like he'd passed out. You'd have to get close and touch the guy to realize his heart was no longer pumping blood.

I returned to the shadows. Crept away from the grounds and followed a footpath up into the nearby mountains. Three hundred yards from the villa, I spotted Ange leaning against a Polaris UTV. She collapsed her sniper rifle and stowed it as I approached.

Climbing into the driver's seat, I fired up the engine and rumbled us around the mountain and down its opposite side. Reached a quiet lake two and a half miles later. Cruised through a tiny waterfront village and parked beside a dock. Handed the keys and five hundred dollars to a local tour guide, then strode down the planks to where our Cessna was tied off.

Ange and I embraced before climbing aboard. Squeezing each other tightly. Feeling the weight lift off our shoulders. The climactic end to a dangerous mess that'd all started on Monte Cristo.

"It's done," I said, then loosened my grip and looked into her eyes. "Time to go home."

FORTY-EIGHT

Rosalind Baptiste's funeral was held the following day. It was late in the afternoon. Key West's historic cemetery was closed and empty. The sun arcing and reddening the sky.

I'd been trying to obtain a plot on the island ever since she'd passed. It'd proved difficult. But Pete had surprised Ange and me upon our return to Key West, informing us that he'd offered one of his family's plots. Blowing both of us away with his generosity.

"If I'd been honest with myself about Delaney, I may have prevented all of this long ago," he'd said, getting emotional. "I guess sometimes you're just blinded by the past. Too blinded by friendships that once were to accept what people become."

I wrapped an arm around him. Thanked him. Told him it wasn't his fault. Told him that he was a good man and that he was doing a great thing helping out a woman he'd never met.

Now wasn't the time for regret or pondering what could have been. Now was the time to move forward.

Besides, if it hadn't been for my talk with Pete and his mentioning Delaney, the man would likely be at large for the rest of his life.

I stood beside the dug-up plot wearing the only suit I owned. The same one I'd worn while getting married to Ange on the island of Curaçao three years earlier. The same one I'd worn at my father's funeral.

Ange wore a black dress. Loose and low, with heels. Scarlett wore a similar number. Jack and Lauren had shown up, along with Pete. Jane was there as well. So was Harper Ridley, a local writer and friend. None of them had ever met the woman before, but they'd still turned up to pay their respects. Some of the best friends a person could ask for.

And Leon was there, of course, with Olivier beside him and Esther in his arms.

There was a picture of their family beside Rosalind's casket. The one she'd given me back in the Tortugas.

A pastor from Key West Church of Christ graciously performed the service. He delivered a brief, but powerful speech. Spoke of courage and love and devotion to family. And of faith. The son of a Cuban immigrant himself, you could feel the emotion and passion in his words.

Tears streaked down Leon's face when the pastor wrapped up a powerful prayer. Esther buried her face in his chest. Olivier just stared ahead. Stoic. Disbelief and heartbreak in his expression.

Ange stepped forward and wrapped her arms

around them. I placed a hand on Leon's shoulder. And Scarlett sat down beside Olivier.

Then the casket lowered into the island.

As the sun sank deeper, a veil of dark, splintered clouds rolled in and the sky erupted with streaks of light. A brilliant sunset. One of the most mesmerizing displays I've ever seen. And I've been fortunate to witness many spectacular sunsets in my life.

It was nothing short of awe-inspiring.

A beautiful send off. A fitting sendoff.

I didn't know the woman descending in the casket twenty feet in front of me. Had barely interacted with her and exchanged only a few frantic words.

But, in another way, I knew her very well.

I've spent a significant portion of my adult life on one form of battlefield or another. Harsh deserts, inhospitable jungles, hazardous swamps. Mountains and tundras. Remote villages and sprawling cities. I've engaged in conflicts all over the world. And consequently, I've witnessed the darkest of human conditions. Witnessed death again and again.

And a human being often reveals a lot about themselves in their final moments. That last flicker of life, when reality sets in and the full scope of mortality can truly be grasped. Fully understood for the first time.

And Rosalind had been strong.

She'd been unyielding and courageous. And she'd been a phenomenal mother. Loved her kids deeply. Cared only for their safety even as the last moments of her life faded. Even as she'd been overtaken with extreme pain.

Ange was tearing up. So was Scarlett. So were

Lauren and Jack and Pete and Jane and Harper. And so was I as the casket reached the bottom, the red sun piercing and blazing through gently rustling palm leaves. Like a beautiful gesture from the heavens.

We took care of Olivier and Esther after the burial. Watched over them as Leon stood alone over his wife's grave. Saying goodbye.

We ate a late meal back at our place. After everyone left, Leon took me aside.

"I can't thank you enough, Logan," he said. "But it's time for us to head to Marathon."

I nodded. "Stay one more night. I'll drive you all to the station tomorrow."

He agreed, and I watched him a moment. Examined him. He was broken, clearly. But there was something else in his eyes. A fire that couldn't be ignored. A mission he needed to perform. For his children. For his wife.

"I'll do whatever it takes," he said. "Whatever I have to do to give them a better life. Even if we're sent back. I'll find a way. I'll work however long it takes, however hard it takes. They deserve it."

I smiled. Asked, "What did you do back in Haiti? For work?"

"I was an electrician."

"Perfect. Far as I know, the laws of electricity work the same here as they do there. Different voltages, but the same principles. I can help you get an electrician license here, if and when the time comes. Not sure you're aware of this, but Florida experiences storms from time to time. Power lines are common casualties. I'm sure you would have no trouble finding good work once you have the proper certifications here."

Then I gestured toward the playset beside us. The one I'd built for his children.

"And when you do, that playground is available whenever Olivier or Esther want. From this day onward, our house is your house."

The man's wife had died in my arms. And moments before she'd passed, I'd promised to look after her children. I'd never back out from that promise. I'd keep up to date on their lives and do all I could to ensure a bright future full of opportunities for the little ones. And I'd do it until my last breath.

Ange and Scarlett rode with us the following day, cruising all the way up to Marathon. There, we met with CBP agents and checked the three of them into the facility.

"I'll do whatever I can to help you, brother," I said, shaking his hand. "Just do as you said. Go through all the hoops. Do all the paperwork. Follow all the rules and work your butt off. You got this."

He smiled. Thanked me for what felt like the hundredth time.

It was an emotional goodbye with Olivier and Esther. Both of them cried again. As did we. But we assured them that this was more of a "see you later." That we'd make sure and stay in their lives forever. Help them however we could. Hopefully, one day, call them fellow Americans.

On the drive home, Scarlett leaned over the center console.

"What do you think's going to happen?" she asked.

It was the second time she'd asked me that

question. This time, I felt better suited to answer it. Now that I'd met Leon and spoken to him a couple times. Knew what kind of man he was.

"I think they'll be just fine," I said. "I think, one way or another, they'll be able to live here long term. Because he's got the right attitude. He's not coming here with his hands out looking to be given everything. He's ready to work. He's ready to earn his keep. He's ready and eager to be useful and contribute."

The sadness I'd felt at Rosalind's funeral faded as we island hopped our way back home. She'd succeeded. She'd given her family a chance.

The sadness was replaced by something else.

Something a lot like hope.

FORTY-NINE

Two days later, hundreds of people packed into the Key West High gymnasium for the graduation ceremony. We sat near the top of the bleachers. Watched as the class of two thousand and twelve were all called out. Clapped for all of them, then let out a riotous cheer when Cameron's name was called.

After the ceremony, we congratulated him and took a few pictures, his uncle, Carl Miller, wearing a proud look that never left his face all evening. Then we all headed over to Pete's where he threw a special party for the graduating class. He grilled grouper tacos, as well as cheeseburgers and bratwurst. Had live music by Stars on the Water. The place was rocking, even more so than usual on a Friday night. And the proprietor was his usual buoyant, vibrant self, laughing with everyone he came into contact with while Tiko stood perched on his shoulder.

While eating among friends out on the balcony, I smiled when I noticed a certain familiar face arrive at the party. Threading through the patrons, I met up with Officer O'Malley as he stepped out through the sliding glass door alongside Jane.

Earlier that day, I'd received a call from Maddox. He'd informed me that, though the evidence against O'Malley had appeared like a slam dunk at face value, an in-depth evidence verification process had concluded that it'd all been planted—staged by someone who'd been trying to frame him. O'Malley had also agreed to and passed a polygraph test with flying colors and had been released that morning.

"Logan," he said, holding up his hands.

I'd been somewhat concerned—worried the guy would hold some kind of grudge against myself, Jane, and the others who'd been involved in the investigation. But the guy seemed chipper as ever.

"I'm just glad my name was cleared so quickly," he said. "And I'm glad that the real culprit has been dealt with. Or so I've heard through the grapevine."

He shot me a sly smile. I just shrugged. "I haven't heard anything," I said. "But something tells me he'll get what's coming to him. If he hasn't already."

O'Malley went quiet. Looked at his shoes. "Hard to believe he was involved in that crap."

"Come on," I said, throwing an arm around him, "you look like you could use a drink. It's a party, after all."

An hour into the shindig, Cameron approached me.

"Do you know where Scarlett went? Her Bronco's not in the lot."

I had a pretty good idea of where to find her. Climbed into my Tacoma and drove as far southwest as you can in the continental US. Pulled right up to the gate of Fort Zachary Taylor State Park. I found her SUV in the lot. Parked right beside it. Then I found her at the highest part of the old fort. Sitting with her back against the bulwark and facing the sea. The spot offered an incredible view. One of my favorite views in the world, let alone the Keys. It was a spot I liked to go to when I needed to think. Clear my head and just enjoy some quiet time. One that I'd shown to Scarlett.

I approached slowly. Just eased over and slumped down beside her.

I didn't speak.

I could have gone into a long spiel about life and how you can always count on change. But I've learned that oftentimes people who are struggling with something don't need you to say anything at all. They just need you to be present. They just need an empathetic shoulder to lean on.

And so, I was present. And I listened. We both did. Each just sat in silence and took in the sounds of nearby rumbling waves and passing gulls and rustling palm trees.

Five minutes passed.

Then ten.

Her breathing slowed. She relaxed a little. Leaned into me.

After nearly fifteen minutes, my phone buzzed in my pocket.

A message from Ange.

A picture of Pete in his restaurant, surrounded by a

sea of happy patrons. Cameron was beside him. So was Isaac. And the happy group was standing behind Oz and Mia, the two staff members presenting the biggest Key Lime pie I'd ever seen.

A caption from Ange immediately followed the picture.

Tell Scarlett they won't slice it without her.

I smiled. Showed the picture to my daughter, along with the text. She chuckled, then I hugged her tight. Stood, stretched and held a hand out to her.

"What do you say, kiddo?"

Tiko was the first to notice our return. The intelligent and observant parrot was still perched on Pete's shoulder when we stepped out to the balcony. His head swiveled back and he gawked and said Scarlett's name.

Then the whole group turned and welcomed us. Pete let Isaac do the honors, handing the young man a steel server. He cut into the pie and it was swiftly divvied up.

The lively, talented members of Stars on the Water lived up to their reputation and had the whole place alive and clapping. Entranced by their tropical melodies. Scarlett returned to her usual outgoing and excited self, celebrating the end of another school year with many of her classmates.

And we ate. And we danced. We sang. And we drank. And we laughed the night away.

EPILOGUE

The following day, we helped Cameron pack his things into the back of his old pickup truck. Once everything was loaded up, the young man shut the canopy. Then he turned and smiled at us.

"Any final pieces of advice sensei?" he said to me.

I stepped closer. Looked him in the eye. "Yeah. Prioritize your studies." I tapped him on the forehead. "Keep this sharp. Keep learning. Question everyone and everything. Hold onto your morals. And when it comes to football, know that high school is over. You're no longer going to be the fastest or the strongest or the most talented guy on the field. Those days are over. But you can be the hardest worker on the field. Never let anyone outwork you. Ever."

I shook his hand. Wrapped an arm around him. Then Ange gave him a hug. Then his uncle gave him a hug. And then he stood in front of Scarlett.

"I'll see you when you get back from your trip," he said. "I'll be home for a couple days at the end of summer."

Then they hugged as well. Then they kissed. And then Cameron climbed into the driver's seat and threw a wave through his rolled down window and began his five-hundred-mile drive up to Gainesville.

Isaac left two days later. His leaving hit me even harder. The young man whose father had died in a car accident and who Jack had taken in at a young age and raised, was moving away. I had vivid memories of hanging out with him in the waves when he was a kid. Taking him fishing. Watching movies with him. Playing video games. Whenever I visited Jack, Isaac was there. My beach bum friend had had help from locals, but he'd raised Isaac mostly on his own. And he'd done a hell of a job at it.

We did our best to help Scarlett take her mind off things after that. With school no longer in session, we spent every day out on the water as a family. Spearfishing. Diving. Exploring. And volunteering for Reef Relief and at the Turtle Hospital.

Then, two weeks after Cameron and Isaac left, the Dodge clan packed our bags and headed to the airport to embark on our great summer adventure.

Jack drove us in the Bronco. He'd already offered to look after Atticus and Boise while we were gone, and we brought our two pets with us so we could say our goodbyes at the airport. Atticus wanted to come along, the energetic Lab leaping from the backseat and prancing in circles near the entrance to the departure terminal.

"We'll be back soon," I said, kneeling and petting

him. Looking him in the eyes and squeezing him tight. "You're a good boy," I added. "You're the best boy."

Boise wasn't quite as animated. Our calico simply rose subtly from her napping position. Purred a little and then collapsed right back onto the car seat.

"Let us know how the election goes," Ange said.

Jack tipped his cap. "Will do."

We'd stayed just long enough to be given the opportunity to voice our say in the upcoming mayoral election. And had slipped in two votes for Pete Jameson the previous day.

"And let me know what you guys discover," Jack added.

After a quick layover in New Jersey, we'd fly to Edinburgh. There, we had a rental car booked and an itinerary to tour Scotland and then all the way down through England. Exploring castles and gardens and beaches and vistas along the way. And, weather and conditions permitting, getting some diving in.

Then we were gonna return the car in London and take the train to Paris. Explore the City of Light, and then tour nearby Normandy, a hallowed place that'd been high up on my bucket list for a long time.

Jack's granduncle, George Rubio, had parachuted into Normandy with the legendary 101st airborne during World War II. He'd fought in many battles and skirmishes and had sacrificed his life on the field just two months before Germany had surrendered.

Jack requested that we inquire about him, knowing that the hero was buried at the Normandy American Cemetery, just up the bluff from Omaha Beach. Jack had also requested that we leave a bouquet of dried sea lavender, a flower native to Key West, at the soldier's grave. And that we speak with cemetery staff members to see if there was anything new we could learn about the man and his courageous deeds.

Jack choked up a little as he handed me the bouquet of flowers.

"Thanks, guys," he said. "I hope to visit him myself one day."

We said our goodbyes. Hauled our stuff inside.

Our plane pushed back an hour and a half later. Took off. Landing gear groaned up into the fuselage. We banked gently and caught a full view of the Lower Keys through the window before turning north and continuing our ascent.

Ange wore a big smile on her face. She'd been planning and looking forward to the trip all year. We all had.

When we reached altitude, I purchased two bottles of Jack Daniels and got a can of ginger ale for Scarlett. We each filled our plastic cups and held them up.

"Cheers to Olivier, Esther, and Leon," I said. "Cheers to their mother, Rosalind. Cheers to Cameron and Isaac. Cheers to George Rubio. Cheers to all our island friends. And cheers to us, and our best summer yet."

THE END

Note to Reader

I hope you enjoyed this adventure. Curious what's next for the Dodge family and company? You can find more installments in the Florida Keys Adventure Series on my Amazon page.

This is the part where I usually write a line or two about the musicians mentioned in this book. As I'm sure many of you noticed, there was a particular artist whose works appeared again and again. Needless to say, Buffett was on my mind a lot while penning this one. And every time Logan or anyone else switched on the radio, it was his voice I heard.

As I'm sure was the case with many of you, hearing of his passing was a devastating shock. It was especially moving for me as I'd just been re-reading a favorite book of mine: Mile Marker Zero: The Moveable Feast of Key West, and had just finished the chapter that describes Jimmy's first time ever visiting the Keys. He'd been in his twenties, riding in the back of a friend's car alongside a baby. His blond locks flowing in the tropical breeze while he serenaded the child with his acoustic and took in the spectacular sights of that unlike any other drive.

He'd been told he'd never make it while grinding away at the Nashville music scene—told he didn't fit into any genre. So, Jimmy forged his own sound. He may have passed on, but his music, stories, and his zest for life will live on forever. Fair winds and following seas, Jimmy.

My deepest thanks to all of you for your support. Your reviews, recommendations of my stories, messages, and comments mean so much to me. And it's because of this support that the series has grown more popular with each new release. Thank you all.

Cheers to the next adventure,
Matthew

LOGAN DODGE ADVENTURES

Gold in the Keys
Hunted in the Keys
Revenge in the Keys
Betrayed in the Keys
Redemption in the Keys
Corruption in the Keys
Predator in the Keys
Legend in the Keys
Abducted in the Keys
Showdown in the Keys
Avenged in the Keys
Broken in the Keys
Payback in the Keys
Condemned in the Keys
Voyage in the Keys
Guardian in the Keys
Menace in the Keys
Pursuit in the Keys
Defiance in the Keys
Treasure in the Keys

JASON WAKE NOVELS

Caribbean Wake
Surging Wake
Relentless Wake
Turbulent Wake
Furious Wake
Perilous Wake

Join the Adventure!
Sign up for my newsletter to receive updates on upcoming books on my website:

matthewrief.com

About the Author

Matthew has a deep-rooted love for adventure and the ocean. He loves traveling, diving, and writing adventure novels. Though he grew up in the Pacific Northwest, he currently lives in Virginia Beach with his wife, Jenny.

Made in the USA
Columbia, SC
22 November 2023

26944100R00209